PRAIS

The Perfe

"Pure fun! A hilarious rom-com that head-fakes you into tumbling headlong into a techno-zombie-survival thriller propelled by banter and plenty of heart."

—**David Yoon**, *New York Times* bestselling author of *Frankly in Love*

"Suzanne Park's *The Perfect Escape* is just that—perfect. Filled with humor and heart, it won't let you go until you're smiling."

—**Danielle Paige**, *New York Times* bestselling author of the Dorothy Must Die series and *Stealing Snow*

"Effortlessly hilarious and super lovable. I hope this is the YA rom-com of 2020."

—**Helen Hoang**, *USA Today* bestselling author of *The Kiss Quotient*

"An adorable, laugh-out-loud YA rom-com with a lovable hero and an action-packed, zombie-themed escape room—what more could you want?"

—**Jenn Bennett**, author of *Alex, Approximately*

"Quirky and hilarious, *The Perfect Escape* has everything you've ever wanted in a rom-com. Suzanne Park has created the perfect mix of humor and heart against the backdrop of zombie adventures guaranteed to keep you laughing. Nate and Kate are absolutely adorable, and you'll be rooting for them until the very end. A must-have addition to any bookshelf!"

—**Sabina Khan**, author of *The Love and Lies of Rukhsana Ali*

"Suzanne Park's debut was a thrilling ride with lovable characters and plenty of belly laughs."

—**Gloria Chao**, author of
American Panda and *Our Wayward Fate*

"*The Perfect Escape* is the hilarious tale of two snarky teens who will win your hearts (and maybe each other's). It is indeed the perfect escape from, well, pretty much everything."

—**Sarah Henning**, author of
Throw Like a Girl and the Sea Witch duology

"The funniest love stories can start in the most unexpected of places. *The Perfect Escape* is a whip-smart, hilarious rom-com that boldly explores classism, family expectations, and how to outrun zombies."

—**Nina Moreno**, author of *Don't Date Rosa Santos*

THE PERFECT ESCAPE

THE PERFECT ESCAPE

SUZANNE PARK

sourcebooks
fire

Published by Sourcebooks Fire, an imprint of Sourcebooks
P.O. Box 4410, Naperville, Illinois 60567-4410
(630) 961-3900
sourcebooks.com

Library of Congress Cataloging-in-Publication data is on file with the publisher.

Printed and bound in the United States of America.
VP 10 9 8 7 6 5 4 3 2 1

For my family.

(Mom and Dad, sorry about all the cussing.)

"Money trees is the perfect place for shade. And that's just how I feel, nah nah."

—*Kendrick Lamar, karaoked by Nate Kim in the shower*

CHAPTER ONE

Nate

I'd recited this blah script more than fifty times.

"Welcome to the Zombie Laboratory. I'm Nate, and I'll be your host for the evening. Can I get a show of hands of anyone who has been to an escape room before?" Near the main entrance, a goateed guy with chunky black glasses raised a hand. Ten tipsy thirtysomething-year-old bachelorette party ladies giggled next to him, ignoring me. They were all wearing strappy, sparkly heels, of course. Who the hell wore heels to a zombie escape room?

"Only one?" I asked. "Okay, show of hands—how many of you have recently been bitten or eaten by a zombie?"

A few titters came from some guys near the front. This time everyone made eye contact with me and smiled. *Whew!* I'd just added that joke in and was testing it out for the first time.

"That's good! Because that would mean we'd be trapped in the room with more undead than our zoning permit allows."

No laughs.

Shit.

I'd have to try out another line next time.

The group chattered as we walked down the dimly lit, flickering hallway.

To my relief, the bachelorettes didn't look drunk enough to require janitorial assistance (of the vomit-cleaning variety). No stumbling backward in those ill-advised heels. No high-pitched, eardrum-bursting squeals. No swaying.

Drunk customers were the worst customers. Actually, scratch that. Drunk-to-the-point-of-puking customers were the *absolute* worst customers. I'd gotten to the point where spotting them was easy, and I had the power to refuse service during the waiver form process.

"Can't we just staaaaart? My heels are killing me!" The pouty bride-to-be swept her hair off her shoulder and crossed her arms. "I'm SUF. FER. ING!" Her girlfriends gathered round and gave her hugs.

Don't roll your eyes, Nate. Don't.

"Not too much longer," I said with a smile.

Sometimes, if the group's vibe is good, I help give clues for some of the puzzles. But this group? Nah, they weren't worth the time. With all the side-eying and sighing, I knew they weren't into it.

The other large party in this group was a bunch of douche-bros from Houzzcalls, a telemarketing software start-up down the street. They wore company shirts with WE MAKE HOUZZCALLS across their chests. Judging by the hooting, hollering, and advanced handshake coordination, I'm guessing these guys were in sales, not software development. They probably found a Groupon or were here for mandatory team bonding, not because they actually liked puzzles or were zombie aficionados. Unlike us dedicated employees, who lived and breathed this stuff.

Judging by the looks of these guys, this sorry bunch would panic after thirty minutes when the halftime buzzer honked, a cue for the zombies to lean harder on the barricaded door. The undead got feistier in the second half, chomping and snapping their teeth as they pushed their way through. The music would speed up, and the clock would tick louder. It was all part of the game. A game I loved.

On the hour mark, I pushed open the heavy metal door and dropped my voice an octave. "Good luck."

Once we entered, the gigantic glowing red digital clock on the wall started the one-hour countdown. The first clue was laid out on the metal laboratory table, a sixty-piece jigsaw puzzle spelling out the next set of instructions. It went ignored by everyone except the trio of Russian exchange students who had signed up at the very last possible minute.

After twenty-five minutes, one of the Russians yelled, "Done!" He was over six feet tall, had a super-chiseled face, and commanded my attention when he read aloud, "Make haste! What you need next is in the attaché case!" His brow furrowed.

"Attaché case? What is that?" He stared at the bros and bachelorettes, who were paired off and leaning against the wall, whispering, laughing, touching, and ready for their post–escape room orgy.

The Russians searched along the walls for a case, not realizing it was in my hand. I could offer help, but they needed to ask me for it. Those were the rules. The attaché case held a key that would chain-lock the door, keeping out the soon-to-stampede army of zombies.

My prediction? This group wouldn't even finish the second clue. They'd be devoured by zombies at the thirty-two-, maybe thirty-three-minute mark.

Just shy of half an hour, a warning alarm went off, and the door with the broken padlock and chain pushed open a little. Grotesque, gray, mutilated arms flailed through the widened opening, and the groaning and moaning commenced.

The bachelorette party switched gears from mad flirting to scream-shrieking, "Oh my God!" on repeat. They retreated back into the far corner away from the door, stumbling over the wussy tech sales guys as both parties ran as far away from the zombies as possible.

I shook the briefcase in my hand, hoping someone would hear the padlock and key clattering inside. Like a giant, adult rattle. *Come and get it! Achtung!* Did Russian people know German?

The room was divided by the zombie arm blockade:

bachelorettes and sales guys on one side, and the exchange students and me on the other.

I rattled the briefcase one more time.

"Is that the attachment case?" one of the exchange students asked, pointing to my hand.

I nodded, and all three exchange students bolted toward me. The girl reached me first and flipped up the clasps. The thirty-minute alarm went off, and the zombies barreled into the room.

Too late.

There were eight zombies in all, and they split into two groups and moaned and groaned as they made their way to their human victims. At thirty-one minutes, the female exchange student was the last one standing, and she jumped on the table with the attaché case high above her head, wild-eyed and ready to use the case as a weapon. One of the crawling zombies behind her tapped her foot. Gotcha. Game over.

The clock froze at thirty-one minutes. The zombies exited the way they came in, and all of the overhead fluorescents flooded the room with intense light. It was the worst escape room effort I'd ever seen.

With eyes filled with disappointment, each of the Russians shook my hand and said they had a good time. "How many clues were there?" the girl asked.

I didn't feel like sugarcoating. "Ten. You guys had a tough group to work with. But thanks so much for coming." I had a pocket full of "Please review us on Yelp!" cards, but I only gave those to winners, people who would rave about this place. Winning groups usually came up with a system, like division of clues, or everyone solving problems together. Losers broke into factions immediately like, say, exchange students versus humping party animals.

Unfortunately for me, losers gave weak tips.

"Let's go get some booze to celebrate our loss!" cheered one of the bros as he walked out with one of the bachelorette partiers, his hand sliding down the small of her back. The rest of the group shuffled out too, giggling and guffawing as they exited.

The bride patted my face and said, "You're adorable! My fiancé is Korean too," then stumbled out. I was surprised she could tell I was Korean. Usually people assumed I was Chinese. Sometimes Japanese. Even kids at school who'd known me forever thought I was Chinese.

"Can I come out now?" a muffled voice cried out from the closet on the far wall.

"Uh, sure? Everyone's gone."

The door creaked open. I backed away as a mutilated female zombie wearing a crumpled witch hat stumbled out.

CHAPTER TWO

Nate

There were entrails hanging out where her belly button should've been.

"I was starting to get a little claustrophobic." The girl blinked rapidly, adjusting her eyes to the flickering radiant lights. "I'm Kate, the new 'spooky seasonal feature' they added last week." She took one quick look at my *Feed Me (Braaaains)!* T-shirt and tattered jeans, then focused her gaze on my face.

My eyes and ears tuned into her every move, my whole body on high alert. I was trapped in a room with a zombie girl. All the other zombies I'd worked with were dudes. "I'm Nate." I shrugged, trying not to cringe at our cutesy rhyming names, not quite sure why I was shrugging in the first place.

Everything on my body that could possibly sweat did. Instant oil slicks involuntarily formed on my palms, feet, and face T-zone, and there wasn't a damn thing I could do to stop it.

Was it weird to think she was cute? She had shining brown eyes and a button nose that crinkled adorably each time she looked at the fluorescent lights. Well, as adorable as a zombi-fied girl could be, with all that makeup, straggly hair, and fake wounds. Why did she take this "zombie girl in the closet" role? She could seriously star in commercials or something like that.

This girl was way out of my league, though. Out of my dimen-sion, even. My heart pounded as my chest tightened, giving me the sensation that my body was trying to choke my heart out of my chest cavity. God, why was I so awkward around girls? And a *zombie* girl, no less.

Not knowing what else to do next, I extended my clammy, sweat-pooled hand, and we shook firmly, like we were coaches facing off in a football game.

"Nice to meet you, Nate," she said, then stretched her arms high above her head. "That closet is way too small for someone my height. And I'm only five foot three and a half." After hopping around on both feet, she added, "My feet are asleep!"

"So, you're the new big finale, jumping out of the closet at the end? You're here from now through Halloween, and then what—are you coming back for Thanksgiving and Hanukkah and Christmas?" I was torn between being ecstatic about her new role and being terrified, knowing she'd be hiding in the closet for fifty-nine minutes of each session, maybe listening to me give my opening spiel. Even with fifty-plus escape room games under my belt, my self-confidence shrank by the second at the mere thought of being in future sessions with this zombie girl.

"Yeah, I'm just a seasonal worker, not a year-rounder like you. Will work for food. Or brains," she said, giving a nod toward my shirt. A boom of thunder rumbled and echoed through the building, taking me by surprise. Thunderstorms were a rarity in Seattle, something to do with the cool breeze on the Pacific Ocean. Something I didn't really pay much attention to in junior high science class, but maybe should have.

"Hey, can you do me a favor?" she asked.

Gulping down my fear, I replied, "Depends. What do you need? If you need a ride home or something, then maybe?" My mom's 2002 Honda was a busted piece of crap and shimmied at fifty-five miles per hour, its top speed, but it got the job done, driving from point A to point B. But if Kate wanted to borrow money, she was shit out of luck. All of my wages went toward my Xbox subscription, college fund, and savings for a business I'd launch in a few years. I had nothing to spare.

"I need you to tell me which black eye looks better." She pointed double-finger guns at her face. "Left eye...or the right one? I'm trying to perfect my makeup artistry for work again tomorrow." Damn, she was working a shift tomorrow, and unfortunately I wasn't. My stomach twinged with disappointment. Or hunger. Maybe both.

"I—I—I like the one on the left. It gives your eye a gaunt, hollow look," I said hesitantly as she raised an eyebrow at me.

She pulled a mirror from her purse and examined both eyes.

"Interesting. I kind of like the other one. It looks more realistic to me. Like I'm not trying too hard to look dead, you know?"

What in the hell was she talking about? Both of her eyes were "dead"-looking. I'd worked at this zombie escape room job for a year. Read every zombie survival guide I could get my hands on. Watched every zombie movie and every episode of *The Walking Dead* more than once. I knew my zombie shit.

"Yeah, I agree," I replied, and motioned for her to come with me to the employee lockers in the break room.

"So, actually, could I get a lift home maybe?" she asked as we opened our lockers. "I didn't really think about how I'd look taking public transportation. And you know, the rain could make it all worse." She removed her hat and smiled, revealing a fake missing tooth and bloody gums. I had to admit, she took her zombie job very seriously. Kate was convincingly, purposefully gross.

I grinned confidently while shutting my locker door, even though my heart was pounding and my sweatiness all over my body intensified. "Sure, my after-hours job is zombie rescue. I retrieve zombies and put them back in their habitat."

She pulled her peacoat from her locker and put it on over her raggedy dress. "Great! There's a Dick's Hamburgers on the way to my house. I need food. I'll buy you dinner and a milkshake if you want."

When we got outside, rain assaulted us from every direction.

We'd already had ten days of straight rain, not unusual for October in Seattle. And the seven-day forecast? Even more rain.

Kate studied the flyers on the corkboard next to the entrance while I locked up. She stared hard at the neon-green Zombie-geddon advertisement, examining every word. Zombiegeddon was a new zombie-themed survival competition with a huge cash prize. It was on the same day as my big-time cross-country meet a month away, so I hadn't bothered to look into it more.

When we finally got to my car, I swiped my accordion folder of college financial aid applications off the front passenger seat and tossed it in the back. I handed Kate a wad of clean tissues from my pocket to mop up her runny makeup and also used some to wipe my forehead's fountain of sweat.

As I turned the key in the ignition, I wondered, *If we are eating hamburgers and it is her treat, does this count as a date?*

Kate took a selfie just before wiping off her cheeks. "I look scarier now than I did before. I might try this look tomorrow. Maybe I'll stick my head under the shower or something."

Her boot thumped hard against something on the floorboard. "Oops," she said apologetically. "I hope I didn't break anything." She bent down to look. "Wow, is this where you keep guns and ammo?"

I laughed. "That's my dad's trusty six-drawer toolbox. It's older than I am." He always liked to consider himself handy around the house, but Mom and I called him Mr. Fixer-Downer.

"He refuses to hire plumbers or handymen. He's a do-it-yourselfer, to save money. Watches YouTube videos and thinks he's a pro."

"Oh, that's cool!" Kate sighed and glanced at the toolbox again. "My dad's not handy at all. He outsources everything."

I wished we outsourced more. "Well, I didn't say my dad was good at it. He once spent three hours building a three-cube bookshelf."

"In his defense, IKEA furniture is a pain in the ass to put together. Don't let those cute cartoon drawing instructions fool you," she teased.

"Yeah! How do they manage to have like forty types of different screws with all sorts of head shapes in an impossible-to-open plastic baggie for just one stool? I should be nicer to my dad."

I drummed my fingers on the steering wheel at a stoplight and snuck a quick glance at her. "Too bad I don't work tomorrow. Do you work any other days too?" Saturday nights were when I played *State of Decay* on Xbox Live with my buddies. There were three of us, and we'd all played together since middle school. I was `z0mbie_killir_1`. Spelling was never my forte.

Kate shook her head. "I'm only working Friday and Saturday nights. It's okay, though. That works out with school and other stuff."

"I usually work Monday-Wednesday-Friday." It dawned on me that the next time I'd see her was the next Friday. "It's cool we'll be able to work together, at least for a few weeks."

Kate shrugged. "I'm a temp zombie for now, but maybe if I do a good job, the guys in charge will keep me around for the whole year."

"Yeah, think about all the holidays after Christmas! Valentine's Day. Saint Patrick's Day. Easter. And who doesn't love an Easter zombie?" I waggled my eyebrows the best I could.

She smiled at me as she grabbed my phone from the center console and typed her address into the maps app. "I live twenty minutes away. Looks like there's a little bit of traffic on the way there. Sorry. But we can do our Dick's pit stop, and maybe the roads will clear up." She leaned forward and peered at the radio. "Mind if I turn it on?"

Heat flushed to my cheeks, starkly contrasting with my rain-pelted, clammy skin. "This is my mom's car. It's super old, so there's nothing automatic on it. You might even have to turn the knob." My ears burned with embarrassment. "And her preset stations are NPR, easy listening, and classical crap, so no judging. But yeah, fiddle with it if you want."

She punched one of my mom's preset stations and "Jingle Bell Rock" came on. Already? It was only October! I thought there were rules against that shit.

"Yes! Holiday music!" she squealed. "Don't you love Christmas music?"

Ugghhh, noooo. Kill me now. "Yeah. It's great."

Mickey's Christmas Carol was the only Christmasy thing I

liked. Scrooge McDuck was rich, focused, and no-nonsense. When asked the question "Who would I have dinner with, real or fictional?" I always answered Scrooge McDuck. I didn't dare tell Kate all this, though, given her affinity for the shittiest yuletide song in history.

When exiting the freeway, she pointed ahead to the right. "Dick's is up there. Let's get milkshakes. Wanna split a burger and fries?"

"Sure," I said cheerily, even though I was sort of lactose intolerant and didn't like the mayo-goop they put on their "Special" hamburgers or their lactose-y shakes. I parked in a spot near the customer walk-up windows, and we both got out and ran up to one of the free attendants.

Please don't order the Special burger. Please don't order the Special burger.

Kate rattled off our dinner request. "We'd like two chocolate milkshakes, a large fry, and a Special burger, cut in half. To go, please." The attendant repeated back the order and said she'd be back with our shakes. She didn't seem fazed at all by Kate's full-on zombie appearance.

I almost interrupted them to change the order at the last second, but I kept my true feelings in check because OMG, I had a girl here on a quasi date with me who, unfortunately, liked disgusting burgers. So instead I shut up and prayed the restaurant would somehow mess up our order and our beef would be free of specialness.

"I love the Special burger. It's sooo good!"

I nodded. Dick's fries were those fresh-cut ones. I kind of hated those too. Kate and I were proving to be polar opposites.

Panic hit me hard as I tried to figure out what the payment protocol was for this Dick's Hamburger pit stop. She'd offered to pay, and I hadn't budgeted for this, uh, burger-binging almost-date. Did she pay for everything because she was the one who wanted to stop here? Did we split payment? Did I pay because I was a dude? Dumb things like this always tripped me up. And it messed with my saving goals for the month. This baby needed a new pair of shoes...plus a newer car and college tuition. Oh, and more Xbox games.

We got our drinks, and as I fumbled with my wallet, Kate shoved a Dick's burger gift card into my palm to hand to the attendant. "It's on me. Thanks for the drive," she said with an appreciative grin.

"Thanks!" I downed my shake in less than a minute, mostly out of relief that I didn't have to pay for everything and she'd handled it so smoothly.

Our food came fast. "I'm pretty full already," I said as we got back in the car.

Kate nibbled on a fry. "More for me, then!" She swallowed with a gulp. "I have a ton of money on that gift card if you want to order something else for later. It's on me."

Wow, she was nice *and* loaded with infinite Dick's dollars.

Things were looking up! The milkshake really did fill me up, though. "I actually already ate dinner and wolfed down a sleeve of Chips Ahoy on the way to work. Not a proud moment for me. I don't even like them."

Kate made a face. "Chips Ahoy? I agree, yuck." She cocked her head. "Stress-eating?"

How'd she know? "Yeah, AP classes, college applications, all of that." I ran my hand through my hair. Twice.

"Oooh, I like salty processed food for stress-eating. Anything with fake cheese." Her eyes brightened as she laughed.

I grinned. "Yes! Anything that can turn my fingertips an abnormal neon-orange color, I'm in."

She handed me a long fry from the paper bag, and I ate it. It wasn't so bad after all. I held out my hand, and she gave me a few more.

"What's your favorite zombie movie?" I asked while chewing. "Mine is *Zombieland*."

She bit her lip. "Tough one. I liked *Zombieland*. Hmmm... maybe *World War Z*? Oh, the Korean one! *Train to Busan*?"

My eyes widened. She really knew her zombie flicks. "Whoa, I just saw that. Yeah, you're right. It's the best one I've seen." I had to watch it with the lights on, but I didn't tell her that.

"Yeah! It was scary as hell, but it made me cry too." Kate pulled her wig off, revealing a matted, sweaty head of brown hair in some kind of netting. "That hairpiece itched too much. Sorry

I didn't warn ya." After fiddling in her coat pocket, she pulled out a bottle and squeezed goop into her palm. "Special lotion. For eczema." She rubbed it into her forearms, wrists, and hands. The faint aroma of lemons filled the car cabin as we exited the parking lot. It was a good kind of lemony smell, not the furniture wax kind.

Google Maps showed I had only four more minutes left of Kate time. I hadn't spoken much after we hit the road, and she would be leaving my car soon. I needed to say something fast. "I never asked where you went to school," I blurted, a slight crack to my voice.

"Seattle Academy," she sighed, and then chewed another fry thoughtfully. "I finally graduate this year. Thank God." SA was the artsiest high school in the city.

"Cool." I don't know why I asked her about school because normal conversationalists reciprocated questions, and I didn't want her to know I went to Clyde Hill Academy. CHA was the douchiest, most elite prep school for grades six through twelve in the Pacific Northwest, and I'd gone there the entire time. I also didn't want her to know I was there on a full ride. Kids like me on full scholarship had a nickname at Clyde Hill. "Skids," short for "scholarship kids." There's no positive association for that word. Skid row. Skid mark. Skids were also trolls on hacker forums, according to Urban Dictionary.

I hated being a skid.

I also didn't want her to figure out I was only sixteen and eleven-twelfths years old. I was a senior like Kate, but I'd skipped sixth grade as soon as I arrived at CHA. Back then, I'd thought it was so great to jump to seventh grade and into pre-algebra. I didn't know that decision came with consequences. I was last to get a driver's permit. Last to get a license. Getting dropped off and picked up by my mom through junior year did wonders for my social life, let me tell you.

Clyde Hill kids were cultured in a "we go to exotic destinations with all-inclusive, five-star vacation packages" sort of way. They waved them off as "quick vacays" to get some "R&R." My buddies Zach, Jaxon, and me, though, we didn't travel anywhere fancy, ever. *Skids* never did. The closest we got to culture was on our eighth-grade trip to Orlando, and Epcot Center blew our minds.

Skids had something the school desperately desired in exchange for free tuition: high test scores, or athletic prowess, or in the case of Zach, they wanted bona fide geniuses to attend, so they would hopefully have the next Bill Gates or Mark Zuckerberg as alumni. My parents gladly accepted the $40,000 scholarship each year for my 4.0 GPA and high PSAT and SAT scores. No way could their IT consultant and Korean tutor salaries cover the expenses of private school.

I turned down Kate's fog-covered street, decelerating as we approached her home. She lived in the remote part of Bothell,

in an area where there was still abundant farmland. Her driveway was a few houses down on the right and disappeared down
a steep hill into a black, foggy abyss. Total horror movie setting.
Cue creepy-as-shit music.

My tires squeaked, and I hesitated before descending into the
dark unknown. Kate opened the door before I maneuvered down.
"I can jump out here. It's fine. It's a pain in the ass to reverse out,
and there's a gate a few yards down." She yanked her bag of food
and milkshake from the center console and shouted, "Thanks for
the ride!"

I grinned. "No problemo, señorita." *Really, Nate? Spanish? My
God.* "It was really fun."

Kate returned my smile, warming my insides. "It was! See
ya Friday." She shut the door and bounded down her driveway,
disappearing into the night.

I'd see Kate in a week! After archery class and work on
Monday, Krav Maga on Tuesday, self-defense and work on
Wednesday, and cross-country on Thursday.

Google Maps let me know there were twenty-four minutes
and eleven miles between Kate's house and mine. So many
questions swirled inside my head as I drove to the freeway.

Did she think I was weird?

Or maybe not that weird?

Just a little weird? Everyone was a little weird, right?

Why didn't she ask about my school?

Would I get to drive her home again?

Why didn't I get her number? *Argh, Nate, you idiot.*

"All I Want for Christmas Is You" blared on the tinny speakers, breaking my concentration with Mariah's high-octave runs. Reaching down to switch off the radio, a mangy, wet pile of dark hair in the passenger seat caught my eye.

Kate's wig.

How do you forget your hair?

I couldn't call her because I didn't ask for her number. Again: *Argh, Nate, you idiot.*

But maybe she'd come to work early on Friday.

Maybe.

I took the wig up to my bedroom because if my mom saw a girl's *anything* in my possession, she'd lose her shit without letting me explain. *What is this? Why you drive girls around in my car? Did she give you gas money? Don't get distracted from school!* I'd never brought home a pile of matted, fake hair before, so this was all new territory for me. I hid it between my mattress and my headboard for safekeeping. After homework, snack, and shower, I was ready for bed.

Kate's fresh, lemony scent, just inches from my face.

CHAPTER THREE

Cold, thick mist enveloped me like fog-machine smoke as I made my way to the security gate. My trembling, frozen fingers made it hard to punch the four-digit key code without timing out. The next gate required my fingerprint and/or face scan, and my full zombie makeup made the facial read impossible. *Oops.* Shivers traveled down my back as sprinkles fell from the sky. I pressed my thumb on the finger pad and waited. After a few seconds, the screen flashed GO in neon-green letters, and a flood of relief washed over me as the iron gate door clicked open.

I dropped my bag in the empty mammoth entryway. My shoes squeaked on the shiny white marble floor as I made my way to the bathroom to take a shower. With a wave of my hand, the automatic heat lamps whirred on, instantly warming my face. In the brightly lit mirror, I examined my runny makeup then glanced up at my hair.

My jaw dropped.

OH MY GOD. MY HAIR.

Where is my hair?

Nate saw me like this! Sweaty hair. In a hairnet. Sans wig.

Then, *Oh, shit! IT'S IN HIS CAR!*

Poor Nate. What a revolting thing for me to leave behind. Not a glass slipper, or a monogrammed handkerchief, or a lipstick-kissed napkin with my contact info on it.

I left hair.

HAIR.

Gnarly, knotted, sweaty hair. And I couldn't warn him about it. He'd have to discover this on his own. He'd drive to Starbucks or something and *BAM*, a nasty pile of hair in his passenger seat. Could I please curl up and die?

Our house phone buzzed at top volume, and my heart nearly stopped. Dad had just installed a new communications system in every room, and this was one of the first times we had an incoming call or message. Was it Nate? Was he a super-genius who telepathically figured out my home phone number from our few interactions?

No, of course it wasn't him. No one called me except for Dad.

Dad, letting me know I'd be on my own for dinner again.

I got some food already, I messaged back on the bathroom wall screen.

For a few months I had a nanny hovering over me, my dad's eyes and ears, but I finally convinced him I was a senior and old enough to handle things myself, which included dinner, something my nanny used to make for me. It was usually just mac and cheese, pasta, or sandwiches, but still, someone else had the job to keep me fed. I had no clue how to cook properly, and those short "easy" internet cooking videos never had measurements, so I usually just got a shitload of Lean Cuisines delivered from the store and ate a lot of fast food. Dad never noticed my no-vegetable-no-legumes diet. He also didn't know about my new job. Hopefully he never would.

Next to the bathroom sink, I pushed my preset shower button: medium hot, strong pressure, low steam. Sprays of water came from all directions and fully warmed my body. I lifted my face to the main shower nozzle, holding my breath as the gray, red, and black makeup streams dripped to my feet and swirled down the drain. I stayed in the shower longer than usual, taking my time through my washing ritual, making sure I'd taken great care washing my eczema flare-ups on my hands, neck, and feet with my prescription soap.

Once dressed, I dumped everything left in the Dick's bag onto a plate and parked myself on the couch. Another Friday night alone, watching AMC's *The Walking Dead* marathons on our eighty-five-inch TV screen. The once-crispy fries were now cold and soggy, and the Special burger sauce had leaked everywhere, soaking both the bun and wrapper. My delicious shake had morphed into thick chocolate milk, which wasn't necessarily a bad thing.

"Jeeves, please turn the lights down!" The lighting overhead dimmed to the default, preset darkness of my liking. "I need a napkin, too, please." Whirring sounds echoed from the kitchen. Within seconds, our cylindrical white robot resembling a four-foot-tall marshmallow appeared by my feet, with a trail of napkins behind it. Little robot arms flew upward and handed me an empty plastic wrapper that once held a twenty-four pack of plain white dinner napkins. "Thanks for trying, Jeeves," I sighed. I logged this delivery error on my dad's company's website.

Dad is CEO of Digitools, and we always test his company's products at home before they were released to the public. It used to be fun, but with the necessity of quickly launching products to beat out competitors, we ended up with a home full of buggy software and hardware. After his company commissioned an elaborate research study revealing that consumers viewed smart-home technology like Google Home and Alexa as "dumb" and "impersonal," Digitools began immediately investing millions of dollars in humanoid robot AI systems like Jeeves. For over a year, Dad had traveled frequently to Japan and China to meet with machine automation visionaries so he could be on the forefront of robotics technology in the United States. This new AI would not only deliver basic, fully integrated smart-home technology, but could also be used for home security, basic eldercare, and childcare, in a 3-D form.

I cringed, remembering the last time I had to log a product

malfunction. Our voice-activated security system had required us to say "suspend the house alarm" to deactivate it, but after a power failure, it switched to Japanese mode and couldn't understand any of my commands. The police were auto-dialed. Guns were pulled. I was home alone. My dad was out of town, of course, and his company's legal representative came to our home in the middle of the night to field law enforcement questions. This napkin delivery error was nothing compared to that.

I closed my laptop and wrapped myself in a comforter, returning to *The Walking Dead*. I'd gotten pretty good at copying their horror makeup. I paused it and pulled out my sketchbook. Next Friday, I'd pick a look that was extra special and extra gory, showcasing visible bone and entrails. Maybe Nate-the-zombie-room-host would like it.

I smiled, thinking about Nate, in his too-baggy jeans and funny novelty shirt. He liked artificially cheesy snacks and foreign zombie horror movies, just like me.

No question about it: I'd look forward to seeing him again.

"Incoming message for Kate Anderson!" Our home communication system squawked at full volume, jolting me awake. "An urgent message from your father: 'Forgot to tell you I'm at the airport on a redeye flight to NYC. I'll be back on Wednesday. Use the emergency credit card for food if you need it.'"

I responded with one of the preset, canned replies on the wall unit. "No problem!"

"Also, happy birthday! I just ordered you a cake. It should be arriving now."

Canned reply: "No problem!" It didn't exactly make sense, but I didn't care.

The front gate squeaked, and one of Dad's company's delivery robots handed me a pink box, a padded envelope, and a bag of napkins and plastic utensils when I opened the front door. "Happy birthday, Kate," it singsonged in a British accent. The Mary Poppins–like voice didn't match the stark-black, faceless veneer of the delivery bot.

The only other person who remembered my birthday was my best friend Zoe because it was hers too. She was a year ahead of me and was a freshman at NYU's Tisch School, studying theater. She'd messaged me that morning on my cell phone that I rarely used.

Happy birthday, bitch!

Bitch, you too!

☺ have fun tonight!

Since she'd started college two months ago, we hadn't talked or messaged much. Maybe it was the time difference. I imagined her hanging out with her new roommates, going to dive bars with fake IDs, snort-laughing her head off, and forgetting me. Kate who?

I put the box on the coffee table and opened it. A midnight delivery of ice-cream cake from Baskin-Robbins. No inscription, just a generic chocolate cake with mint-chip ice cream, which was my dad's favorite, not mine. I hated artificial mint; it reminded me of toothpaste. I plopped down on the couch and pried apart the chocolaty cake layers, leaving the ice cream to melt in the box.

Then I tore open the padded envelope, hoping it was a present from Dad. But no, it was three books he had ordered for himself.

Rich Dad, Richer Dad.

Parenting Out Defiance.

And *It's Not Too Late to Raise a Winner.*

Happy birthday, Kate.

CHAPTER FOUR

Nate

TGIF! Finally.

It had been a whole week, and I still hadn't found a way to explain to Kate that my five-year-old sister had found the hidden wig and gave it some "style" by taking liberties, adding blunt layers with her Crayola safety scissors.

Not only that, but when I tried to tug-of-war it from her little hands, Lucy screeched, "No! *I* fix it!" and glued the cut hair back to the wig with pink, glittery Elmer's. Honestly, aside from the sparkles and random hair chunks that kept falling out, the mangier, matted mess looked much worse, but in a good way. I just hoped Kate wouldn't be mad that the wig had left my chain of custody and fallen into the hands of Baby Vidal Sassoon.

I took the wig with me to my mom's car so that Lucy couldn't do any more damage while I was at school. Mom worked from home on Fridays, which meant it was my day to drive the carpool. I absentmindedly threw the wig in the back seat of the Honda.

Zach was my first pickup. He was standing by his mailbox,

on time as usual. Clyde Hill Academy had a dress code, but Zach always bucked the system and wore the exact same thing every day: black *Starcraft* T-shirt, faded brown cords, and '70s-style metal glasses that he'd had since seventh grade, which were uncool then but somehow had gone retro and come back in style. He practically cannonballed into the seat behind me.

"What the hell?" Zach shouted, pulling the hairy, glittery mass from beneath his ass. As he tried to throw the wig on the floor, not-quite-dried strands of glitter hair clung to his fingers.

I glanced at him in the rearview. "Hey, it's not mine. It belongs to a friend. Pick it up."

"Gross," Zach muttered as he picked the wig back up and flung it at me. I tried to stuff it in the glove compartment, but it was jammed, so I dropped it into the center console drink holders.

Next stop, Jaxon, my best friend since middle school. He stood by his mailbox texting someone, his brown floppy hair nearly covering his eyes. He didn't bother to look up as he plopped down in the front passenger seat and shoved his backpack down on the floorboard. Must be a new game. Or a girl.

"You playing *Noob vs. Universe*?" I asked.

"Huh? Yeah," Jaxon mumbled. "Sorry, actually, no. Not right now. Annie's saying she can't ride with us today. She's getting a ride with her *new* boyfriend." He looked up with a pitying grin. "Sorry to break that to you, Natey. You missed your chance. Again."

Oh.

Annie.

A long time ago, she used to hang out with us a lot more. But then she grew boobs and mostly only hung out with girls after that. We still had classes with her, but that was the extent of our social interaction. She asked us to carpool this year out of the blue. She was a little out of the way, but we still did it.

Annie dated a lot. Even back in sixth grade, she liked to be taken on *real* dates with guys, like ones where you had seafood pasta plus dessert and watched a newly released movie at the neighborhood dine-in theater with unlimited popcorn and seats that reclined.

I shrugged. "So it's just the three of us then, until she dumps him. Whatever."

Zach grunted, "Us three, plus that thing." He leaned forward between our seats, pointing at the hairy mass sitting next to Jaxon and me.

With a full-body recoil, Jaxon nearly elbowed Zach's face. "What IS that?"

"Belongs to a friend," Zach answered, adjusting his glasses, parroting my previous explanation.

"But what IS it?"

I sighed. "It's hair. A wig, actually. And as Zach said, it belongs to a friend."

Jaxon's eyes bulged. "What kind of friend? Like, a *girl*friend?"

"I didn't say that." My face and neck burned so hot that I had to unbutton the top of my shirt. Luckily, neither of them noticed.

Jaxon leaned toward the wig. "But you have some girl's hair in your car," he accused.

Zach chimed in. "Maybe it belongs to a prostitute."

"Thanks, Zach."

Jaxon clapped his hands. "So, girlfriend or prostitute, which is it?"

I needed new friends. And an eject button for my passenger seats.

"It's neither." I sighed. "It's just an escape room prop, okay? I need to bring it to work tonight." I tried my best to make it sound like not a big deal. Not even a small deal. It was nothing. Nothing at all. I wiped the sweat off my forehead with the back of my hand.

Jaxon snorted. "For a minute there I thought you temporarily put aside your Tony Stark tycoon dreams and really had made time for a girlfriend. Honestly, I'd hoped it was true. Then you'd finally stop lusting after Annie."

Behind us, a car revved its engine, and in my rearview, a black Dodge Challenger tailgated so close it was like I was towing the damn thing.

Jaxon turned around. "Is that guy serious?" I hit the blinker to pull over, and Jaxon leaned over and swatted my arm. "Bro, you are *not* pulling over to let him pass. You're going the speed limit, and yeah, you're driving a little grandma-like in a grandma-like car, but you're *not* pulling over. He can reroute." Jaxon's nostrils flared like a bull ready to charge.

To our left, the revving grew louder, like those Harley-Davidson guys who drive around together with those high handlebars, engines fart-blasting for no good reason.

Zach muttered, "Oh God, oh God, oh God," and sank down into his seat.

The Challenger whipped around on my left, driving on the wrong side of the double yellow line, and passed me. With the windows down, the aviator-wearing passenger yelled, "Nice antique!" I couldn't initiate a stare-off because I had the bad habit of steering in the direction I looked.

But Jaxon got a good look. He rolled down his window and scooped a handful of change from Mom's parking meter fund in the glove compartment, which he'd yanked loose.

"Wait, what are you doing?" I squawked.

Jaxon didn't answer. He was too busy chucking the coins out the window with his trusty pitcher arm.

PING! PING! PING-PING! His aim was impeccable, showering the black Dodge with currency. My heart raced as I peeled around the first street I could take on my right. In the distance I heard the Dodge screech to a halt, but I'd already created some distance. If I weren't the one driving, my eyes would have been squeezed shut. My shoulder muscles clenched to my ears from the trauma.

Zach wiped his brow with the cuff on his sweatshirt. Exasperated, he groaned at Jaxon, "You owe Nate a buck fifty. At least."

Jaxon opened his wallet and pulled out two ratty bills. "Nice reflexes, Nate. All those driving games and that quick karate shit you do all the time came in handy." He dropped them in the cup holder on top of the wig. "Keep the change."

Sweat trickled down the sides of my face as I pulled into the one open spot in the Clyde Hill lot, between a Lexus SUV and Tesla sedan. "Okay, assholes. Get out."

"Thanks for the ride." Jaxon fussed with his hair in the window's reflection while I locked the car.

Zach mumbled something, maybe a "thank you." Not much of a talker, that guy. I gave him a head nod in return.

The parking lot on the south side of campus was closest to the senior hallway. The brand-new "coming soon" STEM building was also nearby. Sometime after the holidays, the headmaster would cut the ribbon to unveil state-of-the-art computer labs and science facilities, the best in the nation, thanks to the generous corporate endowment from Digitools, Inc., the largest, evilest tech behemoth in the world that happened to be headquartered in downtown Bellevue. Half of the kids at my school had parents who worked there.

At the school's side entrance, Peter Haskill the Fourth and his preppy gang of other Clyde Hill legacy bros leaned on the brick wall, chatting about how some guy from an opposing soccer team "deserved that punch to the face."

Pete Haskill. The Fourth. Clyde Hill Academy legacy. Captain of every varsity team sport offered. And the guy at school who frequently asked me how my karate skills were coming along and would then do some fake-ass karate chop on my neck, yelling, "Bruce Lee, ha-yaaa!" He'd done it for so many years I didn't even flinch anymore, and lately he'd ended it with a friendly hair muss. Back in junior high, he used to ask me to teach him Korean curse words, but my third-grade Hangul vocabulary couldn't offer him much on that front. I stopped going to the weekly half-day Saturday language classes because I had too many other activities. Something had to go. That something was Korean.

He also joked a lot about my skid status, meaning he did all the laughing, and I took the brunt of his "jokes." Other than this infrequent, ignorant, slapstick racism, he never targeted me, and his friends left me alone too. He wasn't a horrible guy to *me*, all things considered. He could be worse for sure—I'd seen him do worse—but that didn't mean he was a good guy to any of us scholarship kids. On a ten-point asshole scale, he was pretty up there. Pushing above the seven or higher range, into real assholedom.

Pete's boys moved toward the door, creating a bro barrier. Jaxon and Zach squeezed through the body fortress with no altercations.

But Pete stepped into my path when I tried to pass. "Hey, Nate. How's it going?" Most guys at our school called other guys by their last names. But my last name was Kim, and that made me sound like a girl. Thanks to bro courtesy, guys just called me Nate.

I stopped and gave him a half wave. "Hey, Haskill, good I guess?" My voice cracked.

Jaxon and Zach turned around to see if I needed any help. I waved them off. They went ahead to class but kept looking back as they walked down the hallway.

Pete used his massive hand to sweep his tousled Tom Holland hair out of his steely blue eyes. "Serious question for you, Nate." Apparently, we were getting right to business. Enough chitchatting.

"Okay."

"You're probably already done with college applications, right? You were doing early action?" He pulled his phone out of his front pants pocket to check the time.

"Yeah, I'm almost done. I still need to get the regular-decision ones ready just in case, but they're basically finished."

I racked my brain to anticipate his next comment, to get ahead of this line of questioning. Was he going to ask me for college application help? To write his college essays? I wouldn't put it past him.

"Good, good." He forced a smile, and I forced one back in return. Panic inched up my chest, wriggling like a worm.

"A bunch of us friends of yours at school have a favor to ask you. No pressure."

Yes, pressure. Enough with this Tony Soprano shit already.

"Since your early applications will be in soon, and schools are going to make their decisions on last year's transcript, we were wondering if we could pay you to, um"—he shrugged as he spoke—"throw your GPA? So like, some of us doing regular decision have a better chance at getting into college if you do that. It's like in sports, when the top-ranked team gets knocked out of the competition."

"Wait, what?" I balled my fists to stop their shaking. "What do you mean, throw my GPA? Are you talking making B's?" I paused. "Or C's? Or are you talking...F's? And how would this even work?"

He chuckled, the way villains did in movies before murdering someone. "Nothing that would get you in trouble or alert Headmaster Jacobson. A few of us could say we made honor roll and headmaster's list our first semester senior year if you and some other nerds bumped down a few spots. We were thinking a few B's is all, your excuse being getting senioritis. We'd be willing to pay more for C's, though, obviously."

Obviously? Earning money this way hadn't even crossed my mind, though, knowing Pete, maybe it should have. This was shady as shit. He'd found some weird loophole that made this all technically possible. The bulk of the college scholarships I'd applied for would not be compromised because the high GPA requirement was through end of junior year, and not many of them took into account my fall and spring senior semesters. I'd *maybe* be blowing my shot at valedictorian. But could I live with myself knowing I'd whored myself out for some cash?

"You asking Sanchez too?" She was the other person in our class with the highest GPA. But she wasn't on scholarship—her dad was some hotshot executive at Amazon. She didn't need the money.

"I wanted to talk to you first. Seemed like we could come up with a mutually beneficial arrangement. You help us out. We help a skid."

I cringed. In other words, I was poor and needed money, and he and his friends were rich and had lots of money. See? We could help each other, in Pete's simple view of demand-side capitalism.

I went ahead and asked what I wanted to know. "How much money are we talking here?"

"We can talk price later, but the gist of it is, we'd make it worth your time." His gaze traveled up and down my body. "I like you, bro, so I'd like this to work out in your favor. It'd probably be enough to get your mom a new car, one of those that self-park. Depending on how extreme you'd want to go, though, maybe we could get you a self-driving car, like mine."

He had a Tesla Model X. The one with the ridiculous bat-wing doors.

I already knew the cost of a new Accord, around thirty grand. A self-parking one would probably be a few thousand more. I'd hoped Mom's car might last a few more years so I could buy her a newer one after I graduated from college.

Pete was offering me thirty grand, or maybe even more, without having to wait four years. With any leftover cash, I could invest in stocks or put all of that into a savings account. Or just buy Mom a brand-spanking-new sedan and use the extra money to seed my business ideas. Her car could come with Bluetooth and seat warmers and other fancy shit like that.

The warning bell rang. Three minutes to get to first period.

Pete and his buddies moved aside. "Oh, and for my little brother, we could offer twenty thousand for you to take his SAT. But we can talk about that later. It's not as urgent 'cause he's a sophomore," Pete said.

I pushed the door with my entire body weight and exhaled loudly when I heaved myself through.

Damn it. This was a lot of money on the table. It was shady. It was wrong. But it was tempting.

With all the morning's painful events, I tried to focus on the positive. In just ten more hours, I would see zombie Kate again.

....

"This is too hard!" Lucy wailed, throwing her yellow pencil across the kitchen table. She folded her arms and buried her face. All you could see were two short, lopsided pigtails rising and falling with her breath.

She was right. What kind of kindergarten teacher thought it would be a good idea to do a multibranch family tree project for homework? A clueless, sadistic one, that's who. A teacher who didn't realize that Korean families like ours didn't have any relatives living close by to ask about familial history. That families like ours maybe didn't know full names of our great-grandmas or great-grandpas. That both sets of grandparents had passed away and we never got to know them because they lived in another country, across an ocean. Mom's parents died before I was born, and Dad's parents only visited the States once when I was a baby before they passed away.

I helped with Lucy's assignment the best I could while wolfing down my frozen dinner. "Mom, Lucy needs to fill out her family tree homework. It's due tomorrow. She needs our grand-parents' names. Your parents and Dad's parents."

Mom's breathing deepened as she hand-washed the dishes in the sink. The plates clinked against the coffee mugs when she added them to the drying rack.

"Mom, Lucy needs our grandparents' names," I said louder, rephrasing it slightly.

With the back of her right wrist, she brushed her short, jet-black hair from her eyes. "Yi Sung-Soo," she said finally. "That was my father name. Kang In-Sook was my mother." She shook out the excess water from a washed ziplock bag and turned it inside out to dry on the rack.

Lucy scribbled down the names on the blank lines. "How do you spell it? I wish we had an Alexa to ask how to spell stuff. All my friends have one. Mollie's can make fart noises if you ask it."

Mom painstakingly rattled off the spelling, letter by letter. "You don't need any Alexa. You have Nate. He is *almost* as smart as Alexa," she joked.

"And I can make fart noises too," I teased. "Just say the command."

Lucy giggled as she wrote over her words a second time in a black marker, making our family tree more permanent. She asked, "Am I done?" and slid the paper next to my drink.

I shook my head. "We need our other two grandparents on Dad's side."

A glass tumbler slipped from Mom's soapy hands into the porcelain sink. Lucy covered her ears and yelped.

We both knew not to bother Mom while she picked up the pieces of her literal slipup. The number one unspoken rule in this Korean family was that my parents could point out and punish kids' mistakes, but we weren't allowed to point out theirs. We were never, ever allowed to question their judgment. If I'd been the one to drop that glass, Dad would have scolded, *Nate, you never look what you are doing! Jeongshin charyeo!* As if clumsiness could be punished out of me.

Dad walked in just as Mom finished cleaning up. Lucy asked for the grandparents' names again. At the rate this homework was taking to complete, we'd be finished when Lucy was old enough to be a grandparent herself.

He opened the fridge and pulled out a Hite beer that he'd just gotten from the Korean supermarket. With his other hand, he pinched his forehead. "Kim Jung-ho is my father. Kim Jung-hee is mother." The slam of the refrigerator door and the loud crack of the can opening punctuated the end of his sentence.

Lucy paused. "Wait, Appa. You said *is*. Twice. Are they still alive?" She'd heard the same thing I did. But I didn't dare violate the Kim family rule by questioning his word choice.

Dad abruptly left the room and didn't give her an answer. Lucy puppy-dog-eyed me. *Were our grandparents alive?* Mom and Dad had come into my bedroom one night when I was Lucy's age to tell me our grandparents on Dad's side had died in a car accident and that going to Korea for the funeral was too expensive. I cried and cried that night, devastated that I'd never have grandparents to visit, and that no one would visit me. That no grandparents would call me to wish me a happy birthday. No Christmas presents either. Not that they ever did any of that anyway when they were alive. I'd never questioned anything my parents told me about our family. We both turned to Mom for answers, hoping she would explain what was going on.

Mom spoke, finally, crushing my hope. "He mean to say *was*, not *is*."

He'd made a grammatical blunder.

I'd never seen my mom book it out of the kitchen so fast. We heard muffled shouting behind my parents' bedroom door, but the Kim family rule prevented me from barging in there to ask why they were yelling at each other.

Lucy put a smiley face on the top of her paper. "All done! You can make fart noises now."

I watched Lucy slide off her chair, cramming her homework into her open backpack by my feet. Even with my excitement about seeing Kate at work, I couldn't shake the feeling that my parents were hiding something.

CHAPTER FIVE

Kate

Could hair glands sweat? I had to assume yes, because it happened when I wore too heavy of a sweater, or when I got the flu, or when my anxiety took over both my immune and nervous systems, especially before theater performances. Or, in this case, when I knew I'd be seeing Nate again.

My head itched so much that I needed a full dousing in cortizone cream. That's what I got for buying a cheap replacement zombie wig from a nonreviewed third party on Amazon.

In the escape room parking lot, I scratched the hell out of my head using all ten fingernails, from my hairline, to above my ears, to the back of my neck. Note to self: google "scalp eczema relief."

"Fluffing out your zombie hair?"

I halted, fingers midscratch.

Nate propped the door to the building open with his foot, waving me in with a huge grin. Not only had he come early, but he'd been inside the whole time. Had he seen me progressively erupt into a sweat fountain? He definitely witnessed me scratching like a mangy dog. Yet here he was, smiling at me. Making my head sweat even more.

I hurried inside, and he closed the door behind us. "I came through the back. If I had known you were here in front the whole time, I'd have opened the door sooner. I was checking for a package."

Okay, it's your turn to say something, Kate.

"I'm wearing camo. I'm surprised you saw me."

Kate. Really?

He raised an eyebrow. A single laugh burst out. "You're such a clown. I brought your wig back. It's inside."

He'd found it.

Of course he had found it. Seven whole days had passed for him to discover the giant hair mass on his passenger seat. It wasn't invisible.

He led me to his locker and fished around in his backpack. His Clyde Hill cross-country shirt fell out, and he quickly stuffed it back in. Damn, he went to the only school my dad's hefty donations couldn't get me into. Standardized tests were among the highest on my list of things that ruined my life, ranked just above my eczema. My test scores were barely above average, and my grades weren't good enough, the headmaster said, and they couldn't make exceptions. My community theater accolades and national youth screenwriting awards weren't enough to gain admission.

Clyde Hill was nearly one hundred and fifty years old and a feeder into all the Ivys. At night, Clyde Hill looked majestic and impressive, like Hogwarts, but without the magic.

But back to the wig.

Damn it.

"You want it back?" Nate dangled the wig enclosed in a gallon-size ziplock bag. Wincing hard, he added, "My little sister messed with it. I'm so sorry. She was trying to give it bangs. I can pay for it if you want."

"Oh, that's fine," I chirped. "Thanks for bringing it today. Sorry if it scared you." I unsealed the bag and airlifted the tangled wad of hair. Holy hell, it was so matted and hacked up that I couldn't tell which way was the front anymore. "I like the glitter, and the, um, chunks of missing hair." I smiled. "Very grotesque, in a good way." Peering closer, I saw that the avant-garde hairstylist had tried to make bangs for the front *and* the back. "Glittery pink doesn't go with my camo look, but maybe I'll wear it next time. How old is she, by the way?"

"My sister? She's five. There's an eleven-year gap." He paused. "She was an accident."

"Five's a cute age. I bet she's a cute accident." I remembered kindergarten as being one of the best times of my life: new school, new backpack, new outfits. Both parents hugging me and sending me off to class.

He snorted. "Lucy's stubborn and throws tantrums like it's

a requirement for survival, but yeah, when she's not a pain in the ass, she's pretty cute." Nate nibbled his bottom lip. "Um, in case this happens again, maybe you can give me your phone number so I can consult you about which glitter glue color she uses next time?"

He took a step closer and focused his gaze on my face. He had these magnetic, dark-brown eyes that made my knees go wobbly.

How could I explain to him that the phone my dad gave me was collecting dust on my desk because it was the property of his company? Dad could (and did) monitor my location and recorded my calls, so I stopped carrying the phone around. He was more overprotective now than ever before. The iron security gates, surveillance cameras, the GPS tracking. A teenager raised by a single, career-obsessed father who was CEO at a security technology company. Lucky me.

"Um, let me get your number instead." *Think of something, think of something.* "I'm getting a new phone. We've moved around a lot because of my dad's work, and I wanted to get a 206 Seattle number. I swear I'll input your number into my phone once I buy it. It's on my to-do list this week." With a stammer, I added, "Y-you'll be the first new number I enter, so congratulations." My plan was to get one of those burner phones that drug dealers and pimps used. One that Dad couldn't trace. I'd seen it in movies.

Nate pulled a business card from his back pocket. "Cool. Here's my number and email." A matte black card with sans serif font on the front. **Nate Kim, Entrepreneur.** His contact info was on the back.

"How many of these have you given out?"

He shrugged. "Uh, you're the only one. I won them as part of the grand prize of the city's Young Inventors contest."

My eyes bulged. "You're an inventor? Wow!"

A wide grin spread across his face. "Well, sort of. I like to take ideas and make them better. Like, you know how toilet seats are heated in Japan and Korea?"

I shook my head.

"Okay, maybe it's not a well-known fact. Anyway, I invented one for the U.S. market, and it uses a long-lasting, partial-solar-powered battery that you can charge outside. It's still glitchy with limited variable heating functionality. By that I mean, it has an on-and-off switch, and that's it. You can choose between a heated or not-heated bottom."

"I didn't know you had so much passion for toilets," I teased.

"I just picked something easy and useful." His rubbed his chin with the back of his hand. "I don't love poop or anything—"

I interrupted. "I was kidding. I'm not a poop fan either." The heat pulsing in my body went straight to my cheeks, setting them on fire. Attempting more humor, I said, "I'll keep this in a safe place," and slid the card in my bra, like I'd seen sassy, sexy women do on TV shows. What Hollywood never revealed was that the stabby corners on rectangular card stock were extremely painful when poking boob flesh. My eyes quickly filled with tears of agony.

A voice boomed from the hallway, "Can you two stop talking about excrement? The first group starts in like five minutes." One of the zombie actors entered the employee area and slapped Nate on the back. "Hiya, boss man."

Nate glanced at his watch. "Damn it. I have to go. I need to collect waivers. But, uh, message me? And I hope you get to come out of the closet this time," he said, rushing out the door. He turned around, and his eyes widened. "Er, not in a gay way. I mean, not that there's a problem with that at all, but you know, good luck with your role."

The zombie dude and I took the back passage to the escape room and took our positions: him behind the chained metal door, me in the supply closet. I pulled out the business card from my cleavage for immediate relief and shut the door. Slivers of light streamed in from the vents at the top of the locker-like closet. Crouching down, I pulled my key chain flashlight from my pants pocket. I flicked the light on and committed the business card info to memory.

Nate Kim.

Entrepreneur.

NateKimEntrepreneur@gmail.com.

Nate Kim.

And Kate.

Kate Kim.

Nate and Kate Kim. I liked the sound of that.

With some downtime squatting in the closet, my mind drifted to an earlier conversation I'd had with Zoe this morning on video chat.

"Hey!" she'd said. "Sorry I'm calling so early. You busy?" She adjusted her chunky black glasses and pulled the camera back so I could see her newly dyed purple hair. "Whaddya think? Oh, last night I saw a girl at a school Future Filmmakers event who looked just like you, and I got all sad because we hadn't talked in so long."

Zoe was going to fancy film events now. Fancy college girl. "LOVE the purple. I'm glad you called. I miss your face." I'd sighed. "I wish I could visit you. Are you coming home soon?"

She'd shrugged noncommittally. "I'm staying here for Thanksgiving, but probably coming home for Christmas for a few days. You'd love New York. You should visit me! NYU's campus is a little hard to get used to, though. It's all spread out all over downtown. But it doesn't matter. I've found my theater people. None are as talented as you, though." She winked.

She always knew what to say to cheer me up, even at six in the morning. "Thanks. I wish I could go to Tisch. My grades are borderline." I bit back my yawn. "Same with my SAT scores."

"Well, I'm getting more involved in the musical theater scene here. If you wanted to take a gap year or visit this summer, you can stay with me. I have a trundle bed. And my roommates have annoying boyfriends who stay over all the time and don't pay rent. So, whatever. You can be my houseguest!"

"Thanks for the offer, and thanks for calling. I'll think about it. I have to get ready for school."

"Yeah, I gotta get to class. Why'd I think it was a good idea to take Russian at ten a.m.?" She scrunched her nose in the camera. "So think about it. New. York. Freakin'. Cit-aaay! And if you're listening to this conversation, Kate's dad, I'm just kidding about all of this."

If it was his decision, Dad would never let me go to New York to act and write screenplays. *Theater is garbage,* he'd said to me in the parking lot after this past spring performance of our school's production of *Kiss Me, Kate,* not caring that I got the starring female role. It was his first and only time at one of my performances—Mom had gone to all of them before she got sick last year and had been so proud of me. That didn't matter anymore.

It was hard thinking back to those days with Mom. I tried my best to forget them.

That night of the performance, I cried most of the way home. Dad kept flipping the channels between his stupid classic rock stations, filling the quietness between us.

He finally spoke again when we pulled into the driveway. He gave me a life lesson, or in his view, a pep talk.

"Kate, you're almost an adult now. You really need to toughen up." His shoulders straightened. "Crying always shows weakness. You'll never go anywhere in life if you're weak."

I stared straight ahead, refusing to look at him. "I *am* tough. I got the lead role and beat out twenty other girls for the part."

He barked a harsh laugh. "You've got to be kidding me. Theater is the epitome of softness. When I see any job candidate who majored in theater, I toss the résumé straight into the trash."

"Soft? I've been rejected over and over again for so many roles and just kept auditioning. I finally landed a big role this time." I swiped both eyes with the palms of my hands. "I wish Mom were here." My voice broke apart with those last words.

He opened his door and stepped out into the light rain. "Well, I'm sorry. She's not." With a door slam, he'd ended our conversation.

Was he right? Was I weak? Now, wedged into this closet, tears dripped down my cheeks and combined with my zombie stage makeup, forming a gray river delta down to my shirt. Maybe he *was* right.

I'd listened to him and had applications ready to fire off to a few colleges with strong business programs because that's what Dad wanted. He was the one paying for the application fees. But all I really wanted was to be on my own, performing theater, far away from here. If I was going to leave home, leave Dad behind, I needed a plan. I needed plane tickets. I needed money. Untraceable cash money. Dad couldn't track me down then. Dabbing my sleeve cuffs on my face, I made a mental list of all the things I needed to do before I could leave town.

The escape room door drifted open, widening just enough so I could see the fresh new crop of participants through the closet vents. Nate's hands flailed with excitement as he chatted with a few of them. Noticing the unlatched door, he shot a shy smile in my direction just before closing it, making my heart beat double-time.

If I was stuck in Seattle for a while, at least I had Nate Kim—entrepreneur and toilet aficionado—to keep me company.

CHAPTER SIX

Nate

Top three things running through my head:

One, did Kate blow me off with the whole "I don't have a phone" thing? I asked for her number—quite suavely if you asked me—and she basically saw through the ruse and was like, *Hell nah*. Who gives a shit about having a local area code? No one, that's who. Yeah, she blew me off.

Two, if she *did* text me, would it be weird to tell her that she shouldn't send me any huge downloads because I had a very limited family data plan? It would be weird, right? Yeah, it'd be weird.

Third, did she think that I thought she was a lesbian? The last thing I said was something about her coming out of a closet, and she didn't respond or joke around after that. Maybe she *was* a lesbian, and she thought that I was being weird about it.

Damn. She hated me.

Major Kate hate.

But Kate hate or not, I had a job to do. I couldn't let this whole thing rattle me.

Deep breath. "Welcome to the Zombie Laboratory. I'm Nate, and I'll be your host for the evening. Can I...uh...can I..." Oh God. I'd forgotten my lines.

My mind went completely blank. Well, except for those three previously mentioned Kate things occupying 100 percent of my brain capacity.

Fifteen customer service reps from Amazon, there for a management team-building exercise, witnessed me struggling with my lines and immediately jumped in to bombard me with ideas. So helpful, these guys.

"How about you take it from the top, Nate? Start over and get the flow going again."

"Do you have a handbook or instructions? Maybe you can reference that?"

"Is there a problem? If so, maybe we report the problem to management?"

As the Amazonians brainstormed solutions to solve my brain fart on my behalf, a loud, unsubtle "PSSSST!" came from inside the escape room. I opened the door and popped my head inside.

"Um, yeah?"

Kate whispered from the closet, "Your line is 'Can I get a show of hands of anyone who has been to an escape room before?'"

"You...heard that?" *Please just kill me now.*

"Yeah, my hearing's pretty good."

Shit. "How did you know my lines? You remembered them from last week?"

She giggled. "I want to be an actress. To do that, you memorize a lot. It's the only thing I'm good at. Now go back to your group before they ruin all the fun."

Frustrated, I pressed my forehead on the door frame. This was the most embarrassing situation ever. The only positive thing about it was that I got to chat with Kate again. "Thanks!" I shut the door and jogged back to the group to try the game's preamble one more time. What was wrong with me? I was completely out of my zone, like someone let go of a full balloon before tying the neck, sending it sputtering and spitting saliva in all directions.

No more mistakes this time. I couldn't let Kate overhear me screw up twice, and then help me with my lines, even if that would mean visiting her again. I'd rather shrivel up and die in beta dude hell for all eternity than let that happen.

I took a deep breath and took it from the top.

....

The rest of the night passed pretty seamlessly. I still couldn't tell if Kate was mad at me or even remotely interested. So the next night, when my phone buzzed, I did a double take.

Holy. Shit.

Hey. It's Kate. This is my number

YES. She texted me. She actually did it.

"Nate, you fucking cocksucker, we just lost because of you!" Jaxon screamed so loudly my ears rang. A midbattle text distraction wasn't the best game strategy. Sorry, team.

"Guys, I gotta go. Something came up." I tore off my headset and stared at my phone. Multitasking wasn't my forte. And girls trumped this multiplayer shooter. Every time. Especially zombie-loving, funny, cute ones.

My heartbeat raced as I replied to Kate. Hey. Thanks ☺ What's your last name? So I can put it in my contacts. You never told me

Anderson. Immediate response. Yes! *Can you hop on a quick video call? I have a question.*

Was there any downside to this? Couldn't think of anything. The best-case scenario was her asking me out on a seafood pasta plus dessert plus movie date. No, actually, best-case scenario was her wanting to come over, no fancy date stuff.

Fingers crossed.

Sure, I'm around

Only a few seconds to decide the best backdrop for our video call. Preteen Nate had plastered the bedroom walls with Marvel and *Star Wars* paraphernalia, shark drawings, and glow-in-the-dark space decals, decor that I hadn't thought twice about until now. The nautical-themed sheets and comforter on my too-small twin bed were impossible to remove in time. I'd have to avoid them in my video call cinematography.

My parents' room wasn't an option, with their long, Korean-countryside vertical wall hangings, multicolored decorative tassels hanging from their bedposts, and a twenty-four-by-thirty-six-inch framed oil painting of Jesus's crucifixion above the headboard. My sister was downstairs watching *PAW Patrol* and banging on the piano, so the living room was out. The bathroom? Um, no. No more associations between me and toilets.

I had no choice but to position myself on my bed in front of my "Rebel Scum!" poster, a birthday gift from Annie, Jaxon, and Zach last year, the least embarrassing background in the entire house.

BZZZZ.

BZZZZZZ.

BZZZZZZZZ.

I answered on the fourth ring, to make it look like I wasn't just desperately sitting around waiting for her call.

"Hey," I said, my stomach somersaulting.

Kate leaned in and tossed her long, brown hair locks behind her shoulders. "Hey!"

I'd gotten so used to zombified Kate, it took me a second to register this was the girl beneath all the makeup.

Behind her was a super-sophisticated, fancy white backdrop with wall moldings, like something you'd see in one of those house renovation shows that my mom loved binge-watching on HGTV. *Waaaa, so fancy!* She'd point at the screen, mouth gaping. *Jae-Woo, my dream house!*

"Hey," I said. Again.

Oh God. Nate, you suck.

A second or two passed, and my mind went blank. There was only one thing running through my head: *KATE Kate KATE Kate KATE Kate KATE Kate KATE Kate KATE Kate KATE Kate KATE Kate KATE Kate KATE Kate KATE Kate.*

She finally spoke, cutting through my inner *Kate KATE Kate KATE* commentary. "What are you up to?"

Say something normal. "Me? Ah, not much. I just finished up a game with some buddies."

Wow, if I had to rate this conversation, it would get an F minus. Zero stars. The absolute worst. We had no problem chatting in person. What the hell was happening here?

She nodded and pursed her lips. "I like your poster."

Kate KATE Kate KATE Kate KATE Kate KATE.

I turned around, looking at the words *Rebel Scum!* plastered on top of an image of a dramatically exploding Death Star. "Oh yeah? Me too. I was big into *Star Wars* for a while, like, I dunno, sixt—um, seventeen years?" I didn't want her to know I was younger than her.

Her eyes crinkled as she laughed. "Well, I like it a lot."

My speech sped up like a self-conscious auctioneer. "So last year, for my birthday, a-bunch-of-my-friends-got-me-*Star-Wars*-stuff-like-collectible-figurines-and-*Star-Wars*-tickets-and-popcorn"—breath—"Annie-picked-out-that-poster-because-she-used-to-say-I-walked-as-slow-and-stiff-like-an-Imperial-Walker-heh-but-she's-just-a-friend."

Annie and I were barely still friends. Why did I mention her? Beads of sweat spawned across on my forehead. I didn't want Kate to see me wipe them off because then she'd know I was a nervous mess. "Naaaate! I need help!" my little sister cried out from the bottom of the stairs.

Kate's eyes got all puppy-dog-like. "Awww, someone needs you. Her voice is so cute!"

"Yeah, hold on for a sec." I put my laptop down on the bed. Out of the camera's view, I swiped my forehead in a semicircle with my shirtsleeve, like I was on a one-time windshield wiper setting.

I shouted, "Lucy? What happened?" as I barreled down the stairs.

Pointing at the screen, she shrieked, "There's a ghost in the TV!" The DVR recording was choppy and poorly digitized. The characters' askew faces and bodies, formed from blocks of misaligned squares, resembled a Picasso cubist painting.

"Sorry, Luce, it looks like the channel we recorded from didn't air correctly. Maybe something's wrong with the cable connection. Can you watch something else?"

"No, no, no! I want *PAW Patrol!*" By her quick escalation to hysterics, you'd think I'd asked, "You want me to fart on your head instead? Because that's what you're getting. Lots and lots of farts!"

Lucy threw herself onto the couch and buried her face in a

throw pillow. She screech-gasped with shuddering shoulders for nearly twenty seconds, to the point of oxygen deprivation. She looked up from her cry-muffling cushion with red, swollen eyes and asked in a clear, high-pitched voice, "Can I have ice cream?"

"No, you can't have ice cream," I said. "That's a special treat for when you try your best or accomplish something. You need to toughen up, Lucy Goosey."

Probably not the best pep talk for a kindergartner, in retrospect. She went back into pterodactyl mode, screeching and sobbing, while I just stood with my arms crossed. Being the youngest, she got away with a lot. Lucy needed to learn about having thick skin, not taking things personally. She was five and always throwing tantrums. She wasn't going to get anywhere in life by being a crybaby.

At the rate she was going, she'd wear herself out in no time, and then I could put her to bed early.

"Let's go upstairs," I said, scooping up some of her favorite toys near my feet. "You can play in the hallway in front of my room, and I'll come out after my call with my friend, and then we can play Noah's Ark." She had a hand-me-down Fisher-Price toy ark and dozens of pairs of animals that she loved more than anything else in the world. Some belonged to the original set. Other animals she'd added on her own, like her pairs of My Little Ponies and Pokémon. Lucy's face lit up, and she dragged her giant stuffed panda up the stairs. "Coco comes too, to watch me play," she said firmly.

Minor crisis averted, for now. I followed Coco and Lucy up the stairs and dumped the toys I'd collected on the hall floor. "I'll come out and play soon. Knock on the door if it's an emergency."

"Okeydokey!"

For ten years I'd been an only child, and then surprise! Instant little sister. My world changed after that. My parents had less time for me, and I was always tasked with being the babysitter. They constantly scrambled to make ends meet, thanks to having another mouth to feed. Thanks to having more birthday and Christmas presents to buy. Thanks to full-day preschool costs. None of this was my sister's fault of course, I knew that, but there were plenty of times like now when it sure would have been nice to have the house to myself. So I could take a call with Kate without worrying about Lucy.

I hopped back on my bed and was greeted with Kate's smiling face. She stayed on! "Sorry about that. Minor kindergartner meltdown. Where were we again?"

She laughed. "You were gone a while. I was worried! We were just exchanging boring pleasantries, to be honest."

Right. Don't say "hey" again. "Well, YOU wanted to talk to ME, right?" I smirked. "So, what's up?"

She scrunched her nose. "I need your help. It's something I've been researching that sounds like fun. I think."

"That's not quite a ringing endorsement," I joked. "And I

never commit to promises before I hear what the favor is. It's too risky." Honestly, though, for Kate, maybe I would.

Kate smiled, one dimple appeared near her mouth. "It's not like I'm asking you to do some kind of *Ocean's Eleven*–level Bitcoin heist." She took a deep breath. "I want to move to New York one day. To do that, I need money. There's this local contest sponsored by Zeneration, and I need a partner to enter. Remember the flyer at work? It's a weekend zombie survivalist competition, and it starts in a few weeks. The first twenty-five teams to sign up are automatically entered. For everyone else it's lottery. There's an entry fee of one hundred dollars, but the grand prize is fifty thousand dollars if you're the first team to finish. We get zombie-themed swag too." She sat up straight and then leaned toward the camera. "Would you be my teammate? Pleeeeease? I can't think of any team of people who knows more about zombies than you and me."

One hundred dollars was a shit ton of money, but there was also a chance to win a much bigger shit ton of money. And bonus: I'd get to throat-punch zombies, and maybe she'd share a tent with me. Not that anything would happen between us, but even if something did, or didn't, hell fucking yeah I'd do it! *Calm the fuck down, Nate. Be cool.* "Um, sure, count me in, I guess."

"Really? Nate, you're seriously the best! I'll send you an email with all the details. The registration opens tomorrow afternoon, and I want to get one of those first spots."

My sister burst through the door, no knocking, crying, of course. "Nate! My boat broke! All the animals died! They hit an iceberg!"

Oh my God, not now, Lucy! But I had to give her credit for the A-plus dramatic Noah's Ark meets *Titanic* story line. "Lucy Goosey, I'll come out really soon, and we can save all the animals in a special rescue boat." I pushed her back through the door and scanned the room for a pretend ship. The closest thing I found was old baseball mitt. Eh, it would have to do. It was boatlike enough.

"Gotta go, Kate, I have to save some soon-to-be endangered species. Oh, wait! Want me to sign us up for the competition, or do you want to?"

Worry flashed across her face. "Could...could you do it? I'll pay you back. I promise."

"Uh, sure." Whatever spooked her, it wasn't too big of a deal because she grinned and clapped. "Want to come by sometime after school?" I asked. "We can discuss zombie survival strategy. I'll text you my address."

"That'd be great! I can pay you back then."

I couldn't help but mirror the beaming smile on her face. "Cool!"

I closed the laptop to assure she couldn't see me dance. Best day of my life. Ever.

My sister cried out from somewhere down the hallway. "Nate? NATE? Uh-oh!"

"Uh-oh, what?" I flung open my bedroom door.

No Lucy.

No ark.

Shrieks came from the bathroom. "Nate! The animals can't swim! Uh-oh, Noah's stuck sideways in the toilet! I made a flood."

I missed being an only child.

CHAPTER SEVEN

Nate

The next Friday, Kate stopped by my house to pay her share of the Zombiegeddon team entry fee. Due to a plumbing emergency, the escape room was closed for the night. I had let Mom know a friend from work was coming over, but she was out shopping at Target when Kate arrived.

We headed straight to my room and hopped on my computer. "Okay, we're officially registered." I forwarded her the email confirmation. "Damn, that fee was so expensive!" A hundred dollars! Goodbye, Xbox Live game pass fund. You'll be sorely missed.

Kate beamed as she handed me a crisp fifty-dollar bill. "I deposited my first paycheck."

The competition was the same weekend as my regional cross-country qualifiers, but the potential upside of this competition (cash money!) outweighed the benefit of medaling in the regional meet (no cash money!). Truthfully, I hadn't gotten any faster over the last year, and I already had plenty of sports fodder in my early-action college applications.

My Visine-soaked eyes twitched from pulling an all-nighter. I'd spent hours combing through most of the competition's excessively long terms and conditions, studying the campgrounds and the nearby vacant properties on Google Maps, running offensive and defensive strategies (kill versus hide) through my head. The competition had one simple objective: to be the first team to make it to the other side of the campground alive.

I could do that.

We could do that.

She flipped through my printouts. "Hey, did they ask for a team name?"

I clicked on the registration email. "Um. Don't be mad. In the blank space for team name, I wrote 'TBD.'" I shot her a grin-wince. "I should have read the instructions more closely. I thought I could go back to that later. Sorry."

To my relief, she laughed. "Team TBD? Nice alliteration."

"I also forged my dad's signature on the parent consent for—"

I stopped talking when door creaked open. My mom came in with a tray of snacks and juice. "Nuts, apple slice, Cheez-It, and Oreo." Her eyes widened when she saw Kate, but then her mouth curved into a smile, which wasn't a good thing for me. "Nate say you like cheesy crunchy food. He remind me several time to buy at Target this afternoon."

Oh no.

"I always tell him he play video game with same friend. I see he make *new friend*."

Oh no.

Kate said, "Thank you for having me over. And for the food and drinks, Mrs. Kim."

Mom continued smiling.

Shit.

"Nate never bring home a girl before."

I coughed some juice out of my nose. "Thanks, Mom, you can go now."

"You have two cookie each," she said. "No fighting."

She wouldn't leave. Instead, she puttered around, straightening my bookshelf and picking up some dirty clothes I'd stuffed under my bed. She pulled out the pajamas I'd worn that week and some old Pokémon cards from under the dresser.

I cleared my throat. "Mom, can you please leave? I'll clean up later. I promise."

She held up the trading cards and asked Kate, "You play these too?"

"When I was younger," Kate said, amused.

"He used to play all time. Pokémon this. Pokémon that. You know what that make me? His mother?"

Kate shot me a concerned look, and I shrugged. I had no idea what in the hell Mom was talking about.

She took the bait. "What does that make you, Mrs. Kim?"

Mom held her head high and puffed her chest. "I am Poké-MOM!"

Kate snorted hard. Any harder and she would need to see an ENT specialist.

Mom jokes. So grossly underrated compared to Dad jokes.

"Oh God, can you leave please?" The warmth in my cheeks spread through my whole body. I was on fire, and not in the "boy, you got this!" sense. Thankfully, my mom exited quickly, taking the laundry and Pokémon cards with her.

Kate wiped her eyes. "Oh my God, your mom—she's so funny!"

"Yeah, she's a real riot," I said flatly.

She took a small handful of Cheez-Its and popped them in her mouth. "Fank your murm for thith," she said with her mouth full, giggling as she walked over to the short walnut bookcase under my window. Kate examined the trophies my mom had lined up in a perfect row just before I kicked her out.

She swallowed. "Damn. You really do Krav Maga? Isn't that the martial arts where you attack to kill?"

"Yeah, that's the one. But it's more like, defend yourself to the death, for me at least. I have two more belts to go." The last two were basically impossible to get. For brown and black belt, I'd need to master choke holds plus gun and knife disarmament, which would take several years minimum. That was some military-level shit. "All you learn the first few months is how to kick a perp in the balls."

"Well, that sounds handy. Or should I say, *ballsy*? Can you teach me sometime?"

I snort-coughed my juice again. It burned. So painful. "You can lend my mom that joke. And sure. I'd be happy to let you practice pretend-kicking me in the balls. Maybe after work one night."

We smiled, and our eyes locked for a fleeting moment. She glanced down and went back to trophy scrutiny. "You got first place in one hundred meters last month? Wow, you're fast." She peered closer at a small, shield-shaped plaque next to my latest track award. "And only second place in archery?" she smirked. Wiping the dust off my name with her index finger, she asked, "Who got first place?"

"This guy Nate Bishop. He cheated, though. He took an extra turn. But he's not around anymore." Nate moved to Olympia a month ago and I heard he went by Nathaniel now, his full name. Good riddance. He really was a better shot than me, and all around a better, stronger, faster Nate. Way better looking than me, too, the bastard. Nate 2.0.

"No rock climbing or mountaineering awards, Nate? Such an underachiever."

I scratched my brow. "Mountain climbing is on my bucket list. Rock climbing's not my thing. Way too scary. Too high for me."

"I was kind of joking about the last two things. I don't have any awards or trophies like these. I only do theater, and I never win trophies for getting my lines right."

She didn't ask any more questions, a relief really, because no normal person likes to talk about their fears.

By some stroke of luck, I'd moved all of my grade school trophies and other embarrassing old arts and crafts projects to my closet just a few days earlier. She didn't see my cringeworthy honorable mention for fifth-grade spelling bee or my most improved fourth-grade soccer certificate. "Most improved" awards were the worst: you sucked at something and got better. It didn't mean you were actually any good.

"This is so cute," she squealed, lifting my "Fastest Tadpole—Freestyle" medal from the shelf. Crap, I'd thought that I'd thrown that out years ago, or at least had moved it to the closet with my other kiddie awards. I quit swimming the day we tried the high-dive board. Thankfully, she put the medal back on the bookcase, next to my Eagle Scout award.

She bit her bottom lip and glanced up. "Actually, now that I'm thinking about it, I forgot that I got the Gold Award in Girl Scouts. For first aid, starting fires, and setting up camp. I'm good with a compass and stainless-steel cooking utensils too. And I'm excellent at up-selling boxes of cookies." She took a dramatic bow. "I earned patches, not trophies, though. Maybe I'll wear them all to intimidate our competition."

My snort laughter cleared the juice from my nose.

I pointed at her ratty zombie wig peeking out of her tote bag. "Well, if you wear that too, everyone will steer clear of us, even the zombies."

She punched my arm, then jumped. "Argh, shouldn't have done that. Don't put me in a choke hold and snap my neck! Save your energy for the competition."

Stepping back and taking in all of the trophies in their entirety, she asked, "Why do you do all of this?"

"For glory!" I thumped my chest with my fist.

"Har har. No really, why do you do so many activities? You have a job too, and your afternoons and weekends must be packed with lessons, meets, and tournaments. Is it fun? Don't you feel overbooked all the time?"

Krav Maga. Archery. Cross-country. All of these activities were for college applications, but they turned out to be the perfect training for zombie survival. With this victory under my belt, it would add credibility when I jump-started my dream career as CEO of a doomsday survival company, and maybe, just maybe, I could catch the eye of the investors of Zeneration to help me fund the production of my how-to guides and survivalist kits. A guy could dream, right?

All I needed now was a win. And probably an elevator pitch for my business, just in case.

"Well, I'm investing in my future because I want to get into a good college. To do that I need to stand out. And I want scholarship awards. Also, I want to build up my résumé, and having activities would make me seem interesting to the application committees. Ultimately, though, this all leads to my one simple goal in life."

Kate said, "Happiness!"

Simultaneously, I said, "Make a shitload of money." Didn't everyone want that?

Kate shrugged. "Wow, okay. You're the most ambitious person I know. And that says a lot—my dad is pretty intense. He's always working." She gave a palpable sigh of disappointment. "Just do me a favor." She looked me straight in the eyes and put her hand on my wrist. *My wrist!* "Please make sure you don't forget to enjoy your life, okay?"

"Yeah. Okay." I was enjoying life, even now, wasn't I? Being here with Kate was enjoyment. Talking about my future was enjoyment. Money talk? Enjoyment. See? A confetti cannon of enjoyment. *BOOM!*

She smiled. "According to my therapist, it's important to focus on things you want to do in life. Joy will follow."

"Okay. Sure." Total BS if you asked me.

Judging on her dimples alone, Kate was satisfied with my answer. She squeezed my wrist, pumping tingles down to my fingertips. Then sadly, she let go.

"Promise?" she asked.

I nodded, wishing she would grab my wrist again.

Something next to my desk caught her eye. "What's this?" she asked, pulling out a yellow sports Walkman from an old milk crate. "Where'd you get this stuff?" She'd discovered my box of old tech junk my dad gave me, the gadgets from when he was younger. She held up a dusty Nintendo Game Boy, Sony Discman, first-gen iPod, and a Microsoft Zune. My plan was to one day sell them all on eBay for thousands of dollars.

"You probably don't even know what half of that does," I said with a smirk.

She raised an eyebrow. "This plays Mario. These play music." A wrinkle appeared between her eyebrows. "This Zune thing, though, no clue. I'd need to google that."

I burst out laughing. "I'm impressed. You're nerdier than you let on."

More rummaging. "Why do you have a keyboard in here?" She didn't pull it out all the way but wiped off dust from some of the keys. "It doesn't look old."

"My dad used to work at an IT department of a big tech company. He had this IBM keyboard from the nineties and gave it to me. Push down the keys. They're buckle-spring and make a loud clickity-click sound when you type. It's very satisfying."

She laughed and typed her name. "I haven't used a regular keyboard in a while. I've been only doing touchscreen typing lately."

The keyboard went back into the crate as she continued

her detective work. She opened the closet door and yanked the dangling string to turn on the single, low-watt bulb.

"What the hell?" Kate panicked, stumbling backward as the overhead string swung back and forth like a hypnotic pendulum. Her butt slammed into the tall bookshelf inside my walk-in closet displaying my vintage Harry Potter and Minecraft Lego collectible sets, still in original boxes. The bookcase swayed, and my foot-tall Lego Dumbledore toppled onto the carpet, dismembering his head from his body. The damage could have been much worse. I was lucky an embarrassing plume of dust didn't poof from Dumbledore's face-plant into the flooring. I hadn't vacuumed in there for years. Maybe even never.

Directly across from Kate was my autographed, life-size foam-board cutout of my entrepreneurial idol, Robbie Anderson-Steele. CEO of Digitools. The way the color instantly drained from her face you'd think she had discovered my closet was a secret zombie actress murder room.

I let out a high-pitched, nervous laugh. "Meet Robbie Anderson-Steele. I won him at an invention competition. My friends Zach and Jaxon brought the cutout home and put it in my room. It's sort of a joke." *Not really, though. I won a five-hundred-dollar gift card too.* "He's this famous entrepreneur who's written a lot of bestselling business books." *Which I stood in line for at Barnes & Noble for two hours for to get signed. And I watched his recent TED Talk maybe a hundred times.* "I was going to throw that away soon. It's kind of ridiculous because it takes up so much space." *Probably not, though. I kind of love it.*

Kate shook her head like she was trying to knock Robbie's image out of it. She broke her gaze to pick up Dumbledore and put him back in standing position. With a staggered breath, she admitted, "Well, I definitely wasn't expecting that."

"Sorry. Am I weird? You can just say it," I said, shoulders slumping.

"Hey, I like weird. Weird is good. Weird is interesting," she assured me. "And I'm the weirdo who roped you into a zombie survivalist competition, remember? Speaking of which, while we have time, let's go to the army-navy place and see what basic supplies we can get for the competition. They said we're all allowed one backpack per participant, and we can swap things out during the competition if we see anything better lying around."

"It's like in one of those *Resident Evil* games where the player is only allowed to use one weapon at a time." I grinned. "We should read the game rules together later." Grabbing my set of keys from my desk, I shouted, "Mom! Dad! I'm going out for a bit!"

No answer.

Outside my bedroom window, Mom knelt in her garden, wearing thick canvas gloves and a wide-brimmed visor. Lucy was next to her, digging holes with a toy shovel. Farther away, Dad mowed the grass, wiping his brow by pulling up his undershirt and swiping his forehead with the frayed hem. As he trimmed the yard's edges, he leaned his body away from our tilted, humidity-warped back fence. Another broken thing on Dad's handyman to-do list. Fixing the fence was something he just never had time to do. He was always do-it-yourself-fixing something more mission-critical, and Mom and I were always looking up on YouTube how to fix his fix after he went to bed. The Home Depot folks knew us all too well.

Kate tidied up the electronics in the crate and pushed it back into its original spot. "This feels like a setup to a bad joke. A former Eagle Scout and Girl Scout walk into an army-navy surplus store."

I snorted again.

With interspersed fits of giggles, she continued. "Ooooh, I have the perfect setup. Store owner looks at our pins and awards and badges and goes, 'This place is expensive. You're going to need an IOU. You'll come back with more money, right?' The Eagle and Girl Scout say—"

"Scout's honor!" I finished, and we gasped with laughter. We could barely breathe, the joke was so bad. My mom would've loved that one.

CHAPTER EIGHT

Kate

I still didn't fully understand why there was a life-size cutout of my dad in Nate's closet. It was straight out of one of those Halloween carnival fun-house horror movies, when the light flickers off and on and the murdery thing just *appears*. Seeing Dad in his closet made my heart nearly stop. Like Robbie Anderson-Steele had somehow followed me to Nate's, despite the fact that I'd been so careful when leaving the house. Maybe way in the future it'd be kind of funny, but at the time, when sheer terror rippled through my body head to toe, it wasn't funny at all. Not in the least bit.

I sneaked a few glances over at Nate as he drove. His jet-black hair had a jagged part, and his gleaming white scalp line strongly contrasted it. Through his heather-gray Henley shirt, I could make out his lean muscle definition in his shoulders, arms, and chest. When he turned in my direction, heat rushed to my cheeks, and I stared ahead at the road. Rain pounded the windshield as my heart hammered harder and faster.

"So, why'd you pick me to be your partner again?" he asked. "Surely you had other options."

I had three reasons, actually. One, I only had a few friends, and ever since Mom died last year, I pretty much went full-on hermit. Second, to win, I needed someone smart and athletic to be my partner. Ideally someone who knew a lot about zombies. Third, I wanted to pick someone I didn't know too well, someone I wouldn't feel *too* bad ditching after the competition when I hightailed it out of Seattle. Nate was perfect.

"You seemed like the right guy for the job. I'm right, right?"

He puffed his chest and nodded.

I combed my loose locks with my fingers, immediately getting them finger-hair snared. I'd considered chopping all of my hair off and going for that pixie look that was always in vogue, but my very round face structure didn't go with that. "Elongate with a long hair style" was always the advice for me in beauty magazines.

Same for my short, squatty body. My legs especially.

Elongate your look with vertical stripes, never horizontal. Head-to-toe black streamlines your silhouette. Bonus tip: wear fun heels to give you added height!

I placed my hands in my lap, and then moved them to cover both knees, but neither position was natural. What did normal people do with their hands? My palms started to sweat, along with my face and scalp. Oh God. Next was always my upper lip, then armpits. Once the underboob and back perspiration rivers flowed, I'd need to drink electrolytes to preserve my hydration.

To cool myself, I turned up the air conditioner with my damp hand. Nate's hair flopped around in the AC wind stream, but he didn't complain. The air stayed warm and never went down in temperature. I fiddled with the knobs, but nothing helped.

He coughed. "Maybe it needs Freon. Lately it's worked more like a fan than an air conditioner."

No sense pumping his car cabin with unwanted heat, creating sauna-like conditions. I shut off my cool-down operation. My hands were still a problem, though, overly sweaty and flapping like an American flag on a gusty day. I shoved them under my thighs, palms down, hoping that a little body weight could suppress the sweat-gland eruption and stop me from waving my hands around like a fool.

"Would it be okay if you kept all this gear at your place?" I asked. "I don't have any room in my home." It was sort of the truth. Dad would flip his shit if he figured out I'd used some of his emergency cash he stashed in his sock drawer (I mean, who hides valuables in a sock drawer anymore?). He'd return everything, or worse, throw it all away to make a point, and I couldn't do that to Nate.

As we approached my house, my body tensed. Nate pulled into the top of my driveway again. Thanks to the tall evergreens, privacy shrubs, and two iron gates, Nate couldn't see that much other than my mailbox.

He shrugged. "Sure. I'll sort out our two backpacks this week and distribute the weight between us." With some hesitation, he continued. "Can you carry a pretty heavy load? I mean, you're kinda small."

Two ways to answer this came to mind. Both made me look a little crazy.

I'm small? Why, thank you! I try to eat sensibly when I don't eat Dick's Hamburgers.

I'm small? How dare you assume I can't carry as much shit as a dude?

I responded a third way, with my signature awkward approach. I ignored his comment.

"You can drop me off here. Thanks for the ride. So much cheaper than taking an Uber back."

"Did you get everything this time? No more wigs in my car?" He smirked.

I slapped his arm. "Hey! That'll never happen again, lest I be punished by the tiny glitter glue goddess again." *Lest?* Did I just say *lest?*

Nate rubbed his right bicep. "Damn, woman! Go Hulk-smash someone else!" His dark brown eyes gleamed as he teased me. Did he hear my heart thundering? Trying to Hulk-smash out of my rib cage?

Ba-BOOM. Ba-BOOM. Nate KIM. Nate KIM.

Look, heart, I see what you're trying to do here, but I have other priorities on my mind.

"I'll see you at work," I said, opening his car door.

"We should talk before then, to discuss competition logistics. I looked up the contest details, and the competition's getting a lot of press. Like, the Discovery Channel is sponsoring it. It's a bigger deal than I thought."

I chewed my lip. "Okay, message me then, Mister Logistics."

"That can be my code name. We need one for you, though." Excitement flashed on his face. "Hulk Smash!" He said it so winningly.

I hopped out and waved bye. He rolled down the window, and "Holly Jolly Christmas" blared from his tinny car speakers. "Hey, I set the last button to your favorite music station, the one that plays holiday music unseasonably early!" he shouted.

Holiday music, for me! As Nate and the Christmas cheer rolled away, I ran down the driveway and punched in the key code, then at the next gate used the finger pad and face scanner. In the camera, I stuck my tongue out and crossed my eyes.

Unauthorized, the security panel flashed on the screen.

I made my face go back to normal while flipping two birds at the camera.

Authorized. Anderson, Kate.

The front door clicked open and robot Jeeves rolled up to greet me. "Bioscan time, the first one this month."

"Hello to you, too, Jeeves." Yay, my routine bioscan. This used to be manually done by the family doctor, but hooray, now Dad had developed the tech to do basic health monitoring at home. And I was his guinea pig.

I hung up my hoodie and went to the kitchen, where the bioscan machine was set up. It looked like one of those blood pressure and oxygen monitoring machines that the nurse rolls up to the examination table at the doctor's office, and was connected via Wi-Fi to Jeeves's servers. "Temperature, normal," Jeeves said as the device took my vitals. "Systolic and diastolic, normal. Heart rate, elevated. Far above normal. Would you like me to call an ambulance?"

Call an ambulance for my *Nate-KIM-Nate-KIM* heartbeat? Oh God, no.

"Jeeves, I'm fine. Don't call the paramedics. Please don't!" Stupid robot! How embarrassing would that be?

"Heart rate steadily dropping. Verbal command confirmed. I will not call paramedics. Uploading health data to your medical file."

Thank *God*. Crisis averted.

"Excessive perspiration has been added to your file. Possible related health conditions include hyperhidrosis, heart attack, or overactive thyroid. Please let me know if you need me to call nine-one-one."

I wiped the sweat from my face with my flannel shirtsleeve.

Jeeves added, "Your father arrived from the airport at three thirty-seven p.m. Pacific Standard Time."

"Oh, is he home?" I'd forgotten this was one of the weekends he was back.

"He is in the master bedroom. His wristwatch monitor data indicates a resting heartbeat of sixty-eight BPM. Low oxygen levels suggest he may have sleep apnea."

I padded down the hall to his room. There was a *Do not disturb* message on the screen next to the door frame. Deep, rhythmic snuffles accompanied by cartoonish little snort-snores came through the closed door. Based on his slow, heavy breathing, he'd likely sleep through the night. Well-rested Dad was way better than a groggy, sleep-deprived one.

Things used to be different. Dad was different. He used to be the chauffeur, Mom was the trip planner, and I was the snack bringer. I missed our day trips to Portland. Our trips to museum mummy exhibitions. Lazy afternoons watching European films where we would take turns reading subtitles in fake French accents, with all three of us eating Ruffles and French onion dip, my culinary specialty.

Dad had become a major workaholic the last few years, which served him well in the corporate world. Chief executive officer at Digitools at age forty-nine. He'd also become a major snoopaholic, sending me itemized emails on a weekly basis now that required an immediate response (*my house, my rules*) like the one he'd sent me that morning.

Subject: Oct. breakdown so far

From: Robbie Anderson-Steele <ras@digitoolstech.com>

To: Kate Anderson <kaaaaaaaaaateanderson@gmail.com>

Date: Friday, October 11, 5:58 a.m.

My questions:

Home Incoming call: 10/3, 48 min from unknown # (school night). Homework-related?

Home Outgoing call: 10/5, 15 min to Pitstop Pizza. Why was call so long?

Home Outgoing call: 10/6, 5 min to Pitstop Pizza. Pizza 2 days in a row?

Home Outgoing call: 10/8, 1 min Zombie Laboratory. Assume wrong number?

Grocery bill last month: $214.44. $14.44 over your budget. Pls explain.

Credit card dinner purchases: $100.72. 72 cents over budget.

9/4–10/4 daily online average: 1:44. Over by 14 min. Don't make me cut off internet.

Oct. cell phone usage so far is 2 min. Broken? Or did you lose it?

Misc: Workers coming by house on Friday to assess storm damage on the two gates and may install heat-sensing cameras in hallways. Jeeves going through some firmware updates tonight—he'll be off-line at midnight EST.

—R.

No "Hello from Shanghai" or "How's school?" Not even a "Love, Dad" sign-off. Ditching the nanny this year wasn't such a good thing for my independence after all. Instead, Dad just ramped up his security a hundredfold, forcing me to find ways to outsmart his patrol. I never drove my dad's car, which had GPS tracking. I'd opened a secret savings account six months ago. He didn't know anything about my escape room job either. I didn't share any of this with anyone. I couldn't. Not even with Zoe in New York, or Raina, my friend since third grade. She was the closest thing to family I had here, and I barely spoke to her at school these days.

Shooting one last long look at Dad's closed door, I settled on dinner for one. I made myself a ham sandwich and cracked open a cold can of Dr Pepper. I smiled to myself, thinking about how Jeeves almost called 911 earlier. I tossed some chips and grapes on the plate and carried everything to my room.

The house phone ring blasted through the house. "Incoming call! Rohit Mishra!"

I hated how it sometimes announced the account owner's name—in this case, Raina's dad. I whisper-hissed, "Answer call!" because I didn't want to wake Dad.

Raina's booming voice pierced through my room's speaker, sounding as perky as ever. "Mom! I need the car toni—oh—Kate! You're there! Wanna go with me to a movie premiere tonight?"

"Movie premiere" was Raina code for "Want to drive me to a parentless party, so I can get hammered and you can drive my boozy ass home?"

"Errr, no thanks. I have to finish my homework."

"Awww, c'mon. We haven't hung out in forever," she pouted.

It really felt like forever. I'd turned into one of those scary wilderness guys who lived alone in a small, woodsy cabin. I fit the part, except I didn't have a bushy, tangled beard. And the space-age compound I'd been confined in was hardly a cabin.

She announced, "I'm picking you up anyway. We're going out."

I exhaled hard out of my nose. "I don't feel like going out."

"You never feel like going out," she said in a sassy, ever-so-slightly threatening tone. "We haven't hung out in so long. How long has it been? Like, a few months now?"

More than that. Raina was actually at my house the week Dad had returned from the International Robotics Expo and Mom came down with pneumonia, a virus she caught from him. The night he told her that he didn't believe her crackly, wheezing, and wet cough was anything worse than the flu he had during his trip. He still met with investors, wined and dined clients, and raised money while sick. She needed to toughen up, he said that night.

Your dad loves you very much, even if it may not always seem like it. How many times did I hear that at Mom's funeral, from neighbors, family friends, and Dad's coworkers? It was like people knew we weren't compatible on our own and were trying to comfort me. Or worse, warn me.

The last few months I hadn't felt like myself. Didn't want to go out. Or hang out. I simply existed. That was it, the best I could do. Because my childhood died when Mom did.

"Yeah, it's been a while." I added pathetically, "But I see you at school, though, sometimes?"

"Uh, that doesn't count. But whatever, I'll be at your house in twenty minutes. Make sure you're dressed in layers. It might get cold. I heard the party's...uh...movie premiere's gonna be good, and a lot of kids from other schools might be going."

"I'm not really feeling up for a big night out," I complained.

"Shut up and go change. I bet you were just going to watch the Sundance TV channel all night. And you're probably wearing your pajamas already."

Well, okay, to be fair, they were my nice flannel ones. It wasn't like I ate ham sandwich dinners by myself in a dress and chandelier earrings. I wiped mustard from the corner of my mouth with a paper napkin. "Okay, fine. I'll change. See you in twenty."

Click.

Clean clothes needed, stat.

I padded down the hallway to the laundry room and opened the dryer, yanking out wrinkled school uniforms, underwear, pajama tops, and pants, piece by piece. It appeared I hadn't worn any go-outside-the-house clothes, other than quickly-check-the-mail-and-wave-to-a-neighbor attire, in the last week. My zombie wardrobe didn't exactly count as wearable.

My walk-in closet contents were nearly as bad. I swiped through a sea of oversize plaid shirts. Any one of them would've been right for a logging excursion, but none were for "going out." In some of my drawers I found nicer summery tops and pants, hidden away, leftover reminders of my shopping trips with Mom. Back when I went for a cuter, non-lumberjack look. Outlet shopping was our favorite thing to do together. Now, clothing was just utility to me. Something to cover my naked, cold parts. All my clothes purchases these days were made simply out of necessity, to replace worn-out clothes with ripped hems, torn fabric, or noticeable discoloration from screwing up the wash with bleach. I just didn't care anymore.

There wasn't much of a choice for me. A red-and-black-checkered shirt, frayed boyfriend jeans, and UGGs was the best I could offer. To add a little flair, I rummaged through my jewelry box to find a necklace or bracelet to soften my unisex logger look, but its entire contents were a tangled mess of thin chains, tightly knotted and interwoven in ways that defied basic physics, with various rings and earrings secured in the snarled metallic web. In a separate box, a small pair of unworn gemstone earrings lay in solitude on a square cotton cushion, their matching necklace nowhere to be found. The earrings and missing pendant were from Mom and Dad, given to me on my sixteenth birthday. They were so modest that no one else would notice if I wore them, but that didn't matter. It'd been so long since I had even made any effort to get dressed up (other than zombie wear), that even wearing them was a baby step.

As I closed the jewelry box, a flash of shiny redness smack in the middle of the necklace mangle caught my eye. My garnet pendant, trapped inside the chaos. It would take hours to untangle that mess.

My home phone rang. "Incoming call! Rohit Mishra."

"Hey, Raina, you here already?" I glanced at my watch. Exactly twenty minutes had passed.

"Yeah, I'm in your driveway. You have one of those scary haunted mansion gates now. Can you give me the key code so I can get you?"

"I'll just come out. The security system is confusing. Sorry." I grabbed my cross-body bag and navy North Face fleece. "Jeeves," I said loudly, "tell Dad I'm going out with Raina."

"Mishra, Raina. 132 Northeast Sixty-Sixth Street. Information logged and sent."

"Don't stay up too late, Jeeves," I quipped as I headed down the hall.

"I'm scheduled for a firmware update at twelve a.m. Eastern Standard Time, Kate." Right. Jeeves wasn't programmed for sarcasm. "Your father has sent you the following message. 'Okay! Sounds good!'"

So he'd woken up, then. This cheery message from Dad was a prepopulated canned reply, the first option in the drop-down menu. After two weeks on the road, he hadn't even bothered to leave his bedroom to say hello or goodbye to me. Didn't I deserve at least a custom reply if he wasn't going to come out?

I grabbed my things and slammed the front door.

CHAPTER NINE

Nate

"Why does it smell like Fritos in here?" My eyes scanned Jaxon's blue vinyl seats like a helicopter searchlight sweeping for a murder suspect. Where was that god-awful smell coming from? When I dropped off Kate a few hours ago, my car didn't stink like this, so I knew it wasn't me.

Jaxon cracked open his window. "I don't smell it. And I don't eat Fritos in my car."

"Zach, do you smell it?" I asked.

Zach nodded.

"Oh, wait. I know. It's my gym clothes." With only his left hand on the steering wheel, Jaxon leaned down next to my feet and pulled up his mesh black gym bag from the floorboard. Jostling around the contents made the car reek more.

I rolled my window all the way down, even though it was pouring rain outside. "Oh God, I might vomit," I spat out, dry heaving.

Jaxon tossed the bag in the back seat next to Zach, who immediately tossed it back to the front.

An unfriendly game of stank potato. Back and forth it went, till finally Jaxon yanked the steering wheel to the right and pulled over to the side of the road.

Jaxon got out and opened Zach's door. "Hand it to me," he commanded, holding out his palm.

Into the trunk it went. Bye-bye, car anti-freshener.

He got back in and slammed the door. "This is the last time I let you guys ride in my car, you ingrates," he huffed, wiping the rain from his face with a towel in the center console. After pulling his seat belt across his chest, he got back on the road.

A few seconds of silence passed. "Why is this party at a roller-skating rink?" I asked.

Jaxon blew out his cheeks. "A friend of mine heard about this friend's party from another guy. I don't know all the details. He said something about the rent being too high so they're shutting it down at the end of the year."

I raised an eyebrow. "So why would some high school kid have a party there?" I got that the roller-skating-rink industry wasn't exactly booming and the business was failing. But I didn't get why Jaxon had dragged Zach and me to a friend-of-a-friend-of-a-friend's party.

Confession: I'd never been to a roller-skating rink before and was slightly uncomfortable with the whole thing. Okay, terrified was more like it. Frightened of the smelly rental skates. Of falling on my face. Peeing in the bathroom while on wheels. I mean, what if I drift-rolled while pissing in the urinal? I'd gone ice-skating only one time in eighth grade, and I fell on my ass so hard I cried. (In my defense, I legit bruised my tailbone...and for a week I needed to use a special cushion meant for people with hemorrhoids.) My stomach churned, thinking of all the humiliating possibilities.

Jaxon fidgeted with the temperature settings. "Rich people do dumb shit with their money. Especially when they have too much of it," he muttered, pulling his car into the crowded Skateway parking lot. There were open spaces from all these rich kids trying to park their fancy cars and leaving a space in between. The luxury car drivers preferred to find spots far away from cars like Jaxon's (a newish black Accord, with a small dent on the bumper). One Range Rover driver took one look at Jaxon's car, then parked down at the far end of our row instead. Away from the riffraff. Same thing happened in the Clyde Hill school parking lot. We were used to it, sadly. Even if we passed as typical, privileged prep school kids, our cars were a dead giveaway, screaming skid to anyone who knew the approximate CarMax value of a midrange Honda.

Zach pleaded to Jaxon, "Please don't throw coins at anyone today." You'd think he wouldn't have to preface our night out by saying that. And it was the only thing he had said the entire time. He rubbed the top of his head, back and forth, back and forth, his telltale sign he was on the verge of freaking out.

"Okay, grandmas," Jaxon huffed as he locked our doors with a beep. "I promise, no parking lot altercations."

"If this sucks, can we leave and go play laser tag?" I asked. "Or go to the arcade?"

"Okay, but Annie said she might meet us here." He smirked, checking his messages on his phone. "She dumped her boyfriend last weekend. Maybe you can finally grow some balls and ask her out, Natey. Right, Zach? Tell him."

Zach wrinkled his nose. "Annie's not his type."

"Of course she's his type. She's breathing," he laughed, shrinking away from me.

Predictably, I punched his arm, hard.

Jaxon rubbed his bicep. "Owww. Seriously, though, Annie is everyone's type." He was right about that. With her bright blue eyes, melty smile, and blond, naturally highlighted (highlit?) hair, Annie gave off more of an aloof, California vibe than a Seattle one. Guys were always asking me about her, whether she had a boyfriend, or a homecoming or prom date, like I was her gatekeeper. None of them knew her at all. What she liked. What she hated. They just knew her as a pretty face. And sure, she had that, but she was smart and nice too. Jaxon, Zach, and I were a little protective, but even we couldn't stop her from dating some real losers. She never ever went for the archetypical Mr. Right. She always preferred Mr. Absolute Worst Dude Ever.

In the off chance some cute girls might show up, I'd put on a never-worn, forest-green Gap button-down shirt I'd gotten for Christmas, the color of those green army-men toys. But because

I hadn't washed it first, the creases were all still there from the in-store folding. Even worse, I also didn't have time to cut off the label, so the back of my neck itched like crazy. On the car ride, I'd scratched it like an anxious dog with fleas. Why did shirts even have these stupid labels? The smarter companies had that info screen-printed on the inside. Mental note: *boycott Gap.* Terrible labels.

"Nice sticker," Jaxon laughed, pointing at the long transparent sticky label that ran down vertically near my belly button.

L

L

L

L

L

Yet another stupid thing they put on shirts, the sticker size advertisement. I ripped it off and stuffed it in the pocket of my cargo pants.

Jaxon scoffed. "You're a large? Aren't you more medium than large? You're like, lardium."

"Fuck you, J," is all I managed to say, playing mad when all I wanted to do was bust up laughing.

Lardium.

"I'm just messing with you," Jaxon laugh-coughed. "We're skidders for life. We stick together."

Zach spoke. "That sounds like it belongs on the periodic table of elements. Lardium." Snorting hard, he pushed up his glasses to the bridge of his nose using his index finger, in a nerdy, yet nonironic way. Then he hiked up his pants, which were weighed down from his thick leather belt, which was in turn weighed down by all the shit he attached to it, like his clip-on phone holster, his carabiner key ring, and the chain attached to the wallet in his front pants pocket. *It deters pickpocketing*, he'd say every time we teased him about it. He was right. No one ever tried to steal his Velcro wallet. It was like he was wearing a waist-size leather charm bracelet on his hips, dangling his loser charms.

"All right, I'm situated," he announced with a definitive nod.

"Okay then, let's roll!" I battle-cried, realizing only after I said it that I'd made the world's worst skate pun. Jaxon shook his head as we walked to the entrance.

There were maybe twenty kids our age ahead of us in line, most of them in the "two or more Teslas per household" demographic. A lot of them had pairs of brand-new skates casually thrown over their shoulders. Some even had translucent sports wheels. For roller skates? Really?

All around us, people wore '80s-style clothes. Headbands, sweatbands, tube socks, fingerless gloves, and lots and lots of zippers.

"Was this supposed to be a costume party?" Zach asked.

Jaxon shrugged. "I dunno, I heard about this from a friend of an online friend, remember?"

"So, basically a complete stranger." I sighed.

"Yup."

Zach hoisted his belt a little higher and fished his wallet from his pocket. "I think I only have a twenty on me. I hope there's no cover charge." He tore open the Velcro and peeked inside. "Maybe only ten actually." He pulled out a tattered bill and examined it.

Someone's hand fluttered down and snatched the ten-dollar bill away from Zach. "Finders keepers," a familiar voice giggled.

Annie stood behind us, smiling sheepishly, wearing a neon-sweatshirt-type thing that hung off her shoulder.

"That's not how finders keepers works," Zach growled, snatching it back. "What you did is stealing."

"Touché." She broke into a wide grin. "I was just messing with ya. Sorry, Grandpa Zachary."

Jaxon looked up from his phone. "That's *Grandma* Zach to you. Hey, I heard you dumped that asshole soccer team cocaptain, good riddance to El Co-Capitan Loser. You slumming it with us today?"

Her mouth fell wide open, even though she knew as well as anyone that Jaxon was one of the school's biggest gossips, and nothing was a secret at our school between us friends. He participated in both the free market and black market for Clyde Hill dirty secrets. He was a walking *TMZ*.

"Wellllll," Annie said, drawing the word out and rolling her eyes, "he was a competitive dick who sulked when I beat him at anything."

We nodded because we all knew the type. Our school was full of them.

She continued. "He ate less than me, even though he was like fifty pounds heavier. It really bothered me that when I'd eat my whole meal, he'd take half of his home. He said it was because he had to watch his weight for wrestling, but whatever." Her shoulders slumped, and she let out the saddest sigh. "I always pick the wrong guy."

Again, we all nodded. She always did.

She elbowed me gently. "Enough about my love life. What's going on with you? I haven't seen you in a while. You look different. Like, happier or something."

I let out a nervous laugh an octave higher than usual. "Not much, just school, college applications, after-school stuff, work—"

Jaxon interrupted, "He's being modest. And boring. He's been busy inventing, writing business plans, learning how to choke people using his bare hands, hanging out with *girls*." He really emphasized that last part.

Annie shot me another surprised look, which offended me a little. Was it really that hard to believe?

My ears burned with embarrassment. "You skate much before?" I asked, turning the conversation away from me. "My goal is to not crack my head open like a walnut."

"No helmets?" Zach squawked. "Err, no thanks. Maybe I'll just play video games there."

We made it to the front of the line, and we all turned to Jaxon to be our spokesperson. He cleared his throat. "Um, we're here for the party."

The attendant had fiery hair and tiny cute freckles sprinkled on her nose and cheeks. She asked him, "Are you on the guest list?"

Jaxon shot us an "I'm about to lie out of my ass, so just go with me" look over his shoulder, and then turned back to her. "My name is hard to spell, but I see it, right there." He gestured at the pages in front of her, and with a wave of Jaxon magic, she handed him the entire guest list. Skimming quickly, he said, "Here it is, party of four."

She took the list back, and she marked a line through the name. "Okay, enjoy the party, Peter Haskill the Fourth, plus guests. It wasn't that hard to spell." She laughed, under Jaxon's hypnosis. "Oh, one more thing." She opened the drawer by her knee. "You all get VIP wristbands, so you get free Icees and corn dogs."

"Thank you," Jaxon said, and, reading her name tag, added, "Camilla."

She helped us fasten the bands and gestured us to enter the skate center.

We were in.

And Jaxon got her phone number.

As soon as we were out of earshot, we busted up laughing. "You dragged us to a party where we weren't even on the list? Pete's gonna kill you," Zach said, barely above a whisper.

Jaxon grinned. "He won't know it's me. No snitching, Zach!" His eyes darkened, and the corners of his mouth turned downward. "Pete'll be fine. He'll probably slip Camilla a hundred, and it'll all be okay. Everything always goes okay for guys like him."

Out of nowhere, Annie grabbed my upper arm and squeezed it. "Let's go get our skates." My bicep tingled at her touch, and instantly, my blood pumped from my heart at double speed. After a few seconds of walking next to her, I deeply inhaled and exhaled out my nose. I'd forgotten to breathe.

Jaxon coughed and then fake-punched me in the chest (right hook, left hook) in a not-so-subtle way. "You two get your skates. Zach and I are gonna check out the arcade."

He threw a peace sign over his shoulder as he and Zach walked away.

Was it possible to want to kill someone and hug them at the same time?

CHAPTER TEN

Kate

"Wait, whose party is this again?" I asked, pulling out my phone to check the time.

"Hold up. When did *you* get a new phone?" Raina narrowed her eyes at me. "Is it yours? Or one of your dad's?" She dropped her voice down to a near baritone. "Can he hear us?"

It had crossed my mind that maybe Dad's company could bug my phone. I'd just turned eighteen but hadn't done much research on my legal independence yet. "It's mine. He doesn't know about it." I pressed my cheek on the cool window. He had really pissed me off. Why couldn't he just step outside of his room to say hi to me? I didn't care if he'd slept in his work clothes or had BO or eyebrow-singeing bad breath.

The lump in my throat stopped me from saying anything more.

"Well, you know I won't tell, especially not your dad. I'm excited I have a secret way of contacting you now instead of your house phone or one of your dad's company phones. Call me so I have your number."

She recited her number, and I dialed it. "Raina Singh speaking! How may I direct your call?" she chirped into her speaker.

The gloom inside me lifted. "You're so ridiculous," I said, feeling warmer. It was good, being with Raina again. She was familiar and comfortable, like a favorite worn-in hoodie.

Raina laughed and ended the call. "Ooooh, am I the first number in your contact list? I'm so honored!"

I hesitated, so she grabbed my phone. "Wait, who's Nate Kim?"

"Hey, eyes on the road!" Heat flushed to my ears and cheeks. "He's this guy I work with. I bum rides off him sometimes."

"I need more details. Is he tall? Hot? Does he have good hair?"

What if I preferred short, roly-poly guys with prematurely receding hairlines? "He's cute, I guess. Pretty smart and corny funny. Ambitious to a fault. We're just friends." The more I talked about Nate, the hotter my face got. Like space-shuttle-entering-Earth's-atmosphere hot.

She glanced at me at the stoplight. "Girl, you're so red, you look like you're sunburned. There's no way he's just a friend."

Mom used to complain about menopause hot flashes. Was it anything like this? Raina rolled down our windows, and the cool air hit my face, relieving me of my full-body heat flush. She shot me a smile as the light turned green.

Raina had full-blown Kate ESP. In eighth grade, she somehow

knew when I first got my period and gifted me Advil, a heating pad, and some Fran's chocolates. If we didn't get the roles we wanted in the junior high school play, she and I would go share a hot fudge sundae with extra cherries. Last year, Raina was glued by my side when Mom died and eased up contact after the funeral. She checked in to see if I was ready to hang out again, a lot at first, and then only about once a month after that. She hadn't abandoned me. Quite the opposite actually. She was giving me the space I needed because she is such a good friend.

"Okay, I'm clearly making you feel uncomfortable, so let's talk about something else." She turned the corner and bumped the curb. "Stupid turn radius. Did you try out for *My Fair Lady*? I didn't even bother because *I cahn't do the accent*." She said the last part in the world's worst Cockney accent ever.

"I'm Eliza Doolittle's understudy." I sighed. "They're letting me be the lead on Saturday night, to let the primary Eliza rest her voice."

"That's good, though! You get lead role for a night! Want me to take care of her, so you can be Eliza all nights?" Raina spoke in a horrible fake New York (or maybe Jersey) accent, punching her fist into her palm.

I laughed. "I really appreciate the offer, but no thanks."

"Just let me know. That's what friends are for!" Still going with the fake New York–Jersey accent.

In my reflection in the car window, I straightened my shirt

collar. "I can't believe you dragged me out of the house to go skating. Is *that* what friends are for?"

"It's better than you sitting alone at home, right? And I have no idea who is throwing this party, by the way. Someone at school told me about it."

She was probably right. I'd gotten so used to solitude I forgot what socialization was like. At school, I stared at the clock, willing time to go faster, hightailing out of there as soon as the end-of-day bell rang. No activities other than theater and my new escape room job. I used to have more friends and go to parties. But then my life went to shit, and then my number one life companion became Jeeves. Welcome to Hermitville, population: me. Jeeves didn't count in the census, him not being human and all.

I was destined to become one of those sad people you heard about who were eaten by their starving pet cats when they died. But I didn't even have a cat. *That's* how alone I was.

I smiled weakly. "Thanks for dragging me out of the house." *Thanks for throwing me an inner-tube floatie before I drowned in loneliness.*

"No problem." She pulled into the crowded lot and found a spot. "Let's check out this shitty party." Raina pulled a ponytail holder from her purse and dangled it in her pursed lips. With a few swift hair swipes, she pulled the band from her mouth and formed a perfect high pony with her dark, wavy hair. No brush. Zero effort. I'd die to have hair like that.

She passed me some ultra-shine lip gloss. "Here." A discreet signal that I needed a cosmetic tune-up before she'd be seen with me in public. I obliged.

We threw our coats in the back seat and headed straight toward the swarm of high schoolers standing in a nonlinear line. Lots of unfamiliar faces surrounded us as we moved forward in herd formation.

When we got to the entrance, Raina announced, "I'm Raina. Mishra. Party of two."

The pretty strawberry-blond attendant nodded, scouring the first page. I leaned in to see if Nate was on the list. My heart fluttered in my chest like a caged butterfly at the possibility, but "Kern, James" was there and "Kolb, McKinsey," but no "Kim, Nate."

Deflated, I turned to Raina. "You sure you want to go in? We can go to a movie. My dad's treat."

Her warm, copper-colored eyes crinkled with laughter. "No way, not now! Do you hear the music?"

My brain tuned in and listened for lyrics. "Is that Maroon 5?"

"Are you serious? God, how long have you been cooped up at home?"

I was being completely serious. I had no clue about anything when it came to music. Okay, Broadway musical soundtracks, yes, movie soundtracks, yes. Everything else? Nope. No clue.

Raina shook her head and pulled me through the door by the

elbow. "You're hopeless sometimes." Smugly, she yelled over the surround sound, "It's Reverse, the newest, hottest band from Seattle."

"Who?"

"Oh my God, stop it," she giggled.

Seriously. No. Clue. "Okay, let's get our skates. Looks like people are headed that way." I pointed straight ahead, past the restrooms. We followed the flow to the rental counter.

My white cami and Raina's gray-and-white-striped shirt glowed in the black light. Every few seconds, a primary-colored light would strobe by our faces. Red. Yellow. Blue. Repeat. Pulsing to the beat of the song. A lone disco ball spun in the center of the rink, reflecting and refracting colored lights and spraying them everywhere. Most of the skaters rolled in clusters of two or three. The majority were pretty terrible. There were a few people hovering in the center of the rink, dancing alone, spinning like tops, or skating backward to the music, in their own little secluded world.

All four attendants inside the skate rental booth zoomed around, busily handing out pairs in a disorderly fashion. Impatient girls and guys screamed out their shoe sizes (*Seven women's! Eleven men's! Thirteen wide, men's!*) while the employees brought out white-and-brown worn leather roller skates, insides damp with freshly sprayed disinfectant. The weighty artificial lemon scent of Lysol, mixed with the dense, hanging layer of dirty sock smell made my stomach lurch. It was like my unventilated school locker room and the local indoor trampoline park had a baby. And that baby farted nonstop.

Breathing from my mouth, I shouted to the male attendant wearing stacked glow-in-the-dark necklaces, "Size eight please!"

"Same for me," Raina chimed in.

Two girls rolled toward us screaming, "Out of the waaaaay! We can't stop! Sorry!" Raina and I parted like curtains, just in time to watch them slam boobs-first into the rental counter between us. By some miracle, both girls remained upright, saving their dignity.

The attendant rolled back over to Raina. "I'm so sorry, we're out of the eights. And the sevens and nines. I checked those for you too."

One of the traumatized boob-squashed girls said, "You can have my skates. I'm an eight. And definitely returning them. Skating isn't my thing. Totally done."

Her friend nodded. "Me too. I'm done."

They unlaced their skates and leaned on the counter as they wiggled them off. The first girl to finish handed her skates directly to me. "Here you go."

She bent down to help her friend unsuction her foot from the inside of the skate. I whispered to the attendant, "Hi, can you spray these?"

Out came the Lysol. *Psssssssss! Psssssssssss!* A squirt inside each skate. Instant sanitation.

Two squirts and Raina was done too. We carried our skates to a carpeted bench. I got the right one on first. The inside was still warm from the previous wearer. So disgusting.

Raina was having some trouble. "I think my socks are too thick. It's like trying to shove raw biscuit dough back inside the popped can."

After I got both of my skates fitted, I helped loosen her laces. "That should help. The girl who had this before you must've had tiny bird ankles."

"I have Big Bird ankles. Or maybe Snuffleupagus ones." She tried to stand, then held her arms out like a surfer. She warned, "Don't touch me, or I'll bring you down with me. No mercy." Cautiously, she made her way to the wall, toward the metal support bar that new skaters were clutching like their lives depended on it. She wobbled and bobbled as she held herself up. When she tried to let go, her arms would flail like she was talking with her hands. It was hard to believe that she was the one who really wanted to be here.

With small, hesitating steps, I rolled up alongside her.

"How'd you learn to skate like that?" she panted, clinging on to the rail.

"I've only been once before, with my mom, like ten years ago." I remembered kinda hating it then too. I'd begged Mom to leave so I could go home and play games online with my friends, not knowing that my time with Mom would be cut short.

Offering my hand, I waited for her to unclench the bar. Together, we made our way to the rink. Like a new driver merging into traffic for the first time, we found a little pocket of space and rolled into the chaos. Raina used both hands to feel her way along the rink's outer wall. After we reached the other side of the rink perimeter, she said, "Let's exit. I can't do this."

Maneuvering around so many inexperienced skaters trying to enter the arena proved difficult. "'Scuse me, pardon me, sorry!" I pulled Raina off the rink right before the horde of new entrants swept her back into the skating sea.

She tried to make her way to the wall but did one of those cartoon banana-peel slips and pulled me down with her, saving herself from falling alone. I tumbled forward and landed with such a hard force that the wind got knocked out of me. As passersby bent down to assist, I flapped my hand and wheezed, "I'm okay," shooing everyone away. Raina scrambled upright and called out, "Uh, I'll come back!" as she unintentionally rolled away from me.

Slowly, I tried sitting up, still light-headed from the temporary oxygen deprivation. It took me a few seconds to get my bearings. But when I did, I spotted just behind Raina...

Nate. And a pretty blond girl, engaged in conversation.

Damn, she was really pretty. Hot pretty. So much in fact that I had trouble keeping my eyes off her, like she possessed a magnetic force deep within her core. Her roll-out-of-bed, no-makeup beauty was the polar opposite of the zombified, hairnet look I'd shown Nate the first day I met him. She had these Miracle-Gro eyelashes that any girl would die for.

I never understood how a face could launch a thousand ships until now. She even made her ratty rental roller skates look sexy.

Oh God, please don't look over here. Please. No.

"Kate!" yelled Raina, huffing and puffing toward me. "Kate! Make room! I'm coming for you!"

As if his spidey sense tingled, Nate tilted his head and stopped talking to his beautiful companion. He stared at the commotion, a.k.a. train-wreck Raina, and followed her blazing path with his curious gaze.

She headed straight toward me, at ramming speed. She hadn't practiced braking yet. Her face went from smiley to "oh shit!" as she bent her knees, perhaps thinking that being closer to the ground would mean less injury. But all it did was make her speed up.

Shit.

BAM! Her right skate slammed into mine, and she fell face forward on top of me, and I went down a second time. Like a championship lady wrestler, she had pinned me down underneath her with no way to escape. All we needed was someone to count to three and call the match.

"Sorry," she said, blowing a puff of air upward to clear her bangs from her eyes.

"Thanks for the fun night out," I coughed. "Really, this has been great."

"Need some help?" A hand reached down and hoisted Raina up.

Nate's hand.

Damn it, Lord, why have you forsaken me? All I needed now was an embarrassing hairnet and a missing wig.

While he helped Raina to her feet, I moved my legs from a mermaid position to a kneeling one, and used all the upper body strength I could muster to push myself up. My shins pulsed with pain.

Once stable on my feet, I rolled to the nearest bench two feet away and sat with a hard thump. Raina talked to the blond beauty while Nate sat down next to me.

"So," he said with a smirk, "how's your day going?"

"Fantastic," I said, rubbing my right calf, wanting to die right there. "My floor warm-up is done. Time to go out there and slay it." I nodded toward the rink, then I focused on retying my skates, making precise loops and knots, hoping that if I kept looking downward he wouldn't notice my sweat surfacing on my forehead and upper lip. Or the red rashes flaring up on my hands.

Neither of us discussed the girl. Neither of us said much of anything at all. But it was the kind of comfortable silence that was natural between familiar friends. Quiet and relaxed. Easy.

The song medley on the overhead speakers soon came to

an end, and the DJ rattled off a long list of announcements into the crackling mic. Skating ended in an hour. Half-price hot dog special ending soon. Someone had parked their Tesla in the fire zone and it would be towed. Half the crowd booed, half cheered at that last one.

Next came the most dreaded words for any boyfriendless person, just as I finished tying the most perfect bow on my skate. "And now it's tiiiiime...for couples' skate! Where are my couples at? Wooop-woop!"

The lights dimmed, and the rink cleared fast, leaving only a handful of couples still skating, holding hands. A few daring singletons stayed in the center area, twirling and sweeping their arms to some shitty Maroon 5 song. A round white *L* sticker under Nate's shirt pocket glowed in the black light. I yanked it off and handed it to him.

Our eyes met. "Thanks." He stuffed it into his shirt pocket and didn't break his gaze.

One of Nate's guy friends came over to bum some quarters. The interruption gave me a chance to think about my options.

Did I go home, or sit here like a bored lump waiting for couples' skate to end? Did I go all carpe diem and ask Nate to hit the rink with me?

As Nate put his wallet back into his pants pocket, I pressed my palms into my thighs and leaned forward, nearly ready to spring into action. A hard lump formed in my throat, yet one more thing to get in the way of me simply saying to Nate, "Hey, let's go skate!"

A small voice inside my head pleaded for me to just do it. *Get up. Ask him! Go skate with Nate, Kate. Stop giggling to yourself about how that rhymes. Don't make me bitch-slap you later about this.*

A voice cut through my meandering thoughts. "Let's skate!"

But it wasn't Nate's voice speaking to me. It was what's-her-name blond chick, talking to Nate in a smooth-as-silk, velvety voice. Dang it, even her voice was sexy.

Her arm outstretched daintily, like the paintings I'd seen of sirens in Greek tragedies.

Nate breathed unevenly, "Me? Um, now?"

She tossed her hair and laughed, then pointed at the nearest overhead speaker. "Yes, before it ends. I love this song!" Then, she giggled, "Let's skate, Nate. Hey, that rhymes!"

I hated her for pointing out the rhyming. And I hated the song "Moves Like Jagger." And hated her for loving that song.

Nate cocked an eyebrow and shot me a long look, like he was telepathically asking me a question, but I couldn't read him. Was it regret? Sympathy? Damn it. Surely he didn't expect me to throw my hat in the ring and ask him to skate too, now? Compete against the bombshell? I froze, and that was on me. I blew it.

Raina clattered toward me and took Nate's spot on the bench just as he got up. The newly minted couple rolled out to the rink together. She asked so only I heard, "So that's him, eh? Your Nate?"

"Yup," I answered softly. *My Nate.*

She scowled. "He could have asked you to skate, too, you know? It didn't have to be you."

Nate rolled past us in the second loop and waved. Blond bombshell looked over her shoulder and smiled at us. A look of glee. Triumph. Glory.

A sigh escaped me. "He's definitely not my type if I needed to make the first move, right?"

Raina squeezed my arm. "I don't know anything about that girl, except that she was pretty nice when I chatted with her, but I definitely hate her."

I stood up and grabbed her hand. "Yeah. Me too." The little happy flame that had ignited inside me on the drive there had smothered out. Shoulders sagging, I returned my skates at the counter with Raina and put on my shoes. My rubbery legs almost buckled, and walking straight proved difficult. As we passed the bathrooms, I mumbled, "He can have her. I don't want to be with someone pining away for another girl."

As we exited the building, we passed the Tesla getting towed from the fire lane. Even through my misery, it was impossible to keep my mouth from turning upward as the tow truck drove away, dragging the Tesla behind it. Probably belonged to some Clyde Hill asshole. I secretly hoped it was Bombshell's car.

The threatening rain finally broke through the clouds and pattered on the roof and windows of Raina's car. Light at first, then it went into full hailstorm mode. It was so bad we had to pull over until the road conditions improved.

Raina switched on her satellite radio to the "Top Hits" station. A Maroon 5 song came on. She yelled, "You suck, Adam Levine!" and turned it off with a swift, angry palm strike on the radio knob.

"Yeah, screw you, Adam!" I yelled.

We exchanged glances and laughed.

"Sorry it took me so long to come back around," I said. "I missed hanging out with you."

"Welcome back. I missed your face too." She offered me a stick of gum and drove me home.

Raina was the friend every girl needed. Loyal to her very core, standing by your side through anything, even when it wasn't deserved.

CHAPTER ELEVEN

When Annie and I looped around the rink a couple of times, Kate was still there with her friend. I waved every time we passed, but then she disappeared midsong after our third loop. I couldn't blame her. The music in here was terrible.

"Looking for your friend?" Annie asked, an icy edge in her voice.

I stumbled forward when she called me out like that, then tried to focus harder on my strides.

Why couldn't I give Annie my undivided attention? Why was I distracted by Kate when I should be high-fiving every guy in there, like, *Yeahhh! Annie is skating with me! She chose me!* But it didn't occur to me until Annie and I were on the rink that I should have stayed on that bench. To make sure Kate wasn't hurt. To make sure she got home okay.

"Who is she?" Annie's tone softened a little. Just a little.

"She works at the escape room with me. She's one of the zombies. I think she left." I glanced one last time over where Kate had been, hoping Annie didn't catch me.

Annie nodded and skated a little ahead of me, still holding my hand, but tighter now. She said calmly, "Let's go a little faster. You're pretty slow." She smiled, and my innards melted into goo.

I didn't know if there was strong airflow on the rink or if we were just swooshing fast, but Annie's hair whipped back in the wind, sending the subtle smell of spring flowers my way. Her smooth treading made skating look effortless, especially next to my clackity-clack-clacking. My hair would never flow the way hers did. We went around and around in uncomfortable silence. I was uncertain of the rules of couples' skate. Was talking forbidden? Placing my hand on the small of her back...bad idea? Maybe? Probably, especially given how unsteady I was. So we continued silently. I let her tug me along awkwardly like one of those toddler pull toys, my brain occupied with counting down the seconds until the end of the song. There was something about the lead singer's voice that made me cringe. And my balls cringe. No grown man should be able to sing that high.

The end of couples' skate took an eternity to finally come. When the rainbow lights came back on, we exited the rink and rolled straight into Peter Haskill the Fourth and his crew, who were skateless and drenched from rain. Glad they weren't drenched with anger from Jaxon's earlier identity theft.

"Hi, Pete," Annie said, letting go of my hand.

"Hey," I said, using my newly freed hand to do some sort of

handshake/hand-pull/pull-in-hug thing with him. He slapped my back at the end, making me cough.

"Hey, Annie. Nate. We just got here." Pete nodded toward his crew. "There was a front desk mix-up, but I straightened it out."

In the distance, Zach and Jaxon headed our way. I shot them a get-the-fuck-out-of-here look, which luckily Jaxon saw. They about-faced, retreating back to the arcade.

Pete and Annie chatted about school while I glanced around the rink, looking for Kate. Maybe she was still here and could hang out with us afterward. Or maybe she and her friend left to do something more fun, leaving us losers here to stay till closing.

Thankfully we'd be competing together to win that cash prize in a few days. Just the two of us. Kate and me. Alone. And maybe we'd win the whole thing. I could wow her by showing her sporty and strategic Nate. Not the guy in the stiff new shirt who crashed a skate party he wasn't invited to and could barely stand upright on wheels. The chickenshit guy shooing his best friends away because he was worried about getting on Pete's bad side.

Pete still had my hand in his, which was a little weird. I pulled away from him a little, but he pulled me back in like a yo-yo. "Hey, can I talk to you for a sec?"

My muscles in my neck and back clenched, my body reflexively knowing what this was about. *Roll away, Nate! Far, far away!*

"Sure," I croaked, gesturing my free hand toward the bench where Kate and I had sat. "Roll into my office." Bad joke, but my friends would have laughed. Or mustered a pity smile. Kate especially. Pete just stared at me with a blank look on his perfectly symmetrical face.

I led the way. My heartbeat quickened as I sat in the exact same spot as earlier. He plopped down in Kate's spot. How unfortunate to have ruined that memory. At least Pete finally let go of my hand.

"You have a chance to think about what we talked about the other day? All of the other high-GPA skids said they wanted to know what you were doing first—seems like you're the alpha dog in the skid pack," he snorted.

I tried to swallow away the grittiness in my throat. "I've been so busy finishing up applications, working extra hours, stuff like that..." I trailed off because frankly, I didn't know what else to say to him. What he was asking me to do was wrong. I didn't want to do it but didn't know how to say that to him.

"Well, time's ticking," he muttered. "Regular applications will be due soon. Next time we talk, I want your answer."

He stood up and instinctively, I mirrored him, rising to my feet. The nice thing about being on roller skates while talking to him was that I was temporarily taller, so that was good. The bad thing was I was a little unsteady. I wobbled a little by getting up too fast.

Pete's phone buzzed, and he pulled it out of his front jeans pocket, dismissively waving goodbye as he took the call.

I wiped the sweat from my forehead while he walked away.

I texted Zach and Jaxon. When the coast was clear, we all met at the car. Their arms were full of plush animals of various sizes. Jaxon breathed out a gust of wind. "Shit! Thank fucking God Pete's gone. I hate that he was in the neigh-bro-hood." He coughed out a laugh. "Did you know that Zach is king of Skee-Ball and the bear claw game? He's a beast!"

Zach smiled. "Just physics. And practice."

Jaxon tossed over to me a pink My Little Pony with a misshapen butt. "Give that to your little sister." Pinky Pie, her favorite character. She'd love it, mild deformity and all. Christmas was the last time she'd gotten any new toys—for her birthday she'd gotten a fairy costume and wand that would later double as her Halloween costume. Lucy was always sneaking into my room, trying to play with my collectibles.

Jaxon and Zach didn't know about Pete's proposition—they weren't in the top ten percent of our class. Plus, I knew what Jaxon would say: *Pete is a fuckin'-piece-of-privileged-shit-fuck-that-asshole-son-of-a-bitch-mother-fucking-ballsack-selfish-fucker-fuck-him-and-his-money!* Zach would want me to report Pete to the headmaster, but no way in hell was that going to happen. Because you know the one thing worse than being called *skid*? Being called *snitch*.

"Annie got a ride home with Pete," Jaxon continued. "He offered, and he lives a few streets away from her. Sorry you have to slum it alone with us skids, Natey boy."

In a three-to-zero vote, we went to Zach's house for an impromptu movie night. *The Wolf of Wall Street* was on, one of our all-time favorites to watch together. Jaxon loosely quoted from that movie all the time. Zach always corrected him.

I downed my frothy Coke and bowl of microwave popcorn. With the obnoxious, smug Jordan Belfort on screen, my mind drifted to my conversation with Pete and his tempting financial deal. That money could help my family. Get us a new car. A brand-new roof. Newer Xbox console. College tuition. So many possibilities.

Why couldn't I have my turn with conspicuous consumption? My whole life I'd been poor. My parents were poor, and so were both sets of grandparents before them. It was like I inherited a poverty gene. A skid for life. For once, would it really be that terrible to get a taste of being rich like everyone else?

CHAPTER TWELVE

Kate

All of the floodlights flicked on when Raina attempted to pull her car into the driveway.

"Whoa, that's all new," she murmured. "You housing maximum-security prisoners inside your house?"

Yes, the maximum-security prisoner was me. "There are snipers in watchtowers around us that you can't see," I whispered.

She burst into laughter.

"You can let me out here. The codes to the gates are complicated." I scrambled out of the passenger seat and leaped out into the rain. "Thanks for letting me come out with you. Let's do it again soon."

Her brow knitted so close together they almost formed a unibrow. "Wait, you have more than one gate?"

"Yeah, it's something my dad installed a few months ago. We're always testing out his products. We also have a helper robot now, courtesy of Digitools. He pretty much sucks, though. I'll message you later. I'm getting drenched."

Raina beamed. "Yes! On your new phone! And after school on Wednesdays a bunch of us walk to the new diner down the street. It's always empty. I think we're the only ones who keep that place in business. You should come."

It'd been so long since I was part of any group. "Yeah, I guess. Have a good night!"

"I'll take that as a Kate 'hell yeah!'"

She waited until I went through the outer gate before she backed out of the driveway. I slowed my pace down the hill even though the rain pounded down harder, thinking about whether hanging out with Raina and her friends my senior year would even be worth it if I was leaving anyway. Rekindling old friendships and making new friends was a lot of effort. But hanging out with Raina was so much fun and definitely worth doing again. Going out with real people on Wednesdays had to be better than staying at home with Jeeves.

As if he read my mind, Jeeves opened the front door for me. "Welcome back, Kate. Regretfully, I must inform you that you returned after your curfew by five minutes."

"C'mon, Jeeves, are you going to tell my dad?" Jeeves had just undergone a software installation a few days ago that gave him the ability to pick and choose which minor infractions he would upload because the server storage was filling up quickly and getting overloaded with insignificant reporting, like robot deliveries that were only ten seconds late. Birds and squirrels repeatedly triggering alarms. Minor curfew infractions. I pleaded, "I already feel like this is a prison. Please don't send the data. Please?"

"Your home is pleasant, with a steady temperature of seventy-two degrees Fahrenheit and moderately low humidity. The floors are clean. These are not prison-like conditions." He blinked once. "Perhaps you mean the household policies. The rules. But there is no similarity with living here and being in a penitentiary."

"Please don't report this," I begged.

He paused. "This infraction, being your first and being so minor, will not be uploaded." He turned on the lights in the hallway leading to my room.

"Thanks, Jeeves." I puffed my cheeks and blew out.

He rolled up to me. "Your father is awake and in the kitchen, eating a ham-and-mustard sandwich on wheat bread, drinking Yamazaki whiskey on the rocks. Have a pleasant evening, Kate." He whirred to the corner of the room and went into sleep mode.

Japanese whiskey was Dad's BFF when work stressed him out. The last time he pulled out a bottle was when he was unexpectedly promoted to CEO due to a shareholder ousting of most of the executive team at Digitools. But it wasn't the new job title that drove him to drink hard. It was the product launches that were fast-tracked to make the shareholders happy when the software wasn't nearly ready.

The product launch that made the news (in a bad way) was meant to be simple one: when a Digitools security alarm was triggered, instead of alerting the police, it would immediately send real-time texts to authorized neighbors/friends/family so they could check on the situation. Aside from the flood of complaints the company received for false or unwarranted SMS alerts, one snooping elderly neighbor of one of the shareholders was attacked during a home invasion. Startled by the sound of the curious neighbor rattling the back door, the prowler armed himself with a metal rake he grabbed from the utility closet and went on offensive attack. The old woman was hospitalized and sent home, lucky to only have long scratches down her arms. The prowler got away with the rake.

My dad glowered at me. "It's late." Unkempt, with deep, dark circles under his eyes, uncombed graying hair, and a newly formed stomach bulge, he barely looked like CEO Dad. More like a weather-battered, old sea-captain version of him.

He scratched his dark stubble, then looking downward, pressed his palms into the white marble counter. "Where'd you go with Raina?"

I plopped down on a barstool. "We went roller-skating. It was fun."

He studied my face, squinting a little, like he was looking for any sign of lying. "You hanging out together now?"

"More like, I'm hanging out with her again, like I used to."

Surely he didn't need me to spell that the last time we "hung out together" was at Mom's wake.

Dad took a gulp of his drink and winced. "There's something I wanted to talk to you about before I fly out tomorrow."

Something about this didn't sit right with me. His serious tone, his heavy drinking, him wanting to have a conversation. My stomach twisted into pretzel knots.

He poured more alcohol into his glass but didn't bother to add more ice before he sipped. Just straight, zero rocks. "At my company, things are happening. Big things. I'll be traveling a lot for a few more months, but once the ink dries on some of these upcoming deals, I'll try to be home more, hopefully before you go off to college."

He was barely home these days anyway, and now he was going to be gone all the time? Dad was more like a roommate than a parent. He came and went as he pleased, made sure the bills were paid and groceries were delivered. Our relationship had become completely transactional.

Thunder rumbled nearby, and the deafening, roaring crash distracted me from my thoughts. He spoke again, in a booming voice almost as loud as the thunder. "You're guaranteed an internship this summer at Digitools, in whatever department you want. We can work together from this point on, father-daughter corporate dynasty."

"But I was going to do community theater in June—"

"Kate! Be sensible for once!" He plowed over my words. "It's time to take your future seriously. I'm putting you in the leadership program at Digitools before and after college, so you get fast-tracked in management. So you can have a *real* future."

Out of the kitchen window, the sky lit up so brightly that it looked like morning. The thunder crashed again, so close this time it made the walls shimmy.

This internship was an ultimatum. Not friendly daddy-daughter discourse about what my future entailed. He presented it like a business transaction. Or more like a hostile takeover.

He chugged the rest of his drink. "You've got a sharp mind. You just need some grit. When I'm back from Tokyo, I'll be pretty busy, but I can carve out time to talk to you about which summer job you'd want. Maybe you can be in finance or marketing. Or both. Maybe even product development, like how your old man started out."

He made a final attempt to extract lingering drops of whiskey from his tumbler, even patting the bottom to loosen any straggling liquor. With a light clink, his glass went down into the empty sink. His sandwich sat on the white porcelain plate, untouched.

I mustered up the guts to say something. "I...I want to do theater camp this summer."

"Enough with your stupid theater shit. I'm not paying for that." He yawned. "I'm going to bed. I'll see you tomorrow morning. No, wait, I'll be on the phone with the London office for a few hours. Maybe I can get breakfast delivered here before I head to the airport."

"You're not coming to my performance tomorrow night?" My stomach sank. I knew the answer. It was the last weekend performance, and the one time I'd get to be the lead instead of just an understudy.

He made a face like he smelled something rotten. "What? I'll be on a plane. Not all of us have the luxury to do *acting*. Some of us need to pay for the roof over our heads." Before I said anything else, he answered a call on his Bluetooth earpiece and walked out of the kitchen.

After so many years succeeding at his job, he'd learned the art of always having the last word.

A hollowness widened in my chest, so big it could swallow me whole. The thunder outside roared close to the kitchen window, and another bright flash of lightning across the sky soon followed.

The sky boomed at the exact moment I made up my mind. I would go to New York earlier than expected, before the summer began. Staying here would suffocate me.

I took the thunderous applause from the sky as a sign of the universe's approval.

....

"You really killed it tonight," Understudy Henry Higgins said to me the next night. We were backstage, sweaty from the performance we'd just finished. "You ready?"

I nodded. We walked out onstage.

Taxi-hailing whistles and roaring applause filled the auditorium. I smiled and bowed as the crowd gave us a standing ovation.

"Kaaaaaate!"

"Elizaaaaaa! Henryyyyyyy!"

"Encore!"

"Bravo!"

The Saturday show had sold out. The stage director had said it was standing room only, but I didn't expect all of the people in the aisles and in the back near the exits. All of these human fire hazards were there for us. They'd risked getting trampled during an emergency evacuation for *us*!

The entire cast nailed their parts, including me as Eliza Doolittle. The songs, the lines, the accents, all of it—just perfect. I beamed as Henry Higgins and I bowed a second time.

The curtains came down, and the bright overhead lights flicked on. I scurried off the stage to the changing room. No point in lingering while my other proud castmates had their photos taken with their loved ones. Smiling moms, dads, sisters, brothers, and grandparents flooded the stage, many of them congratulating me on my performance as I passed them on my way backstage.

My eyes brimmed with tears while I crammed my belongings

into a canvas tote bag. I'd put this performance on the family calendar when the show dates were confirmed. Posted the school flyer on the fridge for Dad to see in between business trips. I'd even programmed Jeeves to send my dad a reminder a week prior. Even after our conversation last night, there was a part of me that thought...maybe.

But he didn't come.

The loose tissues on the top of my bag grew wet with my fallen teardrops. I dabbed my eyes with them so my mascara and liner wouldn't smear.

Faking a smile, I squeaked brief goodbyes on my way out.

"Nice job, Kate!" Randall, the lighting and sound engineer, saluted as I walked past.

Two of the freshmen in the ensemble gave me hugs. "You were so good! Congratulations!"

"You were way better than the other Eliza," Samuel, the choreographer, whispered to me.

I smiled and responded with an enthusiastic "Thank you!"

As I clip-clopped down the hallway in my painfully high chunky heeled loafers, someone called out to me.

"Pardon me, Kate!" Mrs. Andrea, our veteran theater director, waved me down. Soft-spoken and a grammar stickler, she exuded formality with everything she did. She never laughed, ever.

"Did you enjoy yourself tonight, dear?"

"Yeah. I mean, yes. I did. Ma'am. Thank you for the opportunity, Mrs. Andrea."

She nodded. "Your performance tonight was exceptional. Simply outstanding."

Blushing, I dipped my head and smiled. "Thank you. I practiced a lot." So did Jeeves. He ran my lines with me. At least he was good for something.

"This evening, a fire burned in you that I hadn't seen in a long time—bright, lovely, and warm." A wry smile twitched on her lips. "Your best performance yet. Enjoy the rest of your weekend. You deserve it, dear." She paused, considering, then added, "If by chance you need a letter of recommendation for college applications, I would be happy to help you."

Wow. "Thank you so much, Mrs. Andrea. You spent time in New York, doing theater there, right? Could I stop by after school next week to ask you about that?"

Nodding slowly, she said, "Could I, or may I?" There was that grammar stickler thing. "Yes, please stop by after school anytime. I'd be delighted." With a slight bow of her head *adieu*, she adjusted her silk scarf and headed back to the auditorium.

Giddy from her praise, I pushed open the emergency exit door closest to the auditorium. The buzzer blasted above my head as I escaped into the crisp autumn air.

The door also hit Raina smack in the ass. She turned around and pressed a huge bouquet of exotic flowers into my chest. A fancy one, without any carnations. "Well, Eliza Doolittle, that's the last time eh do anything nice for yeh." *Worst English accent ever.*

"Awww, you shouldn't have," I said, the tears coming back in full force. But these were happy ones. Not daddy-issues tears this time.

Raina grabbed my shoulder. "I knew you'd try to sneak out. You killed it tonight. Your mom would be so proud."

I hugged her tight. Mom would've been front row center, cheering and clapping the loudest.

"Can't. Breathe," Raina gasped. I loosened my grip. "I can take you home if you want. I'm parked in the fire zone. Probably illegal but whatever, maybe not on a Saturday night." She ran ahead of me and opened the front passenger door. "'Ere you go, mah lady."

"Oh God, stop it!" Laughing and crying, I sank into the seat, pulling the canvas bag onto my lap. When she came around the other side, she asked, "Wanna go celebrate?"

Just minutes before, I'd fled out the back door of the auditorium because I wanted to go home and be alone. But turns out I'd actually wanted the opposite of that.

"Yes! But no roller-skating."

She paused to think. "If you're hungry, we can make ice-cream sundaes and nachos at my house."

There really was no better way to end the night.

CHAPTER THIRTEEN

Nate

No way was I imagining it.

People at school were friendlier. Made more eye contact. And from what I could tell there was only one explanation. Couple skating with Annie had made my social status skyrocket.

Jaxon asked during Monday's lunch period, "So...what IS the deal with you and Annie? You're not sitting with her. Are you guys trying to play it cool?" He ripped off all the cheese from his pizza and just ate the crust part but kept his stare on me. Zach lifted Jaxon's discarded cheese off the plate with his thumb and index finger and ate it.

I shrugged. "Nothing since the rink. Haven't even seen her today." I pulled my phone from the front pocket of my jeans and checked for any missed calls or messages. No word from Kate for a few days now.

I broke the silence with a simple message to her. **Hey.** Unblinking, I stared at my phone, willing her to answer me.

Zach swallowed. "You avoiding her?"

"Who?" I asked, still wondering about Kate's silence. I shoved my phone back into my pocket.

"*Annie*, you idiot." Jaxon said. "There! I see her. She's over by the vending machines." He stood up and used his hands as a megaphone. "Hey, Annie! Come sit over heeeeere!"

It took a great deal of restraint not to hammer-punch his nuts. I hissed, "Sit down. Quit being an asshole."

Jaxon waved around like he was drowning. "Yesssssss, she's coming! This is gonna be good."

I had exactly ten seconds to figure out what I was going to say. She was headed straight toward us.

Nine.

Eight.

Seven.

Six.

Five.

Four.

Three.

Two.

One. I had nothing. My mind drew a blank.

Zero words. One tied tongue. And two useless jackass friends.

"How's it going, Annie?" Jaxon asked as she put her tray down next to mine. He lifted his eyebrows, flashing me a message: *You're welcome.*

"Good, thanks for asking." She sat on the bench next to me,

legs slightly pointing away from mine. She gave me a stern look. "You coulda sat down over with me, you know. The bell's gonna ring pretty soon."

"I—I—I didn't see you over there." That wasn't a total lie. But then again, I also wasn't looking for her. Too chicken to scope the place out, I didn't want to discover that she was happy elsewhere, not even thinking about me. That couples' skate was a fluke. Sitting in my usual lunchroom spot was a safe, reasonable plan. She, or anyone else really, could easily find me, if that's what they wanted.

The unfilled silence pained me. My friends were being quiet too, which was also unlike them. She had disrupted our boring, placid ecosystem. Actually, *Jaxon* had. *Thanks, Jaxon.*

Of all people, Zach spoke. "I ate alligator the other day."

I scrunched my face. "What? Why? And where?" I asked, grossed out, but also relieved someone had said something.

"I won a gift card to that new Cajun restaurant last month, and my family and I went there for dinner. I had breaded alligator nuggets for the first time."

"Does it taste like chicken?" We all three asked in unison and burst into a fit of laughter.

He took a sip of chocolate milk before answering. "Eh, actually, it tastes more like rattlesnake."

I spat out a laugh. I'd spent years getting into peak physical shape and memorized every survivalist training guide ever published, but I could never be like Zach, who ate alligator and rattlesnake like it was no big deal. He had a strong constitution, like a billy goat. I got an upset stomach just thinking about Cajun spices.

The bell rang, and I jolted upright. "Well, I don't know about you guys, but I'm on a strict reptile- and amphibian-free diet." After a few pats on my stomach, I took a quick bite of my barely eaten supreme pizza. Bell peppers, onions, sausage, and pepperoni—"supreme" was an overstatement for such a shitty medley of pie toppings.

Jaxon snorted. "Good one, bro. See ya after school." He stuffed in his earbuds and took off with Zach.

That left Annie and me. Alone.

"Walk you to your class?" I asked.

She hesitated, so I hedged. "Or not," I backpedaled. "I'll see ya later."

"No, no, it's fine, I just have to get my backpack from my locker for next period. Let's go." Our metal bench screeched on the linoleum as we scooted back from the table.

In the senior corridor, Pete Haskill IV strolled straight over to me. My upper body shivered as he approached. I expected him to do the same handshake-back-slap greeting he did at the skating rink, but instead he switched it up by grabbing my arm and going back and forth like we were using a two-man saw. Back. Forth. Back. Forth. I'd never seen anything like it. It made me

worried that maybe it wasn't how the handshake was supposed
to go, that maybe I'd forgotten to let go at the right time, and he
was simply trying to pull his hand loose.

His voice dropped low. "You ready to talk about the grade
thing?"

I cleared my throat and whispered to keep out of earshot of
Annie, who was now applying lip gloss in the mirror of her locker.
"Can I have more time?"

Abruptly, he let go of my hand. What was his deal with him
always holding it? "How much more time are we talking about?"
He scowled.

Maybe forever? "Can I get back to you in a couple of weeks?"
I asked, my voice cracking. That would give me time to focus
on the zombie competition with Kate. I could deal with Pete
after that.

Pete smiled, like he had the upper hand. "Two weeks then,
skiddo." He slapped my back hard enough to make me choke on
my spit.

Annie joined us, carrying her overstuffed backpack covered
in purple peace signs. "What're we talking about?"

"Nothing," we both said, him firmly, me in high-pitched
singsong.

"It sounded like more than nothing," she said, narrowing her
eyes. "But whatever, we need to go. The bell's gonna ring." Annie
and Pete exchanged a look I couldn't read and then acted like

they didn't know each other. We walked in silence to her econ class until she stopped a few feet short of the door. "Um, can we study together for midterms?"

A study date...with Annie. Oh man, I would have pinched myself to make sure it wasn't a dream if it weren't such a weird thing to do. When Jaxon found out, he'd high-five himself and say he'd orchestrated the whole thing from the start. Maybe he did.

"So...is it okay if we study together for exams?" Annie repeated with some hesitation. My speaking delay allowed me time to compose myself instead of pumping two fists in the air and strutting down the hallway like I owned the school.

With a steady-ish voice, I asked, "Sure, maybe later this week?" Annie bobbed her head and disappeared into the classroom. That was easier than I expected.

Feeling lucky, I checked my phone again for messages. Kate still hadn't replied.

Time to write again. **Team TBD competition is in a week, let's discuss...Dicks?**

Then, **I meant Dicks hamburgers, not discuss dicks**

Someone please take this phone away from me. **I'll stop typing dicks now**

She responded so fast. *I LOVE DIIIIIIICKS!!! 7pm tonight*

I swear to God, I'd never laughed so hard in my life.

....

"Jae-Woo!"

"JAE-WOO!"

I went around the house trying to track down my dad's voice. Turns out he was on the roof.

"Next time, answer when I call you!" He barked when I came out the back door. If he'd screamed my name a third time, that meant full-on angry-Korean-dad escalation. Added chores. A grounding or two. More yelling. Threats of kicking me out of the house. In other words, the usual.

"Sorry, I was doing homework." Which was a total lie, unless homework involved figuring out what to wear when seeing Kate.

Dad yelled, "I need water! Can you bring to me?" He pulled up his paint-splattered Hanes undershirt tucked into his pants and used the bottom of it as a towel to wipe his face. Dad's face, neck, and arms were golden brown from being outdoors so much, freckled with sun spots. He never seemed to burn, despite his refusal to wear sunscreen. Underneath his shirt, pants, and socks was pasty white, translucent skin. Like a jellyfish, but a little grosser.

"No problem," I hollered, jogging to the back door.

It was locked.

I jiggled the knob and tried again. I'd just come through that same door and deliberately left it unlocked.

A small pair of hands pulled back the curtains in the adjacent window.

"Lucy! Open the door. It's hot out today." It was an unseasonable eighty degrees outside, blistering by Seattle autumn standards.

"No, not till you 'pologize!" The curtain fell straight, and Lucy's hands disappeared.

"For what?!" I banged on the door. "Open it. I mean it!"

"You called me a crybaby again! Say sorry!" True, I called her that a lot, but that's because she was. Seriously, who cried when their toast was too hot? Blow on the stupid thing.

"I'm sorry." I sighed. *Sorry that you're a crybaby.*

"And say you won't call me crybaby again."

Damn it, she was so smart. "I won't call you crybaby again."

"Ever."

Sigh. "EVER. Now let me in, I'm serious. Dad is gonna be mad."

A huge wave of relief hit when the lock clicked.

She scampered away. Good, she'd be out of my hair for a while. I swear, that kid had to be adopted. Or maybe I was adopted. How could two people so different be related? And I wasn't talking just about her crybaby-ness. For Koreans, on the first birthday there's a whole ritual around predicting the future of the one-year-old. Parents typically laid out a stethoscope, ruler, calculator, things like that, and in front of a whole crowd of people, the kid would walk or crawl to the item he wanted, and that would determine what the kid would be when he grew up.

Unsurprisingly, I beelined to the hundred-dollar bill, and all of my parents' friends roared with laughter, saying I'd be showered in riches.

My sister? She picked up a paintbrush and chewed on the brush end. My parents and partygoers gaped when Lucy grinned and revealed two front teeth covered in green Crayola watercolor.

Back then, it was hilarious how different she was from me. She was so unpredictable, stubborn, and full of emotion.

Now, not so much.

"JAE-WOO! *Ppali! Ppali!*" Dad screamed. *HURRY!*

In the fridge, we had kimchi. Pickles. Tubs of tuna and potato salad from Costco. So many apples. Everything but bottles of water.

No bottles of water anywhere, not in the pantry or in the garage. Not wanting to be screamed at again, I put some ice into a large thermos and added some tap water. That would have to do.

Outside, a heavy breeze came through and lifted the tarp from the roof, causing it to flap like a fish out of water before Dad could anchor it.

He cursed in Korean as I approached.

As I rattled the bottle, the ice clinked around. "Appa, here's your water!"

Dad crouched and peered over the side. "I can't come down. You need to bring it up."

"I can't." He knew that. Me, on the rickety ladder, shaking with every footstep, falling to my death. Nope, no thank you.

"JAE." Pause. "WOO." The head shake. The disappointed tone. Him working his jaw back and forth. Translation: how could my only son, my oldest, be so damn scared of heights?

Blinking hard, I tried to push away all the memories that still haunted my dreams. My shoulder muscles clenched thinking about the time when I got stuck up a tree in my neighbor's yard that was too tall to scale. In the pouring rain, it took hours for a firefighter to climb a ladder and coax me down. The time I pissed all over myself standing on the high diving board for the first time (and the last time). Two years ago, when our history class took a field trip to the Space Needle, and I was the only one who stayed on the bus. A rumor went around school that I couldn't go because I was too poor to pay for admission. That was only marginally better than the real reason for not going. That I was too chicken.

I had two choices. To scurry up the ladder as quickly as my legs could go, give Dad the water, rush back down, and piss in my pants. Or I could compose myself, slowly take each step in stride, still piss in my pants, but over a longer period of time. Neither option was "good." But Dad's patience was running out. His disappointment was at an all-time high. I had to make a move.

Panic immediately set in, and my fingers and feet tingled like they were falling asleep. My blood pulsed through my hands as I gripped the ladder.

Pulsing. Hammering. Throbbing. *Boom. Boom. Boom.*

Six rungs. Just six steps. Twelve, if you count the return trip. I attached the thermos's handle to a carabiner and hooked it to my pants belt loop.

Breathe in. Breathe out. Left foot, right foot. Don't look down. Step one.

Left foot, right foot. Don't look down. Two.

Left foot, right foot. Don't look down. Three.

A blast of wind hit the ladder, causing it to shimmy. I gripped it tighter, and my knuckles turned white.

Left foot, right foot. Four.

Left foot, right foot. Five.

Dad had moved to the other side of the roof, unfolding edges of the tarp and weighing them down with broken cinder blocks.

One more step, then Dad could come get the water from me and I wouldn't need to go up any farther.

Unhooking the bottle with my eyes mostly closed, I bellowed, "I have your water!" The thermos dangled like I was doing hypnosis.

"Put it down." No "thank you," "good job," or "thanks for risking your life for my hydration." I didn't care, though. My main priority was to be back on the ground.

I put it down on the roof, then with my eyes fully closed, I felt for the next step down.

"Naaaaate!" It was Lucy again, directly underneath me. Dizziness hit hard when I tried to look in the direction of her voice. *Don't look down. Don't look down. Don't look down.*

"Luce! I'll be down in a second."

She choked back sobs. "I broke it! I'm sorry!"

"Luce, move away! I need to focus." I still had five steps to go.

Now crying hysterically, Lucy took a shaky hold on the ladder. My eyes squeezed shut even tighter. "Luce! Move!"

My body was in full-blown panic mode. Heart pounding, lungs burning, full-body tense and tingling. The burn of bile made its way upward. Ironic, since I was trying to make my way down.

My left foot searched for the next metal platform of safety one more time. Lucy wailed as I made it down a level.

The next time, though, my foot was too close to the edge of the rung, which I would have seen if my eyes were open.

I slipped, of course, banging my knees on the rungs as I lost my grip. The entire front side of my body from the neck down got a metal spanking. I winced as my knees clattered to the bottom.

Lucy had stepped out of the way just in time, thank God, or she would have gotten two boots to the face. Seeing me fall from the ladder made her finally stop crying.

Slowly, I stood to assess the damage. Ripped pants from snagging screws, skinned arms and knees, and a turned ankle.

Terrific.

"Lucy," I groaned, hobbling toward the house. "What were you crying about? You distracted me, you know that, right?"

She gaped at the blood oozing from my elbow scrapes. "I'm sorry."

"I'll be fine. I just need to wash off the blood and put some ointment on it."

She shook her head. "I'm sorry for Hermione too." On the kitchen table, my limited edition Hermione figurine, circa 2002, lay outside her case. The box had been opened carefully, but Hermione was no longer in her Hogwarts robe. She was wearing a ball gown from Lucy's Shimmer and Shine genie collection. "I wanted her to look pretty. With sparkles. But the dress is stuck."

It took a few seconds before it hit me. "Lucy. That was worth five hundred dollars. FIVE! HUNDRED! DOLLARS!" I took her naked Shimmer doll and threw it across the room, so hard that it hit the wall and left a flesh-colored scuff mark on the off-white paint. Irresponsible Lucy, who flushed dolls down toilets, who ate paintbrush tips at parties, who threw away five hundred dollars. It made me so...ARRRRGGGHHHH!

My mom came into the kitchen with bags of Subway sandwiches. Lucy ran to her and hid behind her legs.

Mom swung open the back door and called out to my dad. "*Jagiya!* Time to eat dinner! I buy your favorite! Cold-cut combo foot long!"

"Can you please tell Lucy to stay away from my stuff? She ruined something I was saving!"

"Lucy, don't bother Nate thing. You want him to bother all your toy?"

"Nooooo! I said I was sorry, Umma!"

"Don't you ever go into my room and mess with my stuff," I growled at her. "Mom, I'm gonna go out for dinner. Can you put my sandwich in the fridge? I'll eat it for lunch tomorrow." I opened the freezer and pulled out a bag of peas to ice my ankle.

Mom unpacked the subs and chips and glanced at me. "Why you go out in your zombie clothes?"

I glanced down. "Huh? These are my normal clothes."

She shrugged but didn't apologize. While putting groceries away, she also restacked and pulled out Tupperwares of banchan to make room. She used the Korean mom sniff test to measure edibility before putting it on the kitchen table. Her marinated soybean sprouts, radish kimchi, and sesame leaves made the cut. The spicy pickled cucumbers and spicy squid went straight into the swing-top trash can.

Subway sandwiches and banchan. Two cultures colliding to make culinary magic: this was the Korean American dream right here. KFC with kimchi was my all-time second-favorite combo.

Dad sat down at the kitchen table first, unwrapped his foot long, and crunched his chips. He refused to look at me. Neither of us brought up my painful fall because it brought shame on both of us. I was his "soft" son, unable to climb up and down a ladder.

Lucy still couldn't use chopsticks, so she pulled out pieces of soybean sprouts with her fork. She grabbed a few pieces of spinach with her fingers when my parents weren't looking.

Mom said, "Jae-Woo, your birthday is coming. We can get pizza from Papa John. Maybe I make you brownie cake?"

Lucy lifted a sprout from her plate and dangled it next to her mouth. "Why can't we go have pizza and games at Chunky Cheese?"

Dad grumbled, "Don't play with your food!"

Lucy ate the sprout and picked up her fork to stab at the rest of the vegetables on her plate.

Mom snorted. "Nate is too old for Chunky Cheese. That is little kid place."

Frustrated, I sighed, "It's Chuck E. Cheese's, not Chunky Cheese—"

Mom cut me off. "That's what I say!"

"Me too," Lucy added.

Mom muttered, "What is Chucky mean? Chunky Cheese make more sense."

There was no point in arguing about this. I gave up. "Why can't I have a Ben and Jerry's ice-cream cake?" For the last five years, I'd had Chocolate Chip Cookie Dough plus Fudge Brownie with M&M's and Oreo crumbles on top. It was a custom order, and a yearly tradition.

"Those cake are expensive, Jae-Woo." Dad shook his head, pinching between his brow.

Mom and Dad were back into thrift mode, a cyclical event every few years. Last time it happened was when Lucy was born. My parents returned some onesies and bibs they'd gotten from neighbors and friends just to buy me new running shoes because I'd had a growth spurt, as many middle school boys did. Our groceries went from name-brand to generic. Home repairs went on hold and were never resumed. Though I became aware of our circumstances over time, the Kim family rule prevented me from asking or arguing with them about it. Not that my parents would open up about personal matters anyway. It wasn't something they ever did, even when they directly affected me. Like, say, being too poor to afford an ice-cream cake and party, and not just saying that directly.

Lucy looked up at Mom with watery eyes. "But I like that cake too, Appa. Umma." Tears popped out and streamed down her cheeks.

I glanced at Mom and Dad, but both sat with pursed lips.

"That's okay, Luce, Mom makes amazing brownies," I said, trying to defuse the Lucy time bomb. Mom's brownies were straight from a box, but Mom added chocolate chunks into the batter, making it gooey and extra-chocolaty. "And maybe this time we can add a scoop of ice cream on top."

The two things Lucy loved most: chocolate and ice cream. Her crying stopped instantly.

I looked at Dad, hoping to catch his eye and give him a reassuring "Lucy crisis averted" smile, but he was too busy staring at the stack of mail on the counter. After putting his beer down, he opened one of the letters. Color drained from his face while he read. When he finished, he ripped the note in half, threw it in the trash can, then stormed out of the room, leaving his half-drunk Hite beer sweating on the fake marble-top.

When Mom ran after him, I fished the letter out of the bin and skimmed it fast.

Seattle Mutual Savings and Loan

1200 Broadway

Seattle, WA 98104

Dear Mr. Kim:

We are writing to inform you that your request of loan modification for your home mortgage payments has been reviewed. Regretfully, we are denying your petition. While we understand that you have recently been terminated from your IT consulting position with Zeneration, Inc., we do feel that there is a possibility of you being hired elsewhere with your strong credentials.

Per your request, we have deferred your payment for the next month, as a courtesy, but late fees on the previous months of nonpayment will not be waived. We hope this will provide your family with some financial relief.

Sincerely,

Bernie Akins

Chief Loan Officer

Dad had lost his job? And no one told me? The guys in the IT department loved him, so none of this made sense. He could probably get a job at another company, right?

Now there was way more at stake for winning the zombie competition. We could lose the house.

Lucy broke my concentration. "Nate! What did the trash note say?"

Think quick. "It says...be nice to your brother on his birthday. It's from Santa."

She raised an eyebrow. "Can Santa give you an ice-cream birthday cake if Umma and Appa don't?"

I smiled. *Oh, Lucy.* If there was any leftover prize money, I'd definitely buy myself an ice-cream cake. And fine, maybe I'd get Lucy one too. And maybe take us all to Chunky Cheese to celebrate. A joint gift from Santa and me. What an amazing birthday that would be.

CHAPTER FOURTEEN

The Uber dropped me off a few minutes late, thanks to a backup on the freeway caused by a six-pack of Coors Light that had fallen from (or been thrown out of) someone's vehicle and landed into the express lane of I-405. I'd seen blown tires, broken hubcaps, and glass littering the road, but there was nothing more infuriating than a domestically mass-produced beer road hazard.

Nate was already there, and not only that, he came straight toward me with a tray full of food and drinks, the same order we had from that first day we met, but with an extra burger. I'd initially been annoyed that he'd broken days of silence with a meaningless, "Hey," but this more than made up for it.

He motioned with his head to follow him. We walked to the "stand and dine" area, or rather, I walked, and he limp-hopped, holding our tray. A section of a counter opened up, and we swooped in to take it.

"Confession time. I don't like special burgers," he said, unwrapping the second burger. "I hate mayo. And aioli. And pretty much anything creamy or oily that drips off a sandwich. Plain, boring burger. Yum." Nate took a big, satisfied bite.

I grabbed one of the shakes off the tray. "What happened to your leg?"

"It's my ankle. It's nothing, I just fell down a ladder."

I leaned forward. "You WHAT?"

His mouth was full of burger bits, but he answered anyway. "I fell down a ladder. Actually, just halfway down a ladder. It's a long story, and embarrassing because it deals with my fear of heights and my little sister blackmailing me, so can we not talk about it, please?"

He took another bite.

The special sauce soaked my burger's wrapper, leaving a damp circle on the paper mat. "Thanks for getting the food." My stomach relaxed after gobbling down a pinch of fries and a few bites of soggy burger. Maybe dry burgers were the way to go.

Once I took a long sip of milkshake, we got down to business. "I have so many questions about the competition now," I said. "Online, all the descriptions about the game conditions are really vague. There was a whole section in the rules of participation about advanced AI technology systems. Do you think that means it's all virtual reality?" More fries. More milkshake. "You think the zombies are part of a video game? Or maybe I'm overthinking it and it's just a bunch of minimum-wage actors, dressed up as dead people? Maybe our strategy should be no sleeping, no eating, just straight-up kicking zombie ass, mercenary style, till we make it across the campground."

"That was my plan, you know." He smirked. "Drink Red Bull and decapitate zombies. Repeat."

"Not with that ballooned-up ankle of yours you're not." He bent down and propped his leg up with his backpack, and I could see how swollen it was—puffed, like what happens when you microwave marshmallows.

"I'll be fine in a couple of days," he said with a quick wave of his hand. "I've gotten pretty beaten up in my Krav Maga classes. This is nothing."

There was not a single sporty bone in my body, so I couldn't relate. I lived a life-in-a-protected-bubble existence, surrounded by robots and robust security systems. I was the person who ducked when a ball came within peripheral view. The teammate who would bend down to tie my unlaced shoe just as someone scurried past me to score a game-winning goal. The one whose body sunk in water when it should be naturally buoyant. I never got close enough to harm's way to result in any injury, sports-related *or* ladder-related.

"You think you'll be okay in time for the contest?" I hated to ask, but with the competition so close the following weekend, he needed to tell me straight up if he was going to bail on me because of this injury.

He rolled his eyes. "Are you trying to ditch me already? I'll be fine by the time the competition starts. It's very temporary, I swear. Scout's honor." His face turned blazing red. My cheeks were hot too. We both laughed and chewed our burgers. Was this how it would be during the competition? Us together, always next to each other, awkward but weirdly at ease?

He cleared his throat before he spoke again. "I don't like that there's not a lot of information, either, and what they have online is cryptic. Maybe it's because it's the first annual one. Now all I do is run through a gajillion scenarios in my head about all the potential what-ifs. What if there's no food or water? We should bring enough to hold us over a couple of days just in case, right? Maybe some energy bars because they're light and easy to pack." He bit his bottom lip, lost in the turnstile of his thoughts. "We might need to layer for frigid weather. And we should bring headlamps."

Headlamps?

He wadded a napkin and threw it on his tray. "I guess we should bring a tent too. Or should we assume we're not sleeping? Should we bring bear spray?" Nate gave me an earnest look, like he wanted me to answer all of his rapid-fire questions.

Bear spray? Wildlife threats hadn't even crossed my mind. I'd only considered hiding from the undead.

"Let's table everything and decide later," I said. Translation: let me go home and google "best bear spray." I finished the ketchup for my fries and looked under the fry container for another packet. Nate smiled and handed me some from his side of the tray. "You want any fries to go with that ketchup, Miss?"

"Can you bring some of these ketchups in your backpack? I may need them for sustenance," I said. "To put on some tasty bear meat."

He made a blech face, one eye closed with his tongue hanging out. "Probably not what Heinz or Hunt's had in mind."

"Okay, let's be serious now. If you fall behind with that balloon animal leg of yours, you may be sacrificed to Smokey and his bear posse so I can make it to the finish line."

"You'd use me as bear bait?" He winced. "That's harsh. I had no idea you were so competitive."

"It wouldn't be personal. And I'm not usually competitive. I just really need the money right now. I don't think teams can split up, though, so you're safe."

"Yeah. Good. I need the money too." His eyes locked on mine.

Blushing hard, I looked away. *Focus on the mission. Eyes on the prize. New York City.*

I cleared my throat. "We should get to know each other better, since we'll be attached at the hip all weekend. Your likes, dislikes, worst fears. You go first."

He stroked his chin. "I'm a Ravenclaw. Scorpio, my birthday is actually coming up soon. I like romantic walks on the beach."

Tilting my head, I shot him a narrow-eyed glare.

"Okay, fine, fine. I love BLT sandwiches, no mayo. My best friends are cool, Zach and Jaxon. I hate mayo. Did I mention that? I am scared of heights and dying by quicksand."

"Quicksand?"

He laughed. "I've watched a lot of old, bad TV. Quicksand is hard to escape. It used to give me nightmares. Your turn."

I tried to clear my throat but coughed instead. "I'm Slytherin. A Libra, my birthday just passed. I hate the beach. The salty, fishy air is gross. I like BLTs but love Cuban sandwiches even more. I hate horseradish and love mayo. I'm scared of..."

A brief wave of panic hit me. Did I tell him the truth? That I was scared of losing my chance to do theater in New York because of Dad? That since Mom died, I'd been desperately lonely, but scared to stay close to anyone because I didn't want to risk losing them too?

"I'm scared of nothing."

I liked him, but Nate wasn't reason enough to alter my plans. He was a means to an end. That was it. Eyes fixed on my tray, I focused on my straw making a "hee-haw-hee-haw" sound when pulling it up and down in my milkshake cup. No one knew I'd already started looking into GED studies and was ready to bolt right after the survival competition. Not even Raina. What I needed, above everything, was to stay focused, so I could succeed in what I wanted most. To be free.

Sorry.

Goodbye, Nate Kim.

Hello, independence.

....

"NO! NO! NO!"

Panting hard, I slapped the bedroom wall. trying to find the manual light switch. These recurring bad dreams had really screwed up my REM cycles. When I went to a therapist, she'd told me to keep a dream journal. It made me laugh at the time, but now I wondered if that would have stopped the nightmares.

This time, I'd dreamed that a room full of humanoid robots—like Jeeves, but more advanced—had turned me into one of them. My skin glowed, but not in a radiant, free-radical, moisturized way, but in a luminescent, eerie, LED-light way. I had circuitry where my eyes had been.

Sweaty and heart drumming, I gave up on finding the switch and yelled, "Illuminate!"

My entire room flooded with eye-wincing light. It made me sound like a rip-off Harry Potter, sans cool magical wand, but that was the command programmed by my dad's company. The command to yell in the middle of the night to relieve myself of terrifying darkness.

How many times had I woken up from a dream like this? Ten? Fifteen? Maybe even twenty? Dad's technology had infil-trated my life so deeply that even in my dreams, I was no longer my own self. Was this my conscience letting me know it was time to leave?

I knew I wouldn't be able to get back to sleep after that. Deciding that snacking was a good way to kill time, I shuffled to the kitchen without turning on the hall lights.

"It's two forty-one in the morning, Kate. You should be asleep."

I nearly screamed. Jeeves's silent sneak-roll in the darkness pretty much woke me up for good. "Damn it, Jeeves, you scared the crap out of me." I flung open the pantry door and took a look at my crunchy food options.

"That was not my intent. I apologize. Your father has sent you a rather urgent message. Would you like me to read it to you?"

I pulled out a new can of Pringles and popped open the metal seal. It hissed as Jeeves played back my dad's words.

"Two twenty a.m. Kate, call me back when you get this. End of message."

With half a chip dangling from my mouth, I asked, "Uh, okay, can you call him back now? Let's get this over with."

A dial tone came from the speaker on Jeeves's midsection. Then my dad's voice boomed, "Kate! I'm busy at work!"

I rolled my eyes. "Jeeves said you had an urgent message for me. Trust me, I wouldn't bother you otherwise."

"Hold on." The silence filled with the familiar "swish-swoosh" sound from Dad's wool-silk blended suit pants. A door closed. "Okay, I can talk now, but it'll be brief. I've heard from reliable sources that your chances of getting into your top-choice colleges are slim. Early-action candidates are stronger than ever this year, and applications are way up. So rather than applying to second-tier schools, right after you take your finals, you'll come with me to Asia, where I really need to be to oversee R and D. You can do a gap year early. I can line up some charity work in Japan and China. With some intensive East Asian language studies, bam! You'll get in anywhere."

The way he spoke to me was like how he talked when he was raising capital from investors. Like he was selling me this grand plan and wouldn't take "no" for an answer. Did he realize that I was his daughter, not a business investment?

My throat closed, preventing me from speaking immediately. How could he possibly think that yanking me out of school right after final exams would be good idea?

Dad continued his rapid-firing speech. "I've already spoken with your headmaster and guidance counselor. They said it's not ideal from a social perspective, but you're only really losing a semester. Plus, it's not like you hang out with your friends anyway."

I took a deep, unsteady breath. "Dad, this is what *you* want, not what *I* want. You know why I don't hang out with friends anymore? Because of Mom. Mom *dying*."

He plowed on. "This isn't a discussion, Kate. This is

happening. It's for your future. And don't you dare bring up Mom again or any of that useless theater nonsense—"

Steady tears trickled down my cheeks. "We already lost Mom. Do you really want to lose me too? Because you will."

He sighed. "Look, I have to go. This is the end of this conversation, Katherine."

The line cut. Then silence.

He'd never called me Katherine before. Somehow, the distance between us had grown so wide that we were using formal names. The rift between us was now a chasm.

Could you close a chasm?

I did the only thing I could think to do. With my can of Pringles in hand, I grabbed my backpack and rain gear by the door, and took off in the dead of night.

CHAPTER FIFTEEN

Clink. Clink-clink. Clonk.

With the wind howling and kicking up debris, it was hard to tell someone was actually outside, purposefully throwing shit at my window.

"Psssst, Nate!"

That *psssst* was so familiar. Heart thumping hard, I raced to the window, unlocked it, and yanked the handle up.

It wouldn't budge.

With few more huge heave-hos, it wouldn't move, not even a millimeter.

I cupped my hands to the window, hoping to get a better view of her. There Kate stood, a story below me, backpack on one shoulder, raincoat damp from the drizzle. Her face glowed from the light of her phone. She pointed at her screen. Then pointed at me.

It took a second to click. She was calling.

I lunged for my nightstand. My phone lit up, but there was no ringing, thanks to "do not disturb" mode.

"Hullo?" My voice rumbled with a low-pitch baritone. Better than squeaking, I guess.

"Hey," she sniffed. "Can I come up?"

I walked to the window and saw her wipe her eyes with her rain-soaked sleeve.

"Uh, sure," I whispered. "Let me unlock the front door."

"Thanks." The light from her phone flicked off. Her shadowy figure walked toward the front of the house.

A quick glance down revealed I was wearing an oversize Mariners shirt and tattered boxers. I grabbed a crumpled pair of gray sweats from the floor and pulled them on as I simultaneously walked to my bedroom door. It creaked as I opened it. Waiting for a few seconds, I made sure there was no stirring from the other bedrooms, then continued down the stairs and opened the front door.

We stood there for a second, facing each other. Me, dry with massive bedhead. Her, sopping wet with clumpy brown curls. She didn't look physically harmed, but when Kate gave me a weak smile, even in the dark I could sense her intense pain. All I wanted to do was make her feel better. Nothing else mattered.

"Come here," I whispered. I pulled her body forward and gave her a bear hug. One of those long ones where I worried if she could breathe after a while. Her damp hair smelled nice, like expensive shampoo.

Her shuddered breath calmed. "My dad and I had a fight. I...I couldn't stay there."

"It's okay," I said. "Want to go upstairs where we can talk? We have to be quiet because, you know."

She nodded. After taking her shoes off, Kate tiptoed behind me to my room upstairs. Once I closed my door, she said, "No offense, but your Harry Potter collection looks way creepier at night."

I flicked on my desk lamp. "Gee, thanks. Last time I let you into my room at three a.m."

"Thanks for taking me in." She peeled off her backpack and jacket and plopped down on my bed.

"Why were you and your dad fighting in the middle of the night?" My brain woke up to full realization that I had Kate in my bedroom again, and I sat down in my desk chair, several arm lengths away.

Her shoulders slumped. "He called me from Japan. He wants to pull me out of school. It's a long story." Tears trickled down both cheeks.

I leaped over to her with a box of tissues in hand, then sat down on the floor near my bed instead of retreating back to my chair. "I'm sorry." What else could I say? The more I said, the more danger I was in of overstepping somehow. Or worse, saying something stupid so she'd hate me forever. She was airing shit out. I needed to let her do that.

She told me about her dad's plan to bring her to Asia just for the sake of college admissions. Wow, he was just as bad as Pete and those guys, trying to rig our GPAs. Maybe even worse.

Her life sounded so awful. No mom. A conniving dad. I stood up just so I could sit next to her and gave her a side hug. She yawned and leaned her head on my chest. We stayed like that for a while, until Kate turned her head up and looked at me. She had stopped crying, but streaks remained on her cheeks from the dried tears.

Her soft brown eyes no longer looked pained. I'd never noticed her long, dark lashes and the smattering of freckles on her nose before. With her so close, right next right to me, I couldn't think of anyplace I'd rather be. Not playing video games, not even hanging out with Annie.

I whispered, "Need to re-up on bear hugs?" Kate smiled as I pulled both arms around her again. She leaned into me, tucking herself into my chest. Soon, her shoulders relaxed, and her breath grew slow and heavy. Kate was asleep, safe and sound.

I slowly maneuvered out of my dual-arm-hook hug position, letting her curl into a side-sleep on my bed. She murmured something unintelligible as I pulled my comforter up to her chin. Something about Pringles. Something about sharing them with me. I set my alarm to some ungodly time and turned off the lamp.

Rolling out my sleeping bag on the floor and using one of Lucy's large freaky Beanie Boo stuffed animals as a pillow, I focused on slowing down my breathing. But my brain kept jumping to the fact that Kate was here. In my room. Sleeping near me. Inhaling the same air as me.

Deep breaths. *Sloooow dowwwwn, Nate.*

It took a while, but once Kate had fallen into a deeper sleep, and I knew she would be okay for a while, my eyelids finally grew heavy enough to drift away.

CHAPTER SIXTEEN

Nate

Guess who showed up at work on the night before the big competition? Pete Haskill Numero Cuatro and two of his bro-magnons, both of whom had resting bitch face. When they locked the door to the outside to make sure no one entered or left, I knew they were here just to see me. Thank God Kate took the night off, just in case I was about to get a royal ass kicking. Since she stealthily slipped out of my house earlier in the week, we'd texted a lot about the competition, but she never ever mentioned the whole middle-of-the-night "sleepover." And leave it to Pete to be the only one in the world who could get me to stop thinking about Kate being in my bedroom.

He whistled as he glanced around the waiting room. "So, Natey boy, this is where you spend all your time when you aren't nerding it up at the library? *Interesting.*"

"It's a good job. Some of us need jobs. Not everyone has four-car garages to hold our four Teslas." *Smack, take that, moneybags.*

"We have only two Teslas. One Bentley. And a Lexus SUV

for camping." Correcting my Tesla count was idiotic, but the fact that he took a Lexus SUV out to the local campgrounds made him the biggest douche in the entire douchiverse.

"How'd you know I worked here?" I couldn't imagine Jaxon or Zach telling Pete any shit about me.

"A little birdie named Annie mentioned it." He threw back his head and laughed, cartoon-villain-like.

My stomach rolled. *Damn it, Annie.*

He continued the torture session. "I bought out the rest of the tickets for the entire night, so it's just you, and us." He made a sweeping hand motion, and his amigos stood at attention and gave him one of those smug jock nods. "I just wanted to see if you had time to think about the business proposal."

I puffed my chest. "I've had some time to think about it, yeah."

"And?"

"I have a pretty good shot at coming into some money soon. So thanks, but no thanks."

He raised an eyebrow. "How much are we talking?"

"Fifty grand," I gulped. Sweat beaded on my forehead, thinking about all there was at stake. I was losing my cool. Not that I'd ever played it totally cool with Pete.

He shot a look at his two buddies, who backed up to the door. "It's higher than what we paid some other skids, but we can go up to fifty large. I'm not sure you get what's happening here, but I'm not leaving till you say yes."

My throat constricted, and I couldn't get any air in. His two bros were positioned by the exit, preventing my escape. There were no windows in the waiting room. The escape room down the hall, absurdly, had no way to escape, with no entry or exit to the outside world. I balled my fists, ready to swing if needed. I could get a few punches in before these un-Incredible Hulks took me down.

The door to the escape room creaked open. We all jerked our heads in surprise.

"Hey, uh, Nate? You're late. We should get started." Damon, one of the longest tenured zombies, peeked his head out and surveyed the situation. Pete and his buddies relaxed their shoulders. Mine stayed tense.

Damon pulled out his phone from his tattered lab coat and straightened his black costume glasses. "Is everything okay here? Need me to...uh...call the owner? Or the police?"

Pete narrowed his eyes at Damon, my nerdy savior. "We stopped by to say hi to our buddy Nate here and were just heading out. No way are we wasting our weeknight playing some stupid shitty zombie game." He turned my way and hissed, "We'll see *you* later."

Each word hit like rapid sucker punches to my stomach.

From his embossed leather wallet, Pete pulled out a crisp fifty-dollar bill and threw it at me. "Here's your tip, skid." He spat that last word at me. The money fluttered at first, then spiraled straight to my feet. In normal circumstances I'd be thrilled with any gratuity for my gracious hospitality and well-paced comedic monologue. Clearly this was not that kind of transaction. He'd thrown his "fuck you" money at me like I was a slum dog, small and pathetic.

He unlocked the entry door, and his buddies followed him outside. When it clicked shut, I exhaled slowly. How long had I been holding in my breath?

An excited look crossed Damon's face. "Wow, big tipper! Does this mean we get the night off?"

With a sad smile, I picked up the bill and focused on the positive. "You and the rest of the guys can split the tip." I sighed deeply. "And yeah, let's call it a night. It's been a long day." I released the zombie talent early and locked up.

Rain pelted my windshield on the drive home, making the white and yellow lines on the road nearly impossible to see. Lucky for me, I'd taken this exact route home hundreds of times, so the trip home was essentially on autopilot. Full-body numbness set in during my ride, and at first, I assumed it was from nerves about the looming zombie survivalist competition. But the feeling of doom rising in my chest, the unmistakable urge to throw up, well, that wasn't anticipation. Or excitement. That was fear, of the unbridled variety. Pete's plan was not actually a choice; it was a mandate.

The downpour continued as I pulled the car into my driveway.

In the streetlamp light the fuel gauge was dangerously close to *E*, and I was driving on fumes. And, more visibly now, it was clear that my hands were shaking violently.

....

Annie messaged me just before I crawled into bed.

Hey, she wrote.

Hey back

I'm coming to the cross-country meet. Good luck!

My stomach clenched. *I'm not going. Got other plans.*

I accepted a video chat request. "Whaddya mean you're skipping the meet? Is everything okay?" Her bedside lamp glowed so brightly that it took over half her screen, partially obscuring her face. She was wearing a tattered Adam Levine shirt. I couldn't tell if she was being ironic or not, so I kept my mouth shut. I also didn't feel like mentioning that Pete had paid me a visit at work. No need to add even more stress the night before the big competition.

"Everything's fine. I've already sent out most of my college applications, so this meet isn't that big of a deal to me. And I qualified last year. Because I'm so awesome."

She moved her head so the background light gave her an angelic halo. "So what are you doing instead? Masterminding a new product release in your basement? Going on a hot date with a girl?"

Did competing in a zombie survival contest with a cute girl count as a hot date? "Well, because you asked, Zeneration is sponsoring a survivalist competition tomorrow and Sunday. There's a huge cash prize, and I think I've got a good shot at it. I need to be there bright and early in the morning, though." I bit my lip. "So, actually, I'd better try to get some sleep."

Annie's eyes widened. "Oh wow, good luck! That sounds so cool."

"Thanks. I'll let you know how it goes." We said our goodbyes, and when the call ended, I let out a deep breath and turned off my lamp.

Sliding the comforter to my armpits, I closed my eyes and prayed for sleep.

It never came.

....

In our front hall, I wrestled with the laces on my hiking boots. My mostly deflated ankle barely fit in there. I needed an ankle girdle, desperately.

A few yanks of a double knot, and finally, I was ready to go.

The weather forecast predicted no rain, but a chilly forty-three-degree low and sixty-two-degree high for each day of the competition. I put on my trusty Patagonia thermal jacket and hoisted my backpack. Carting around an extra fifty pounds on my backside turned me into a human packhorse.

A door down the hall creaked open, and a pitter-patter of tiny feet echoed in the darkness.

Lucy, in her *PAW Patrol* pajamas, padded toward me holding a ziplock bag. She rubbed her eyes and asked, "Where are you going?"

"Luce, go back to bed. I have to go on a quick trip." I didn't have time to chat. I had to meet Kate at the campground location at five a.m.

"But, your birthday. We were going to have pizza. And I have a present." Her bottom lip jutted out, and her eyes brimmed with tears.

I reached out and ruffled her hair. "We can celebrate when I get back, I promise. Mom and Dad think I'm going to a track meet and staying over at Jaxon's this weekend. Can you keep a secret? It can be my birthday present."

"I already got you a present." She held out the bag. Inside was a mix of play money (a few fake hundreds) and real currency (maybe about four bucks in coins). She gave me a firm midsection hug, the kind I'd imagine an octopus used to suffocate prey.

"Thanks, Lucy Goosey. Now go back to bed. I really have to go. I'm already late."

Through the window on the front door, lightning brightened the dark sky. So much for the zero percent rain forecast.

Lucy loosened her death grip and cried all the way back to her room. Once her door clicked, I unzipped the plastic bag she gave me. Inside was a handwritten Post-it note in smeared washable blue marker: "ish creem cake munny."

She'd drawn a picture on the back of both of us standing in jumping-jack formation, smiling ear to ear, with a giant birthday "ish creem" cake between us. I laughed and wiped my eyes with the palm of my hand. Thunder crashed again, drowning out the sound of my heart exploding into pieces.

Sometimes I liked being a brother.

CHAPTER SEVENTEEN

Nate was late.

In the back seat of the Uber, I reread the driving directions on my phone. This was the right place. SUVs and RVs pulled into the parking lot around the same time I arrived. A procession of hardcore hiker-camper types walked northbound in the freezing rain.

And here I was, running up the tab, squatting in the back of a cherry-red Corolla. But that was better than standing out there like an idiot in the rain, waiting for late Nate.

My pulse mirrored the seconds ticking rapidly by. The competition started in less than half an hour—was it possible that my partner was not just tardy, but had abandoned me? In a remote campground. During a thunderstorm.

Maybe my middle-of-the-night visit freaked him out. Maybe my super quick, awkward, barely audible goodbye early that morning shouldn't have been so super quick and awkward. Maybe I should have texted him a thank-you.

When Nate's Accord rolled in, high beams blazing, I let out a deep sigh, partly relieved, partly angry that he could have ruined my chances in this competition.

"Thank you, that's my ride!" I said to my driver. He popped the trunk for me to retrieve my backpack. Assaulted by the precipitation, my parka and gear darkened as I splashed my way to Nate's car.

Banging on his windows in the dark wasn't a good strategy. Nate startled, but when he saw it was just me and not some roving campground serial killer, he unlocked the doors and waved.

"Good morning," he chirped.

"You're late." I threw my pack in the back and plopped down in the front passenger seat.

"Not a morning person?"

I cleared the frog in my throat. "I am, actually. But you're late." *Don't you dare wave this off and distract me with one of your cute, coy smiles.*

He shrugged. "I'm sorry about that. My sister woke up and kept me home longer than expected. I tried to leave as soon as I could." He mustered an apologetic look, and my heart softened. His sister was so little.

"Okay. You're forgiven, but only because Lucy is cute. And it's your birthday." I threw a small package into his lap. "Happy birthday. I should have bought you a watch with an alarm."

He shot me a lopsided grin. "Hopefully I won't piss you off

anymore this weekend. I'll open it later since we're running so late."

My floppy, drippy bangs fell into my eyes as I retied my shoe. "Good call with your priorities."

When I sat upright, my head whooshed. The car cabin tilted, and I steadied myself by grabbing something stationary.

That something was Nate's hand.

Regrettably, I'd skipped a sensible breakfast. I'd been too worried I might toss it during the start of the competition, not thinking about the ramifications of low blood sugar.

Oh God.

His hand was a little calloused in some parts, but soft to the touch in others—a nice hand to accidentally squeeze, all in all. Warm and strong. Not like my clammy grip. Tingles ran through my fingers, and the sweat in my palms threatened to push to the surface. I let go like we were playing hot potato, just as Nate pushed my damp bangs out of my eyes with his other hand.

I searched for words. "Your present was on sale."

He coughed and laughed at the same time, just as some chipper dude with a megaphone made an announcement in the parking lot. "Participants need to load onto one of the three charter buses! We leave in five minutes! Cinco. Minutos!"

Nate cracked a smile. "We'd better go. We don't want to be late."

I blew out my cheeks, letting out a big breath. My eczematic hands itched and burned, and my palms were sweating buckets by that point. I could single-handedly solve California's eternal drought problem with my leaky glands.

We left Nate's car and swished through the muddy puddles, loading our gear beneath one of the two remaining buses. Then we stood in line and boarded bus number two. The aisle and seat lights were off, making it hard to find an empty row. My eyes hadn't adjusted, so making out any faces was virtually impossible.

We took some open seats toward the back. Across the aisle were two vaguely familiar people, a guy and girl in their midtwenties, both with approximately zero percent body fat. It took me a few seconds to remember where I knew them from. They were the grand prize winners of the *American Muscle Hustle* show, which had just been renewed for another season. The red, white, and blue star-spangled parkas should have tipped me off.

I leaned in and whispered, "Hey, don't look right now, but those guys are the winners from that life-or-death obstacle course reality show on CBS."

Gah. He looked. "Well, obstacle courses are one thing. Outdoor survival is totally different." He closed his eyes and leaned his head on the window. Staring at the unremitting rain, I tugged on my garnet pendant on my necklace and slid it back and forth on the chain.

Nate opened one eye. "And I bet their cheap-ass parkas aren't even the good temperature-controlling kind." I nodded in agreement, though I wondered if my all-weather jacket was anything more than a low-end raincoat.

The emcee on our bus rattled off rules, regulations, and changes to the event schedule, not even caring that almost everyone was asleep. Some of the information was brand-new to us, like the fact that we were being driven to the middle of God-knows-where in a storm instead of having the event at the campground. Other details were not—like bringing automatic weapons or handguns would warrant disqualification. After a few minutes of him "warming up the crowd," I'd completely tuned him out.

Thanks to the twisty-turny roads, I completely lost my bearings. The bus hurtled along through the forest, around and down, then up again. Our phones barely got any reception. Unable to pinpoint our precise location, GPS was showing that we could be anywhere within a five-mile radius of the campgrounds. Google Maps showed us in a large green area in the middle of nowhere.

Nate was fast asleep, so I stuck in my earbuds, cranked up my playlist, and stared out the window. The condensation made it hard to see, so with one horizontal arm swipe, I cleared the glass.

Straight ahead, thousands of majestic evergreen trees touched the heather-gray sky. Far away, they were compact, but next to them it was hard to peer upward to see the emerald tips without knocking our heads fully back like Pez dispensers. The dark clouds in the distance never drew any closer. Maybe we'd be lucky and the rain would pass.

Nearly an hour later, the bus turned into a gravel parking lot and pulled in next to another charter bus. "Okay, last stop! Everyone off!" the bus driver boomed. He let us know this was the last chance we had to use a civilized bathroom, either in the back of the bus or the portable one a few feet away outside. The rain had finally let up, and a handful of people were braving the drizzle to use the facilities.

We descended the bus's steps. The emcee-turned-luggage-handler opened up the storage in the belly of the bus and held up each pack for the owner to retrieve. He held mine up, and Nate grabbed it for me.

"Thanks, partner," I said. Without me asking, he helped me with the second strap, lifting it so I could pull through my arm.

His backpack came out, and someone behind us whistled, "Whoa, that looks heavy!"

Nate hoisted his pack on before I could offer my help in return. He smiled at me and placed his hand on the back of my upper arm, pushing me gently toward the fence opening. A tingle ran down my entire spine just as my arm warmed to his touch. My face flushed, overheated despite the cool weather.

By some miracle, the menacing rain clouds passed over us and sun breaks streamed through the tops of the trees. In the distance, the sound of a running brook caught my attention. If we weren't about to spend up to forty-eight sleepless hours in the freezing cold, being massacred by biting insects and possibly bears, fighting off zombies for a minuscule chance of winning a competition, I'd say it was a picturesque Pacific Northwest day.

The final bus pulled up, but rather than wait any longer for them, the event organizers—discernable from their whistles and walkie-talkies—ushered us to the left side of the lot, where we collected our team T-shirts. Unfortunately for us, we got the hideous magenta ones. Mine was a men's XS and hung huge on my frame, even when tucked in. Nate was issued one in an impressive XXL, passable as a wind sail. Hardly the outfit I would have chosen to wear in a survivalist competition, where blending in was key.

We were each handed electronic wristbands, similar in style to a high-end Fitbit. "What are these for?" I asked.

The guy at registration demonstrated for us. "It's weatherproof, has GPS, tells time, and it also has a half-mile-range walkie-talkie for your team." His voice dropped deeper. "If it's removed from your wrist, or tampered with, your team will be disqualified. The ops teams will be deployed and will collect you, along with your belongings."

Nate and I practiced using the walkie-talkie function.

"Breaker one-nine. Testing, testing, one-two-three," I chirped.

"Copy," he responded. "Should we go join the others at the start line?"

"Affirmative."

"Roger that. Over and out."

Speakers blared above our heads on the large wooden poles lining the parking area. "Bus One, you'll start the competition at the red marker. Bus Two, you'll start at the blue one. Bus Three starts at green, straight ahead."

Nate put his hand back on my arm. "You ready to win this?"

"Affirmative."

CHAPTER EIGHTEEN

"How do we know when it's time to start? And where do we line up? Do they blow a whistle or something?" There was an unfamiliar edge to Kate's voice.

"Hey, do I look like a zombie apocalypse competition brochure to you?" I smirked. "I know about as much as you do." The atmosphere buzzed with confusion. "Don't worry. Everyone here looks as clueless as us."

She punched my upper arm just as a horn blasted over the airwaves. "Good luck, Zombiegeddon participants!" a cheery voice said. "For more information about the event sponsor, go to www.zeneration.us."

What the—?

The two guys next to me asked, "So we just...go?" They were identical twins, with extreme muscle definition and arms almost the size of their legs. Maybe they drank protein shakes and worked out together or deadlifted each other. Both wore matching red bandannas on their heads, tied the same way. Like loser pirates.

"Yeah, probably. Good luck," I said.

"You too, Team Hot Pink. Hope the zombies are color-blind!" They jogged to join the masses, heading straight into the eight-foot-tall hedge maze directly ahead. The opaque, vibrant green walls were fashioned from entangled, dense huckleberry and honeysuckle bushes, trimmed back to let people through.

"We're Team Magenta actually!" I shouted after them, but they were already too far ahead to hear me. "Team TBD!" I tugged Kate's arm. "Let's go too!"

If we didn't move fast to join the others, we might miss out on something, like better weapons or some sort of extra-life bonus. Or money. Maybe they'd get better snacks. We sprang forward to catch up to the masses, leaving the designated marker behind us.

BOOM!

Smoke came from above the hedges. Burning-eyes-and-lungs smoke, not smoke-machine smoke. Shit just got real.

Shouts.

Moans.

Screams.

What had we gotten ourselves into?

No way were we walking straight into whatever was happening in front of us. Those first movers had encountered something scream-worthy, and we weren't about to join them. A quick scan of the area revealed a separate dirt path running adjacent to the hedges. A hand-painted wooden sign on a nearby tree read,

Beware! written in reddish-brown script. Blood, presumably. Nice touch, Zombiegeddon.

"Okay, let's go over there!" I said to Kate. She jogged along next to me, both hands holding her backpack shoulder straps. My ankle had mostly healed from the ladder incident, but it was still stiff.

We reached the foot of the trail and exchanged looks. Kate asked, "Wanna do the honors and go first?"

"Nah, I think we do 'ladies first' this time."

She shook her head. "Fine, you chicken." She ran ahead before I could even tell her I'd been joking.

I caught up to her and was surprised by how winded I was already. The packs were heavy, and walking at an incline made me insta-sweaty. My heart pounded from the cardio and the sheer excitement and terror of everything happening around us. "Well, if there are any zombies on this path, they should be plenty distracted by all the noise going on in the maze." Gray plumes of smoke wafted in our direction. My eyes watered from the sting.

Kate nodded and started walking northbound. "Hey, maybe we should go to the brook to fill our—"

My eyes widened, and instinctively I jerked her arm back. Hard. Like, dislocation hard.

"Ow! What the hell, Nate?" she snapped.

"Trip. Wire," I panted. She'd almost walked straight into it. We needed to be more careful. Who knows what would have happened if we triggered it? Maybe hundreds of zombies would fall from the trees. Swarms of bees instantly released from captivity. Feces catapults. My imagination ran wild with possibilities.

"Holy shit," she whispered as she regained steady breathing. "Trip wire? We've only walked a hundred feet."

Holy shit was right. But winning this thing wasn't supposed to be easy. My anxiety was at an all-time high, but as the wind blew toward me and the smell of Kate's lemon eczema cream wafted my way, it reminded me that she was here with me. We were a team. And we were here to win.

Her brows scrunched together. "After you," she said, gesturing ahead. With a quick glance back, the starting-line marker already out of sight, we trudged deeper into the forest.

....

I pressed my index finger to my lips. Kate nodded, staying silent. The heft of my pack sank my heels into the damp soil. I shifted my weight so I didn't topple backward.

"Let's go this way!"

"Up there! I think I see a sign!"

We'd been crouching on the ground a few minutes as streams of people passed by us, shouting back and forth, not giving a shit about drawing attention to themselves. Leading the pack were two drunk guys, punching each other's shoulders, guffawing as they took turns swigging from a bottle of whiskey. The competition rules and regulations stated nut snacks were prohibited due to contestants with food allergies, but all other food and drinks were allowed. Whiskey was apparently okay. Good for them.

Our plan was to come out onto the path and continue the journey once the crowd died down. After the trip-wire incident, it was probably better to have these other contestants be the booby trap guinea pigs, not us.

"I think now," Kate whispered, popping her head out from behind her tree.

But then, new voices approached. She quickly hid again.

A familiar voice passed by. "Let's catch up with the others in our group. This map is so useless." A girl. Our age. My breath grew unsteady as a slow realization hit me. I knew her. "Knowing Nate, he's probably gone a whole different way that's not even on here."

She passed by, and Kate and I both peered out to get a better look. Instead of a climber pack, the girl had on her oversize school backpack covered with purple peace signs.

WTF was Annie doing here?

CHAPTER NINETEEN

Kate

"What is *she* doing here?" There was a tinge of iciness in my voice I instantly regretted, but this wasn't the right place and time to discuss tone interpretation.

Okay, it was more than a tinge of iciness.

Fine, it was a hate tsunami.

But that girl was here. Stalking Nate.

"I...I don't know," he stuttered. And he genuinely looked confused too. "I'm just as surprised as you are."

I swallowed away the dryness in my throat, remembering why I was there in the first place. New York City. I needed this win. "No one else is coming. Let's head in their direction." I unzipped my jacket and let in the cool air. All of my layers of clothing were overheating me.

Maple leaves crunched under my boots. We walked side by side in silence, at first marching at different speeds, but then falling into the same stepping rhythm. Like Imperial Guards, but no backdrop of ominous music.

Crunch. Crunch. Crunch. I'm. So. Annoyed. I. Could. Scream.

Nate pulled out his map, already weathered from the damp climate and crumpled from catching the occasional gust of wind. "Somewhere up ahead there should be a fork."

"You mean...here?" While he was looking at the map, mindlessly walking, we'd encountered a split in the dirt trail. There were at least twice as many muddy shoe prints on the main path versus the one on the right.

"Isn't there some poem about this exact situation?" Nate joked. "What would Robert Frost do? WWRFD?"

Nothing like a nerdy poetry joke to lighten the mood. It worked, though. I snorted. "Let's not trust a cryptic poet in a zombie survival situation." I pointed to his hand. "What does the map say?"

Nate chewed his lip and studied the paper. "On the left, there are a few buildings, cabins maybe? Ranger stations? It doesn't say. On the right it's pure nature. A giant waterfall is the main obstacle before the finish line."

We were already so behind. We needed to pick something soon to make headway before nightfall.

I tried to use the map on my phone, but there wasn't any signal. "You think there are zombies hiding in those buildings on the left?" Getting outnumbered was a huge risk, especially since we'd fallen so behind the others and were essentially all on our own.

He nodded slowly. "Maybe we go right then? Fewer people, hopefully fewer zombies in the forest?"

"Sounds good. You go first as, you know, my zombie body shield."

We examined a few of the footsteps on the trail. The imprints were still fresh, so we weren't terribly far behind. Kneeling too close, I lost my balance and toppled to my side into fallen leaves and mud.

"You should have handed me your backpack," Nate said, hoisting me up by my nonmuddy hand.

"I hear mud is a natural remedy for eczema." I wiped my filthy palm on a nearby tree trunk, taking most of the filth off. Neon-green moss stains replaced the caked-on mud, which now didn't seem so bad.

After wiping my mossy hands on the thighs of my pants, I pulled out a bottle of sanitizer and squirted my hands.

"Seriously, you have hand sanitizer?" He burst into laughter. "It's not even trial-size. You're such a precious snowflake."

I corrected him. "A germ-free snowflake."

The footprint frenzy ahead of us slowed us to a stop. There had been some kind of skirmish. A fight maybe, between contestants. Or a zombie attack?

A twig snapped behind us.

Nate and I spun around to see a figure lurching forward, about Nate's height, maybe taller, standing twenty feet away.

Chills ran up my spine as I took a few stumbled paces back.

Nate stood his ground and slowly, from his backpack pocket, pulled out a stick. Or...a flashlight? A wand? Had my partner gone mad?

The figure drew closer and so did the rancid odor. Dead rats, sewage, outhouses, all rolled into one putrid package.

Our first zombie.

Was it real? And by real, I meant was it a human? Something about his movements was strangely familiar. Was it...could it even possibly be...a robot? Maybe it was just my mind playing tricks—the by-product of me seeing robots everywhere, both at home and in my dreams. The zombie was too far away to tell for sure.

"Gaaaaaaaaa."

It talked. Actually, gurgled, like he was gargling Listerine. Though he certainly didn't smell like Listerine.

The zombie drew closer, and Nate took a few steps toward it.

"Nate!" I warned, but he didn't listen. He continued his movement toward the undead figure, holding his flashlight-wand with two hands, like a lightsaber.

"Gaaaaaaaaa!"

Closer now, I could see the zombie, with his ragged clothes, body gashes, and open wounds on his bashed-in face. My heart hammered in my chest. He was missing an eye.

Oh God, the smell.

It turned me into a statue of fear, too scared stiff to gag. I couldn't even yell Nate's name again.

Nate, though, was the opposite. He jolted into action and charged ahead. "Gaaaaaaaaa!" he yelled, but it was more of a swashbuckler battle cry, mocking the undead's mouthwash gargles.

They collided. Nate's feet were springier, but the zombie overpowered him. They both fell to the ground in a tangle of limbs.

"Nate!" Jolted out of my paralysis, I ran to help.

Sheer terror pulsed through me as I tried to yank the zombie from him. The overwhelming stench made me want to vomit, but I pulled and pulled, determined to free my partner. The zombie turned to me and bit toward my face. Horrified, I fell backward.

Nate took his stick and jabbed it on the zombie's neck.

"ZAP!" A cracking sound. Then dead silence.

It flopped over. There was metal under his ripped flesh.

The zombie *was*, in fact, a robot. Holy shit. The burned plastic stink made me dry heave. Thank God I'd skipped breakfast.

We stared at it for a while. Finally, I asked Nate, "Where'd you get a zombie zapper?"

He wiped his brow with the back of his hand. "It's a stun gun. I couldn't find a good bear spray, so I bought this just in case. Nothing in the rules and regulations said it was illegal." He handed the stick to me. "Here, you can have it. I brought two, just in case."

Relieved, I took it from him. "Just in case you ran into a bear or robot zombie?" I hugged him. He smelled like rotted fish that had vomited their own rotten guts out. "I didn't bring you anything as good as this. I have Cheez-Its and cheese puffs we can share. But I don't even have two hand sanitizers."

He laughed. "That's okay. After smelling that"—he swept his hand at the lifeless, undead robot—"there's no way I can eat. Maybe even for days." He sniffed his forearm and cringed. "There's a river up ahead. We can wash up there, ditch some clothes, and then get going. It'll be dark before we know it."

Our wrist devices alerted us that sunset was in couple of hours. Behind us, the moon was already visible. "Hey, a full moon! Maybe if we're lucky more weird shit will happen tonight." I meant it to be a lighthearted joke, but it came out as a panicky whimper.

He punched me on the shoulder. "Now you've jinxed us! You know that, right?"

I totally did.

We scampered ahead as the sun started its descent along the tree line. We had no time to waste.

CHAPTER TWENTY

We built an impressive fire. Or rather, Kate built it, and I sat there with my mouth hanging slightly open, like she was doing a magic trick. She had brought this flint striker that made fire production look effortless. Seriously, it was like she was peeling a carrot and then *bam!* Fire.

There was a huge risk of having a campfire, of course, but we needed warmth. The night chill descended fast, and we concluded it was better to be warm and mauled by robot zombies than freezing and mauled by robot zombies. We set up a few simple traps around us so we'd be warned if anything, or anyone, approached our campsite.

Pleasant crackles and pops filled the silence, so we ate our hermetically sealed dinners, drank our bottles of water, and stared upward at the bright moon in companionable quiet. If we were the only two people in world, would it be like this?

Kate threw a small handful of twigs into the blaze. "You think we have a chance?"

She meant winning the competition, but part of me wanted to think she was talking about us.

To answer both, I said, "We're gonna win. K-A-T-E. That's how we spell victory!" *Oh God, why, Nate?* Eyes fixed on the ground, I rubbed some dirt off my shoe, hoping she'd just ignore my mortifying cheer.

I stole a quick look at her, and she caught me midglance. My heart nearly stopped beating.

Shit.

She didn't call me out, even though she totally should have. "When we win," she said, pulling on her pendant, "I'm going to buy you something."

"Really? Like a deluxe pyro flint striker?"

"Um, nooooo." She smiled. "Your very own hand sanitizer."

"Wow. I was going to say that next."

Kate shivered. "After that, I'm going to New York. I've never been."

"For winter break?" I asked softly.

She threw in more sticks but didn't respond. But maybe she didn't hear me.

"I need the money for my parents. But if I have any cash left over, I might put capital toward my business," I said, louder this time.

"You have big dreams, Nate. I like that about you."

I threw a broken branch into the blaze. "Well, when you're poor, dreams are really all you've got." I sighed. "I see my parents barely scraping by, and it makes me sad. There's no way we could have afforded school without my scholarship."

"Your parents seem happy, though," she said. "At least, from what I know of them."

"Yeah, but...Dad's an IT consultant, and he's out of work. If we win this competition, we can keep our house."

Anguish flashed across her face. "I didn't know finances were so tight. I'm sorry."

I'd blathered on way more than I'd intended. But being around Kate was comfortable. Talking with her was easy. "What about you? What are you doing with our vast winnings after your trip to New York?"

From the jagged cliffs above us, an eardrum-piercing howl echoed. The hairs on my arms shot up straight.

"Maybe the coyote wants to visit New York too," I said in a nervous whisper.

She giggled and gave a thumbs-up in the coyote's direction. "I bet the coyote could eat all those subway rats I hear about. It's perfect, actually."

I grabbed a hunk of wood and poked at the fire, sending embers into the night air like fireflies. The only way to keep it going through the night was to take sleeping shifts to tend it. A way to stay even warmer was by sleeping together—not sleeping with each other in the biblical sense, but just, sorta, spooning without groping. Maybe I'd hold off on mentioning that.

Kate cleared her throat. "I'm wide awake, and I don't know how I'm going to sleep. I'm a little wired. What about you?"

I nodded like a bobblehead on speed. She mentioned sleep arrangements first but didn't suggest cuddling. Damn.

I stood to stretch my legs, which had stiffened from the uphill climb.

She reached both arms in the air and straightened her shoulders. "Well, maybe one of us should try to sleep." Standing up too, she added, "I'll go first. Since I made the fire and all."

"Yeah, no problem." I yawned.

"Um, one more thing." Kate shifted, smiling awkwardly. "I'm actually moving to New York, not just visiting," she said, resuming the conversation I thought we'd ended. "My dad doesn't know. We're not exactly talking right now."

"So, you're like every teen hating their parents?" I joked. Her smile turned sour. "Or, wait, how bad is it? Other than the fact that he wants to ship you off to Asia."

It took her a while to answer.

"Well, for one, I blame him for my mom's death," she said quietly.

For one? There was more than that? That was a fucking big one. "Oh wow. How'd...how'd it happen?"

Kate crossed her arms and shivered again. "She had pneumonia. She got it from Dad." She paused, her eyes brimming with tears. "She was a bit of a hypochondriac honestly, so she tried herbal supplements, but when none of her home remedies worked and she got worse, Dad didn't take her to the doctor. He told her to sleep it off and went on another business trip. He said when he was sick he'd still gone to work and didn't take any sick days. When her fever spiked to a hundred and five degrees, I drove her to the ER. I'd just gotten my driver's license. She passed out in the waiting room."

"Oh God, I am so sorry, Kate. That must've been so...I'm sorry." I didn't know what else to say. Words weren't forming. My brain was numb from the cold. I walked over to Kate and hugged her tight.

She sniffed. "Mom fell into a coma later that night. She died the day after my dad got back from his trip. It's like she held on so he could see her go." Her tears beaded on my chest and dribbled down my waterproof parka. "He should have been there," she murmured. "For her. And for me. I miss my mom so much."

We stayed like that for a while. Kate fit perfectly in my arms. She tilted her head up, and our eyes met. "I'm sorry I dumped all of that on you. I just wanted you to know why I needed to leave home so badly."

Another howl echoed from above, but it was much closer this time. Directly behind us, a loud rustle came from the brush. Kate and I hugged and drew in close.

Her breath quickened. Mine stopped.

A tiny rabbit tore out from behind the bush. Then another one shot out and followed. Relieved, we laughed and relaxed our grips.

Two more rabbits ran past our camp area, skirting around the fire. We laughed again, but when the chilling realization hit me that the adorable bunnies were running away from something, I let go of Kate and hollered, "Shit, we have to go!" We hadn't laid out our sleeping bags or tent yet, so I blindly grabbed things around me and shoved them in my backpack.

We bristled when the perimeter trap jingled around us. Color drained from Kate's face, like she'd seen a ghost.

"GAAAAAAAAA!"

"GAAAAAAAAA!"

"GAAAAAAAAA!"

"GAAAAAAAAA!"

Shit, shit, shit. Nothing worse than a reeking zombie choir to ruin the night. They smelled worse than a hundred of Jaxon's gym bags.

We grabbed our packs and ran deeper into the pitch-black forest, through the frigid, thick air. Tightly holding her hand in mine, we ran for our lives.

....

We eventually reached a clearing.

"Well, I'm certainly not sleepy now," I huffed. We both chugged water because we had sweated so much. A hint of daylight lit the woods around us with a hazy, faint-peach glow.

My heart pounded so hard it nearly burst from my chest. By the sound of Kate's panting, her heart was exploding too.

Though she'd been the one to suggest doing this competition—and, you could even argue, dragged me into it—I had a strong sense of responsibility to keep us both safe. Even though she was plenty capable on her own. Kate used her body weight to pull down two dead tree branches to make us makeshift torches while I waited on the trail. Was there anything she couldn't do?

She'd been quiet since we abandoned our campfire. I figured that our encounter with zombies warranted her some uninterrupted "me time."

I checked my phone for a signal.

Nope. Nada.

"That's why we have these." Kate's tinny voice came through the speaker on my wristband. "Do you copy?" She shot me a mischievous grin.

"Roger that," I responded by pushing the talk button. "Copy."

She crouched and lit both torches with her flint. Handing me one, she said, "Let's take advantage of our fright-induced insomnia and get moving."

"We have flashlights, you know. And I think I packed a headlamp somewhere. We don't need torches."

She spun the tip of hers in a circle. "Yeah, but torches are badass."

I swung mine like a Jedi.

She was right. Torches were pretty badass.

CHAPTER TWENTY-ONE

A dense fog fell just before sunrise, ruining our visibility. It was the kind where you hold your hand out to see if it disappears in the thick haze. The kind of fog that people describe as having the consistency of pea soup. The kind you see in scary Halloween movies, when someone's about to die.

God, please don't let us die.

The forest was mostly quiet. We'd become accustomed to the normal bustle around us, sensing what was ordinary and what should put us in high alert.

The *krrrrecccckk* of the tree frogs surrounding us, for example. That was totally normal.

The weird hoot that sounded like a mash-up of a rooster crow and toddler crying. That was the barred owl, Nate had said. Very normal.

Not normal, though? Running into a veil of fresh bug spray lingering on the dirt trail, one so pungent it made us both cough. We stopped cold in our steps, our skin prickling with alarm.

Someone was here.

I jumped back into Nate as the *American Muscle Hustle* TV show winners dropped down from nearby trees and landed on our path. The woman was unarmed but stood in an elbows-out, ready-to-choke-us stance. In contrast, the dude was weaponized, holding a long wooden staff. It looked like a bo staff, but it was hard to tell, because it was so blurry from him showing off his rapid side-to-side and up-down kill strikes.

Nate rolled his eyes. "Do you have a riddle for us so we can pass?"

I shot him a look. *Not now.*

Bo staff guy sneered. "You have no idea who you're dealing with."

"You're the *American Muscle Hustle* guys," Nate said.

"So you've heard of us!"

"Not really, the show's logo is embroidered on your jacket."

Bo staff guy scowled, and I swallowed my laugh.

"Hey!" The woman took a few moseying steps forward. "It's exactly who we're looking for." Her eyes narrowed as she approached us. Closer up, it was hard to miss her glowing skin, perfectly sleek ponytail, and mega-shine lip gloss. How could she look this good out in the wilderness?

Screw her.

The fog made it hard to read the name on her parka. But she kept creeping closer. And closer. Natalie. Her name was Natalie.

Bo staff guy said, "Get their wristbands. Maybe if we hurry we can catch up to that girl, the one with the reward. She said she'd pay us in cash."

These guys were bounty hunters. But for what? And why?

Our torches had died out, but I lit mine again with a lighter, then tapped Nate's torch head to set his on fire too.

He laughed. "You had a lighter the whole time?" His torch blazed bigger and brighter.

Natalie took a few steps back when Nate swooshed his fire stick around. Yeah, bitch. That's right. We have fire.

The guy, on the other hand, laughed maniacally and stepped forward.

I'd seen him use the exact same scare tactics on that reality show. He was the aggressor, trying to steal our attention through intimidation. He'd also made us look away from Natalie. The sneaky alpha bitch ran behind a tree and came back with something concealed in her hand.

Bo staff guy sprinted toward us. Nate instinctively took a swing, making a whoosh sound with his torch, almost putting out the blaze. Mr. Bo Staff took advantage and used his weapon to knock the torch from Nate's hand. It fell with a clunk between Natalie and me. We both dove for it, but she was faster. Luckily, the fire smothered out when it rolled on the ground. In our rumble, I managed to knock the thing from Natalie's hand. It fell to my feet, but I didn't dare bend down to grab it. Instead, I waved my lit torch around like a blindfolded madwoman. "This fire, plus your ridiculous amount of hair gel, and all that bug spray? Bad idea, lady. Back off."

I tried to keep my eyes only on Natalie but kept glancing over at Nate.

Bo staff guy charged like a bull again. Nate removed himself from danger by doing a quasi-back-roll. *Nice.*

Bo staff guy swung hard. Nate ducked.

Bo staff guy swung again. Nate ducked again. Why was this guy trying to behead my partner?

Bo staff guy growled and ran full force with the staff held like a bat. Nate disarmed him by jumping out of the way and tackling his midsection. Grabbing the bo staff, Nate pushed the guy down hard with an eye-wincing thud.

Now Nate had a weapon.

The gladiators both staggered and then took off running, disappearing behind the veil of mist. Just like in those scary fucking horror movies.

Once I knew we were out of danger, I squatted down to pick up what Natalie had dropped.

It was a folded paper.

More specifically, it was a folded color printout of a wanted sign, with Nate's senior class picture front and center. Cleanly designed with beautiful hand lettering, it didn't look all that sketchy, even though it was. A $5,000 reward for the retrieval of Nate's wristband. Plus $1,000 extra for his partner's, a.k.a. mine.

Why?

Nate's face grew paler the longer he stared at the paper.

"What is this?" I asked.

Nate stammered. "I don't know what it is. But I know who. That's Annie's handwriting." He handed me the paper but wouldn't look me in the eyes. I shoved it inside my backpack.

"How many of these flyers do you think there are?"

He plopped down on a nearby weathered, mossy log and held his head in his hands. "I have no idea. But if there are a lot, we're pretty much fucked."

Damn it.

Annie.

She messed up my plans when I tried to ask out Nate at the skating rink, and somehow she boomeranged back into my life to wreak more havoc.

Well, *Annie*, there's no way you're going to screw me over again. No fucking way in hell.

CHAPTER TWENTY-TWO

None of this made any sense.

And we had no time to contemplate.

The sun had risen, and the haze finally lifted. Kate and I followed the winding footpath until we came across an abandoned fire pit filled with charred firewood. Half-drunk Capri Suns and full beer bottles littered the area. Crushed graham crackers, trodden marshmallows, and unopened chocolate bars were strewn across the dirt. What kind of monstrous people would abandon their s'mores?

More alarm bells rang in my head when we discovered trampled canisters of sunscreen, bug repellent, and unused sleeping bags farther down in the woods.

"Maybe zombies?" Kate asked.

I popped a straw in an unopened Capri Sun and sipped while we surveyed more of the grounds. The sugary water coated my dry mouth and throat, relieving the dehydration I didn't know I had.

Kate picked up a few things and stuck them in her pack.

"Snacks?" I asked.

She handed me some Black Cat firecrackers, a fancy lighter engraved with initial "H," and a foil condom single-pack. I lifted my eyebrows, making her laugh.

"You think they ran off, and these guys are maybe still in the game? Or you think, you know, they were—?" I made the universal "finger slit across throat" signal.

"Hard to say," she said, chewing her bottom lip. "Whatever happened here, it took place in the night. These ashes are damp."

Walking on the far perimeter of the campfire area, there was more evidence of struggle. Broken branches. Trees with large, chipped-off chunks of bark. Stampeded brand-new cigarettes and joints ground into the dirt. No way someone would willingly leave unsmoked weed lying around.

Scattered footprints made it look like a wild dance party had taken place. By the looks of the sleeping bags and quantity of food and drinks, though, there were five, maybe six people there tops, hardly enough to make all those prints.

"Okay, let's move on," I announced. "This place is creeping me out. It's like the aftermath of a shitty dystopian movie."

We walked ahead, finding broken glass bottles, torn clothes covered with zombie flesh goo, and four inactive wristbands just past the campsite. Another quarter-mile down, we came across the two gladiators on the side of the road. Assholes Natalie and No Mo' Bo Staff Guy. Their once pristine jackets were filthy and torn, but physically, they were picture-perfect. Infuriating.

They raised their hands in the air.

"We're out of the game. No wristbands, see?" Natalie took a step forward. "We just want some water and any food while we wait for pickup. The game officials are on their way to get us."

I threw them two juice packs we'd taken from the campsite. "But the bo staff's mine."

They agreed to the terms with eager nods. I gave them each a Pop-Tart. A modern-day olive branch.

Kate glared at me. "You're helping them? That guy tried to whack your head off."

"I believe in karma," I said, shrugging. "Plus, I like the staff." In a low voice so only she could hear, I whispered, "And I gave them the unfrosted ones."

Natalie took a cigarette from her pocket. "You guys have a light?"

Kate rolled her eyes when I pulled out the fancy lighter from my pants pocket and threw it at Natalie. "You can have that too. We found it at the campsite back there."

Natalie squinted at it. "Hey, this is the lighter that guy had." Natalie lifted it so her partner got a better look. "The one who gave us the flyer. He was with that really pretty blond girl."

Kate's shoulders stiffened at the words *pretty blond girl*. She turned and stormed back to the main path, pushing through tall ferns to reach the clearing.

I ran to catch up to her, my bulky pack growing heavier with each step.

A gentle breeze carried Natalie's voice our way. "Watch out for that guy, though. You think we were bad? He's a real primo asshole."

....

"Cool Ranch or Nacho Cheese?"

It was my third time trying to start up a conversation with Miss Grumpy McGrumpface, who continued marching in silence, eyes locked forward, making it a mission of hers to avoid all eye contact.

A message flashed on our wristbands. **24 hours remaining. 70 contestants eliminated. 30 participants still in the competition. Good luck!**

I marked the message as "read." Kate glanced at her watch and continued down the trail.

"Kate, we need to stop. I have to piss! Too many Capri Suns." One last try to get her to slow down and talk to me.

Please, just talk to me.

She shouted over her shoulder. "Hurry!" Slowing her pace, she added, "I have a rock in my shoe anyway." Hallelujah! No more silent treatment.

A nearby Douglas fir, over a hundred feet tall with a green, thick, moss-covered bottom akin to Treebeard in *The Lord of the*

Rings, was as good a place as any for a long watering. I unzipped and relieved myself for a full minute, honest to God. Eyes firmly closed, I basked momentarily in my man versus nature glory moment.

"Hey! Bruce Lee. How's the karate coming along?"

Terror jolted through my entire body, and a voice inside me screamed for me to run. But I couldn't—Pete was standing only a few feet behind me, my pants were unzipped, and my guy parts were hanging out.

This encounter wasn't going to go well.

"Give me a second," I said. *Think, Nate. Think.*

"It's not like I haven't seen your *skid* dick before in the locker room, Natey boy."

Hands shaking, I zipped up quickly and turned around.

Pete wasn't alone. Annie was standing right next to him, eyes wet with tears.

"Annie, did he do anything to you? Are you okay?"

Pete barked out a laugh. "Me, hurt Annie? Nah, Nate. You got it all wrong. She's been instrumental in this whole plan."

"What plan?" I asked, panning my glare from Pete to Annie.

She sighed. "Why couldn't you just take the money? If you'd done that, we wouldn't even be here."

"What plan? Why are you here?" I repeated. "I don't understa—"

Pete cut me off. "I thought you were a smart *skid*, but

apparently I have to spell it out for you. Guess you were too dumb to see the coincidence of *your* dad losing his consulting gig at the company where *my* dad's a VP. What was *supposed* to happen was you would tank your grades, take our generous skid donation, and it would be a win-win for everyone. But *now* look." He pulled something out of his pocket that was sort of like a stun gun, but more pistol-shaped.

Shit, a Taser. One of those expensive high-voltage ones that shot needles AND electricity at you. "*Now* we have to make sure you lose this competition. Then you'll have to take my money."

I turned to Annie. "You knew about this? You were in on it?"

She took a step closer. "I wasn't at first. You have to believe me."

"So...you mean, you at the roller-skating rink?" *Nate, you fucking moron, don't make her answer that.* I knew couples' skate was all bullshit, way too good to be true.

It was a ruse.

She scammed me in the worst way possible.

Using my pathetic skid heart.

I instinctively recoiled with her next step forward. Acid reflux kicked in just thinking about that night at the rink. It was one of my best memories too. And it was a lie.

She wiped her eyes. "Pete recruited me that night, on skate day, when he drove me home. He saw me with you at the rink and thought I could help you change your mind." Eyes pleading, she added, "I didn't think it was that big of a deal, and he recruited me *after* we hung out that night. I swear. He said you were already on board with everything, I just needed to help pull you over the line." She hung her head and closed her eyes. "He said he'd pay me what he paid you. I needed the money for college."

Pete had his Taser pointed right at me. The neon-green laser dot danced across my chest. "You're an econ whiz, right, Natey? It's simple, really. You have something I want, and I'm willing to pay top dollar for it. I still am because I'm a charitable guy. It's not personal, skid. No hard feelings." His cold eyes searched my face for a reaction.

I winced. "But how'd you know...I'd be here? How'd you get in?"

Annie's face went pale, revealing so much.

She'd video chatted with me.

She knew I'd be at this competition instead of the track meet. Damn it.

Pete snorted like an angry bull. "My dad's a big deal, you idiot. He knows everyone on the board at Zeneration. He pulled a few strings. Now, hand over your stupid fucking wristband. Let's not let this get ugly." His green laser dot traveled down to my crotch.

Sadistic son of a bitch.

I had nothing on me to protect myself. My bo staff was by my backpack, near where I'd taken a leak. *Good job, Nate. Bringing bare hands to a Taser fight.* Pete had a good two inches and twenty pounds on me, and he was quick as fuck in every school sport. I didn't see a way out of this.

"C'mon, Bruce Lee. Show me some karate moves first, though. How do you say *skid* in Korean? Or does that not translate?"

Something inside me snapped.

Fuck you, Pete.

You.

Fucking.

Asshole!

The voice inside my head cheered, *Beat the living shit out of that privileged, racist, silver-spoon-fed mufuckaaaaaaa!*

Adrenaline-fueled, I lunged straight into him, in brute-force tackle mode.

"Oooof!" Pete coughed as I rammed his upper body, smacking the Taser out of his hand, and knocking the wind out of both of us as we crashed to the ground.

I wheezed and stumbled onto my feet. Pete played football and was used to tackles worse than this. Child's play. He cracked a smile before he rushed me.

I fell back into piles of rocks, landing backward on big, jagged, skin-puncturing, skin-scraping limestone. A lot of it.

Shit, I think I burst my own appendix.

There was minor blood spill on the limestone, presumably mine.

"Just give me the wristband, Nate," Pete said, wiping his

bleeding lip with his left hand as he picked up the Taser on the ground with his right one. I wished he looked as battered as I did, but no, he looked great. Fantastic, in fact. I'd tousled his hair and made his shirt a little askew, and that was it. He looked manly with that cut lip. Somehow, I'd made Pete look hotter.

Fucking asshole.

I scrambled to my feet again.

He charged, and I reacted faster this time. I grabbed his arm, twisted it, and struck him hard in the side of the face with a headbutt. A basic Krav Maga move, one I'd never imagined using. I'd added the headbutt at the end, just because he pissed me off.

He collided into Kate, who appeared right in time to zap him in the ass with her stun gun. As he crumpled and fell, she blew the top of the stun gun and put it in her holster. "I was aiming for his lower back, I promise." She shrugged at me.

I burst out laughing, then replied with a pun, because I couldn't stop myself. "What a total pain in the ass."

She smiled in return.

I loved this.

Kate took away his Taser. "I'll admit, I eavesdropped on that whole exchange between you two. Your bathroom break was way longer than it should have been, so I had to come back to investigate." She moved in closer. "What you did, turning down his money? When he almost Tasered your nuts? That was pretty brave."

Our eyes locked again. *Nate. Don't be a moron. And don't you dare say what you're thinking: not all heroes wear capes.*

Annie interjected, exploding our bubble of happiness. "Nate, I hope we can still be friends. I'm so sorry about all of this." With a five-digit code, she disabled her wristband, and Pete's, and put them both on the ground. Pete was still in fetal position, lying in a bed of brown leaves, semiconscious. Some drool trickled from his parted mouth.

Kate spun me around to look for any injuries. "Lift your shirt," she ordered, and I complied. "Some scrapes and bruising, a tiny bit of blood, but not as bad as it seemed." She side-eyed Annie. "Let's go, partner. The crew will come get them."

I glanced down at Pete again. "But I kinda want to show him some Bruce Lee moves."

"Not advisable." Kate tugged my arm, adding a squeeze. Her arm hooked into mine, and we began our walk.

Annie shouted to me, "Hey, Nate?"

Over my shoulder, I asked, "Yeah?"

"I really did like you. At the skate place. That was all real for me." A soft sigh escaped her mouth. "And...I really hope you win."

So many years I'd pined after Annie. *Years.* Jaxon told me to get over her because she wasn't all that. And Zach never said much but he nodded in agreement when Jaxon urged me to move on. It was infatuation, not love. Annie wasn't right for me, or better than me. I knew that now.

"Goodbye, Annie." I hesitated. "Uh, and one more thing."

"Yeah?" she brightened.

"I fucking hate Maroon 5. Cannot. Stand. Them."

Kate snorted and unhooked her arm from mine. She held out her hand for me to grab.

I reached for it, but she giggled and ran ahead of me. We did this over and over. A simple game of "Kate keep away" that ended with me sneaking up to her, grabbing her backpack waist strap, and pulling her right toward me.

A scream from Annie ruined the mood. "Nate, *run*! Zombies! Headed your way!"

I'd limped a little before from my stiffened ankle, but had no problem breaking into a full-blown panic sprint after Annie's zombie alert.

Adrenaline was a funny thing. It usually signaled mind-blowing excitement or outright terror. Two ends of a spectrum, same bodily reaction. In this case, it was terror. Definitely terror.

....

Our boots pounded into the dirt and gravel path like sledgehammers. A zombie herd had formed behind us and kept adding new members to their undead tribe. No time to contemplate a safe place to hide. Or rest. Running was our only option.

Kate tripped on a tree root and tumbled to the ground. "Shit! My ankle!"

I backtracked to her and hoisted her up under her arms. "We need to keep going. Are you okay?"

"Yeah, I twisted it, but let's go." She continued jogging with a slight limp. Her fall looked pretty bad. We needed to elevate her leg, stat.

But of course, we had no time for that.

The moans grew louder by the second. They were barely visible, and their god-awful stench hadn't reached us, but with Kate's bum leg we'd be under siege in a few minutes. Not even a hundred stun guns would help us then.

Panic climbed its way up my chest, and I choked out a nervous, high-pitched cough. It almost came out as a shriek, but I stifled it, because there was no way I was going to freak out in front of Kate.

We'd slowed down to a casual jog.

We were as good as dead.

The trees surrounding us were too high to climb, especially when one of us had a twisted ankle. There were no bushes, or brush, or anything to hide behind. No miraculously placed hollow tree logs large enough for two that always appeared in fantasy movies with forest adventures.

Up in the distance, there were a bunch of boulders and...could it be? A cave? The first one we'd come across the entire competition.

I motioned toward it, and through her long winces, Kate nodded. "Yeah. Let's hide there."

The cave turned out to be great, except for one critical thing. Nothing covered the cave opening, so zombies could stream inside and trap us in there with no way out. In all the books and movies and shows, regular zombies could smell live humans. And their sweat. And possibly, their terror. Zero clue what robot zombies could do.

We needed a diversion.

Down in the side pocket of my backpack, I slid my hand in and pulled out the string of Black Cat firecrackers Kate had given me. They were shitty, unspectacular fireworks for the Fourth of July, but perfect for creating a distraction for a zombie herd.

Kate's eyes grew wide. "Oh wow, good idea. I found some matches."

"Of course you did, fire goddess," I said.

She handed me a small box, along with a roll of tape. "Tape them to a rock." She winced. "Physics, to get some more distance."

I nodded. "Here's hoping my shot-putting for track comes in handy."

I MacGyvered the shit out of the firecracker rock and lit the green wick. Immediately, I launched the Black Cats down the path, past the cave by about seventy feet. "Okay, let's go in."

Crouched silently in the darkness, we waited.

POW! P-P-P-P-POW! POWPOWPOWPOWPOWBAMPOW!

I took a deep breath and closed my eyes, fighting the urge to throw up. Between the exhaustion from sleep deprivation and dehydration, a wave of nausea passed. Kate nuzzled into me, and I wrapped my shaking arm around her quivering shoulder.

Over the next few minutes, maybe twenty zombies staggered by. Not as many as I'd anticipated, but still more than two people could've handled in an undead ambush. When the groans and moans tapered, Kate flicked her flashlight on and off and let out a deep breath.

"I nearly peed in my pants," she said in a trembling voice. "I'm so glad we're in this together."

"Me too." I exhaled. "We got lucky. That was way too close."

While the zombie swarm thinned, Kate's body remained pressed against mine. My heart hammered faster and harder and with more force than from our adrenaline-fueled zombie chase moments before.

Kate tilted her head upward, her lips parting to say something. But at that moment, our eyes locked. She stayed quiet. Her brown eyes glinted with the reflection of the light from outside the cave. I could look at her face every day, all day, until the end of time. I lifted my hand to sweep her hair from her cheek, and she responded by rubbing her cheek up against my fingers, slowly and softly. The warmth of her skin against mine lit a fire inside me. Intense heat ignited through my entire body.

My hands trembled. This was all pretty new to me, and there was so much at stake.

I gently lifted her chin, and Kate breathed deeply. Focusing on her soft, full lips, I brushed mine against hers. Kate leaned in, sending electric currents straight through me. Our mouths met again, this time with a single dizzying kiss that made my entire body float in the air, like a kite soaring in perfect wind conditions.

I took a deep breath and kissed her again. And again. "Damn, I've wanted to do that for so long."

Her hands ran down my chest and wrapped around my waist. "Yeah?" To my surprise, she kissed me right back, long and hard.

A couple of zombies passed the cave entrance, and we hugged each other tight. Once we were in the clear, Kate looked at me. "Maybe we could stay here a little while longer. To rest."

I nodded.

She loosened her grip and turned on her flashlight again, aiming it toward the back of the cave. "Might as well explore, right? Make sure it's safe for a quick nap?"

And hopefully for kissing. Maybe more than kissing.

She added, "You stay here in case we need another diversion." Hobbling, she moved deeper into the cavern.

After a minute of silence, I called out, "Kate?"

No response.

"Kate?" I repeated with more urgency, trying to be loud enough for her to hear, but not so loud that the zombies came for us.

I paused. Listening, breathing, panicking.

"NATE! Help!"

CHAPTER TWENTY-THREE

Nate

The last thing I remembered was running to the back of the cave. That, and someone throwing a hood over my head. Then... darkness.

Through my brain fog, there's a fuzzy memory of a shadowy man shoving an oxygen mask on my face, forcing me to breathe in God-knows-what.

How long had I been knocked out?

The hood had been replaced by a blindfold, which made breathing a lot easier. From the air-conditioning blasts above me, chilling me to my core, I could tell I was indoors now.

Groggy and sore, I tried to stand. Something tied to my waist, wrists, and ankles held me down.

"Nathaniel Jae-Woo Kim," a thunderous voice said, circling me. "We finally meet."

"Where's Kate?" It came out sounding like a whine. "And where am I?" I cleared my throat, trying to get my voice to stop wavering, and I dropped it to a lower pitch. "Tell me where she is!"

"Please, Nate. Stop shouting. You're being disruptive in our work environment. Kate's safe and you are too. You're going to give me a headache with all your racket."

This made me want to annoy the man more. I shouted, "Fuck you! Take this blindfold off, you asshole!"

His voice went down a few decibels. "I will, but you have to stop shouting. And cursing. You're disturbing the workers."

The band came off my eyes. Uncontrollably blinking, I tried to take in my new environment. I'd expected an interrogation chamber or a windowless, cinder-blocked room with a singular incandescent bulb swinging on a string above our heads. But no, I was in an executive office, with sleek IKEA-looking office furniture. Directly across from me sat a familiar-looking older man in a stylish dark gray blazer, blue button-down shirt, and no tie.

Through his interior office window, he had a clear view of a few dozen people buzzing around in front of four enormous computer screens. Each one projected linear graphs, topographical maps, weather conditions, and live feeds of the forest.

I glanced back at the man, and it clicked. He was Robbie Anderson-Steele, my idol. Here, in the flesh. Far more impressive that the 2-D version of him in my closet.

"Why are you here?" I asked.

"Well, how about this? Let's play a little game. To test your deductive reasoning." He placed his elbows on his desk and folded his arms in front of him. "Let's start with, why are *you* here? I'm talking about this competition, not here in my satellite office. What made you enter this competition?"

Before I answered, I tried to loosen the zip tie securing my right wrist. Whoever tied me up had done a good job. "I'm here with Kate. She's the one who wanted me here. To help her win."

He leaned back a little into his chair. "Interesting. Kate's not the outdoorsy type. Why would she want to do this in the first place?"

This familiarity with Kate set off sirens in my head. *Serial killer! Perv! Obsessive community theater junkie!* I needed to proceed with caution.

"She and I are both into zombies. We love them. We thought it would be fun." There was way more to it, but I didn't want to discuss this anymore. Not with him, Mr. Pervy Pants.

My heart thumped harder than ever before. My spidey sense tingled as he took a slow sip of water from his Evian bottle.

On his desk, he had a recent school photo of Kate.

Holy shit.

It clicked. Robbie Anderson-Steele was Kate's dad. Kate Anderson. Her house with the creepy iron gate. Her freak-out when she ran into her dad's cutout in my closet. It made sense now.

"I've done some research on you, Nate. You're very talented, I must admit. And smart too. Makes sense that Kate would use you to win." His words stabbed little holes in me, but the way he spat my name reminded me of Pete and all those rich shits at my school. Now I knew what Pete would be like when he grew up.

"We're *friends*," I hissed back. Even though we were maybe more than just friends, this was not exactly the place or time to ask Dad's permission to date.

His cold smile sent a shiver down my spine. "Good, good. That's what I wanted to hear. Then as a *friend*, you'll want to consider Kate's best interests." He unfolded his arms. Through his glass desk I saw him place his palms on his thighs. "Kate's in a bit of a bind, you see. As of tomorrow, I will be merging *my* company, Digitools, with Zeneration, the sponsor of this competition. It will be publicly announced in a month. Since you signed a nondisclosure agreement as part of the registration process, you can't talk to anyone about any of this. Especially Kate."

The NDA.

Damn it.

He continued. "Technically, since Kate's part of the Zeneration family as of tomorrow, she can't win this contest. She'll be disqualified because family of full-time employees are not allowed to compete. Your case is different. Your father was a contractor, not a full-time staffer. And with his job loss, he's no longer affiliated with the company anyway."

While I wanted to punch his face off, I hung on to his every word. I had no idea where this was going.

"Kate can't win this competition. It'll be a PR nightmare. We originally planned to ask you to throw the competition so she'd lose, but now the Zeneration and Digitools PR guys are telling me you're the only American team left in this contest. We can't have a non-American win, not for a competition of a large-scale U.S. military contractor. Zeneration's been plastering this contest all over our website and social media. It would ruin us. And ruin the deal."

I narrowed my eyes. "And these wristbands? What's the deal with them. Are they yours? Digitools?"

"Yes. We've collected biometric data on all of you to show us how people respond to threats in poor weather conditions, while lacking food and water. The GPS is a little spotty, though. We need to work on that. Those robots are ours too. Now that we're merging with Zeneration, the government will have access to all this data when they build out their military robotic technology."

That didn't sound good. "So what do you want from me?" My stomach sank with that question. A lot of this mystery had been answered or solved. We were now at the part where the evil person disclosed the malicious plan. Like Pete did when he almost Tasered my balls.

He scooted up in his chair. "This is the good part. Effective momentarily, we're changing the rules to allow teams to break apart into solo participants. A single person can win the whole grand prize."

He grinned at me like an overzealous game show host. "That's where you come in. According to our analysts studying the video camera data, for a while Kate and you were projected to be in first place getting to the finish line. But now, with her leg injury, they're expecting you two to come in fourth. Team TBD would lose anyway." He took a deep breath in, then exhaled from his nose. "You need to drop her and win, by yourself."

My mouth gaped, but no words came out. My chest tightened at the thought of doing this competition without Kate.

Robbie Anderson-Steele leaned back farther in his chair, making the wood creak. His steely eyes narrowed. "For you, under the condition that you will never breathe a word of this to Kate, declaring yourself independent would grant you a twenty-thousand-dollar bonus. So essentially, you'll be compensated another twenty thousand on top of the fifty thousand you'll earn if you win the whole thing. You get to keep it even if you lose. But if I find out you've told her anything"—he pulled out a manila folder from a pile of papers on his desk—"I'll sue you for contract breach. And your parents will be left to beg on the streets."

I shook my head. "Why don't you just tell Kate? Why make all of this so complicated?" The words barely croaked out.

He sprang forward in his chair, making my head reflexively jerk back. "Kate and I don't see eye to eye on a lot of things concerning her future happiness and well-being. She's already upset with me for acting in behalf of her own best interests. And this will just make her think I'm taking more things away from her. Simply put, she wouldn't understand. I'm protecting her from embarrassment and even more hostility. It's best to avoid this conversation with Kate altogether."

He stood up. Meeting over. No handshake. "I can tell from our conversation that you're not an idiot. I'll have my guys take you back to the cave. Kate will regain consciousness in an hour or so. We checked out her ankle a few minutes ago, and it's lightly sprained, so we injected some anti-inflammatories and steroids. She won't remember a thing, so it's up to you to act normal and break the news to her when she wakes up."

Telling Kate about any of this would mean her dad would sue me, and my family would lose everything.

But Kate needed money. She'd made that crystal clear to me. I wanted to help her. There was only way to guarantee that would happen. She could follow her dreams, but it could mean that she would never talk to me again. I'd get us a shit ton of money, but...I would also lose her. A win-lose situation.

Before he walked out the door, an idea popped in my head. I blurted, "Go ahead and send the bonus in cryptocurrency. I'm in."

He slowed his step and whipped his head over his shoulder. "What?"

"I want the bonus payment in cryptocurrency, the fee for breaking up the team. Right now. Twenty thousand. My wallet info is in the registration information."

"If we have ourselves a deal, then I'll honor that request." He opened his office door, and waiting outside, two swole dudes in army fatigues marched in and threw the black hood over my eyes again.

His phone bleeped. "The payment's been put through. You're now a lot richer, Mr. Kim."

Funny, I'd dreamed about moments like this, when money came easy, with a snap of the finger. I expected to feel euphoric, but what I felt was something much different.

Sadness. With an extra helping of shame.

Muffled in the hooded fabric, I mumbled, "You should've been there for Kate."

He was still in the room, near me. I heard him pacing and breathing hard.

"You should have been there," I repeated. "With Kate at the ER. She told me about that. You really should apologize to her."

"How dare you! Get. Him. OUT OF HERE!"

The opaque fabric prevented me from seeing Robbie Anderson-Steele's reaction, but I didn't need my eyes to know how furious he was. His body radiated anger.

The hood lifted, and a hand securely affixed the gas mask to my face. Blackness came quickly.

CHAPTER TWENTY-FOUR

Coldness woke me like a hard slap to the cheek. The icy air made my lungs ache.

"Nate, what happened?"

My head.

Pounding.

Hard.

Flat on my back, arms and legs sprawled on the ground, I contemplated my next move. Heaving my body left, I rolled over and curled down to touch my injury. My ankle was puffy, like a balloon. Sore to the touch.

"Nate?" My voice echoed in the cave. Sluggishly, I sat up and felt around for my backpack. I pulled out my water bottle and chugged until it was almost empty.

"I'm here." He was close by. But somehow, he sounded distant. "Waited a while for you to wake up." He paused. "What's the last thing you remember?" A few feet away, I could see his silhouette, but not his face.

I squeezed my eyes shut. "It's fuzzy and in pieces. The zombies and firecrackers. And...that's it." *Why couldn't I remember?*

"You don't remember unrolling your sleeping bag? You complained that you wanted to rest," he said gently.

Something was off in his tone. The niceness was there, but the friendliness was gone. It was hard to explain, but it didn't feel right. This wasn't the Nate I knew.

"How long did I sleep?"

Nate turned on his flashlight but aimed it downward. His face was still hard to see. "A couple of hours maybe? I slept a little too."

I wanted to look into his dark brown eyes. To kiss him again and feel his body heat against my skin. But we were in the home stretch, and this wasn't the time to get distracted.

"We should head out." I pushed myself up to a crouching position and rolled up my sleeping bag. It was still warm from my body heat.

Nate checked his wristband. "If you're tired, though, we can hang out here a bit. It's raining out there."

A light drizzle fell outside of the cave opening, but nothing we couldn't handle. I hoisted on my backpack, which added extra weight on my inflamed ankle. From the first aid kit in my backpack pocket, I pulled out two Advils and swallowed them.

Our wristbands lit up and buzzed, grabbing our attention with the incoming message. I scrolled down the teeny screen.

Eight teams remaining. Congratulations to the final-
ists! And surprise! We've changed the rules (See appendix B,
Section 2 that you initialed, accepting all conditions listed
in that section, including, but not limited to, altering
terms of the competition).

Effective immediately, teams are allowed to disband and
participate as individuals. Grand prize remains the same. See
you at the finish line!

I reread the message again. It was a lot to process.

Nate spoke first. "Your ankle, from here it looks pretty
swollen, like a float in the Macy's Thanksgiving Day Parade. Can
you walk okay?"

Based on the limited data I had, standing in a cave with a
backpack, the answer was "sort of."

"I...I think so."

"Can you run?"

I bit my lip. "I can try."

Nate's shoulders stiffened. "Okay, can you outrun zombies,
and other contestants, with your leg like that?"

"I don't know," I whispered.

He breathed deeply. "Yes or no? Which is it?"

"I—I—I don't..." My eyes filled with tears. "No."

"You don't know? Or just no?"

"No." Anger shot through my veins. "NO. Okay? NO. I *can't*
run. And if I can't run, we can't win. I get that. Is that what you

wanted to hear?" My voice wavered. *Do NOT cry, Kate. Don't you dare cry.*

He waited for me to finish. "I can still win, though." He cleared his throat. "It's still possible for me to win."

"By yourself?" I barked. It came out more harshly that I'd expected.

"Yes. By myself," he said, barely audible. "If we stay as a team..." His voice trailed off.

If we stayed as a team, we'd lose.

If he left me, he could win.

I wasn't an idiot. Cutting him loose was the logical answer. But let's face it, I wasn't really letting *him* go. He was letting *me* go.

Abandoned again. A memory flashed of my mom, wildly clapping for me in the front row of the auditorium. Then another, of her casket being lowered into the ground. Did she know how much I loved her? How it hurt so much when she died? I hated being alone, but love inevitably turned into heartbreak. There was no point in going through that again. My heart couldn't handle it.

"Go," I whispered.

"Kate? Are you sure?"

Louder, I hissed, "Just go. Now. I'll be fine."

His wristband buzzed. "If I win, I promise—"

I cut him off. "Stop. Talking. Just leave while you still have a chance to win." Nate wasn't complicated. Money was the only thing that drove him. I was so stupid to think there was more to him than that.

Nate nodded. Standing up with his heavy pack on one shoulder, he walked to the front of the cave. "I left you extra food and water," he said before he took off jogging into the rain. The wind had picked up, rattling the trees and blowing debris every which way.

If he'd shone the flashlight back at my face, he would have seen tears tumbling down my cheeks as the fire inside me blew out.

CHAPTER TWENTY-FIVE

Kate wouldn't let me finish talking, but honestly, I wasn't sure what to say.

I wanted to tell her this was the only way to win the prize.

I wanted to tell her I'd split the money.

I wanted to tell her this was the hardest decision I'd ever made and there wasn't a way out without losing everything.

But I didn't.

I couldn't.

I'd woken up only a few minutes before Kate, and barely had time to think of a cover story. Lying to her made me queasy, like at any point while we were speaking I could have projectile vomited. I tried to keep my cool and not say too much. She knew me well enough to know if I was hiding something. I didn't turn on the light because she'd see my usually-under-control restless leg syndrome in full swing, and my eyes brimming with tears when I suggested I'd go the rest of the journey alone.

I hated this.

I hated myself for this.

But what was most important now was to win, so I could make it all worth it. She'd have money to go live in New York, and I'd have money for my parents, college, and my business. The knot forming in my stomach told me that I was doing something wrong for the right reason. Or maybe I was doing something right for the wrong reason. What scared me was I couldn't tell which was which.

There was no one to discuss this with now. I was on my own. In this freezing, rainy gloom, I was all alone.

I would win alone.

....

Behind a barely-wide-enough pine tree, a deep feeling of unease set in as I watched a group of contestants pack up their camp stuff. There were four of them, and only one of me.

"We don't have much farther to go. We might finish this evening, possibly even late afternoon," the girl with the long braid and blue bandanna said. She had a thick German accent.

Her partner, a raggedy wilderness man, had a grizzled beard so bushy that forest animals could be hiding in there and he wouldn't know it. As he took down their tents, he grunted to his campmates, "What're you gonna do with the money if you guys win?"

The other two scruffy guys laughed. One yelled, "Coke," as the other shouted, "Hos!" They fell back in laughter on their sleeping bags.

Bandanna Girl and Grizzly Beard Guy didn't show any signs of repulsion as they packed up their cooking gear. They didn't even notice when the two scruffalumps stood up and came around from behind and smacked them both in the wrists simultaneously with these bug zappers that looked like tennis rackets. The jolt made the couple yelp in pain. More importantly, though, their wristbands unclicked and fell on the ground.

Comrade betrayal, for coke and hos. These guys were brutal, attacking their own pack like that.

The woman screamed, "What the fuck, Hans? Andreas? We had a pact!"

The scruffier, doughier dude scratched his belly. "We did what we needed to win. Fuck the pact."

Without hesitating, Bandanna Girl and Grizzly Beard Guy both jumped him. He went down hard, and they took turns pummeling his face. Instead of helping his partner, the coke guy grabbed his backpack and ran down the path as fast as any stoned person could, partnership be damned. Coke and hos all to himself. Too bad he didn't have his map, which had been next to his bag but had blown toward me when he left his former tribe. He would've figured out he was running full speed the wrong way, heading in the direction of the cave.

I folded the map in my hand and stuck it in my cargo pants back pocket.

With these four contestants accounted for, it meant there were only two others left in the competition other than Kate and me. I didn't know if they'd be together or competing separately. But with the coke guy heading the wrong way, I did know that these two other people were the only ones who could stop me from winning.

My heels dug deep into the muddy path, making me adjust my backpack every few steps and use my bo staff as a walking cane. Gnats and mosquitoes took turns landing on my face like it was a runway, so I took a brief break to douse myself in deep woods bug repellant. The smell of decaying leaves, pine, sweat, and Deet filled my nose with each inhale.

After a couple of hours of walking, I crept into the woods to break for water and food. Parking myself under a fir tree, I leaned against the soft bark and closed my eyes. I'd gone through nearly all of my water reserve and was relying mostly on the Capri Suns to keep me hydrated.

Twigs crunched nearby, startling me awake. Before I reacted, Kate came around the tree and held out her palm, in a "stop right there" formation.

She unsheathed the stun gun I'd given her. Irony at its best.

"You're here?" I gaped. "How?"

She snapped. "I followed your footprints. Surprised I made it this far?"

No point in lying now. "Yeah, I am. How are you even walking?"

"This German guy came running up to the cave and saw me wrapping my ankle. I traded him my map for some heavy-duty painkillers. And steroid tablets. He was a walking dispensary. He grilled me with questions and assumed I wasn't a threat since I was injured. I didn't bother to tell him he had the map upside down when he walked away in the wrong direction."

A roar from my stomach reminded me I hadn't eaten anything before I passed out from exhaustion. "Well, good for you." My tongue was chalky with those four words. I needed water. Not Capri Suns. Badly.

As if sensing my thirst, Kate pulled her canteen from her side and took a long swig. "I'd offer you some, but you know. You're an asshole."

Kate was smaller than me. It would be easy for me to take everything she had, along with her stun gun and backpack of supplies, with a swift tackle, headlock, or choke hold. But I couldn't. I wouldn't. Because it was Kate.

I swallowed hard. "It's still the best this way." Her dad sure as hell made that crystal clear with me. "When the steroids and pain meds wear off, you'll slow down."

Her chin thrusted up. "I don't want you back, anyway. I'm leaving. May the best person win." She took a few steps and turned. "After all of this, I never want to see you again," she spat. The look on her face said everything. She loathed me.

Her words pierced through my heart, and air left my lungs. I was doing this for her, but she could never find out.

Up and over the hill, with her back to me, she disappeared.

CHAPTER TWENTY-SIX

Kate

Walking was easy now.

I'd dumped most of my gear and supplies in the cave to lighten my backpack load. Everything except water, food, bear spray, matches, and a stun gun. And, of course, my hand sanitizer.

I'd wrapped my ankle tightly in my boot, and the swelling had finally subsided some. That German guy gave me really good painkillers too. Even if both of my ankles had twisted, I could probably speed walk a 5K without any physical pain. I'd taken a few breaks off the path to rest and refuel so I didn't push my body too hard.

Emotionally, though, when I saw Nate resting in the woods, pure anger flared inside me, compressing my heart and squeezing my lungs so hard I could hardly breathe. It pushed me to confront him. Made me want to fight. Made me want to win. Just to see Nate lose.

Nate. Him kissing me was one of the best moments of my life. I squeezed my eyes shut and tried to push the memory out of my mind. Every time I thought of zombies, or roller-skating, or campfires, I would think of Nate now. He tainted them, forever.

I'd taken a photo of the map on my phone, which was why trading it with the German wasn't a big deal. The longer route to the finish line was a hiking path that wrapped around the side of a narrow cliff. There was a slightly shorter route, but it was steep and slippery, following a boulder-strewn path to the waterfall where you had to cut across a fast-moving stream. Surviving that, you would take the Indian Falls trail to the end. Slippery stones and sprained ankles didn't go well together, so I had to take the road less treacherous.

Sunlight gilded the tops of the swaying trees, sporadically blinding me as I walked. The trails had been easy to follow up to that point, but now I found myself winded as I climbed over or around fallen trees to stay on course. Was this nature's doing, from the storm? Or were these tiring obstacles placed there on purpose, to wear us out so we couldn't fight the zombies?

Buzzing winged insects circled around my head and nipped my cheeks and neck. Swollen bug bites and eczema left the backs of my hands inflamed, sore, and irritated. In my hasty cave departure, I'd remembered to douse myself in OFF! before leaving, but the spray was ineffective: it was as if these bugs were attracted to my spray, not repelled by it. I hoped the bear spray didn't have the same effect. Last thing I needed now in my exhausted, sweaty state was bear magnetism.

Walking alone in the forest was much creepier than walking alone in Seattle, even compared to the rough parts of Pioneer Square after midnight. Here, every animal rustling, pitter-pattering, or rooting around made my stomach churn and the hairs on my arms stand on end. Someone could murder me out in the wilderness, and no one would even know. Not even Nate.

Past the thick, droopy tree limbs, the dirt path continued up the side of the jutted cliff. I placed each foot carefully, one step firmly in front of the other, so my ankle wouldn't buckle in the slippery, muddy terrain. One small misstep and I'd send stones (or myself) tumbling off the edge.

The sun was positioned at exactly the wrong angle for this last leg of our competition, the cliff just high enough to get plenty of direct light. Blinding, disorienting sunlight, smack in the eyes with no relief.

One small step in front of the other. Like a tightrope walker.

Left. Right.

Left. Right.

Up the incline I went, taking in the occasional breathtaking view of the forest below. Perched high above the woods, quietness and stillness surrounded me. The path wrapped around the cliff, out of immediate view, and protruded out again farther down on what appeared to be a second cliff.

I made my way around the first bend and stopped cold.

In the middle of the trail, sitting with his knees tucked to his chest was nemesis Nate. Backpack off, eyes squeezed shut, trembling too hard to be meditating. How long had he been there? Probably more than a few minutes. Maybe an hour or two—no doubt he'd been moving faster than I had.

Not wanting to startle him, I said in the calmest, quietest voice I could muster, "Nate? Um...are you okay?"

He kept his eyes closed. "Hey. I just need a little break."

"But...here?"

Nate was sitting just past a critical juncture in the trail's topography. The path narrowed even more up ahead, and where we were now, no greenery shielded the outer edges. Here, a simple slip meant you'd plummet straight down into the forest and meet a certain death.

It was funny to think that a few hours before, Nate was hurling firecrackers and sprinting ahead of me. Fearless and confident.

"Are you sick? Is it the height?"

He took deep, calm breaths, eyes still closed. "Yeah. And there's at least a quarter-mile left on this cliff. I...lost the bo staff. I dropped it, and it rolled off the side of the cliff. I couldn't hear it land—that's how high we are."

He continued. "I've been here for maybe an hour, in this exact spot. I can't move, forward or backward. If I take off my wristband, they'll come get me. Maybe I should just do that."

My mouth hung open. "What? You're giving up?"

He opened one eye and focused it on me. "You can't get

around me. It's too narrow. I can't let you meet the same fate as my bo staff. When they clear me out, you can keep going then. I haven't seen anyone else on this trail." He closed his eye. "That could mean we're smarter than everyone—"

"Or we're idiots for taking the plummet-to-our-deaths path?"

"Yep," he mumbled. "If you're in a real hurry, there's one way you can keep going. You'd need to crawl on top of me and then get off. I can try to help you with that." His face flushed, and both eyes popped open. "I meant it in an obstacle course sense, not a 'let's have sex right now' way."

"Yeah, I figured. You don't seem to be in a very sexy mood," I deadpanned.

Squeezing his eyes shut again, he shook his head. "Oh God. Ignore me, please. The high altitude's messing with my brain."

I took off my backpack and sat down next to him. It was a good time to take a rest, anyway. "I'll pass on your generous humping offer. Maybe another time."

Here we were again, falling back into conversation. Just like old times.

We were almost around the first cliff bend. Nate was too wide to get around, he was right about that, but I still risked slipping off the edge by straddling him wrong. And who knew how long it would take for someone to pick him up once he'd pulled off his wristband?

The right way to handle this mess was far from simple. We

both needed to keep going. After he and I made it across, I had just as good a shot to win as he did.

"Nate, do you trust me?"

No hesitation. "Yes."

"Good. We're going to keep moving, together. My therapist used to work with me on my fears, mainly stage fright and night terrors, especially around my mom's death. Maybe some of those tips can help you." I took his pulse. "Your heart rate is way too fast. You need to slowwww down. Are you breathing okay?"

Eyes still closed, he took a series of deep breaths. His frenetic pulse went down a little.

"It's better," I said. "But try breathing in and exhaling even deeper."

He did a few and grumbled, "I feel stupid doing this."

"It might feel stupid, but your pulse is close to normal now. That's great! Okay, now you need to tell me what we can dump out of your pack. It's weighing you down and might be contributing to your unsteadiness on this ledge."

"Anything but food and water can go. The competition should be over soon anyway, so I don't need a lot of stuff."

His pack was stuffed full, and we didn't have room to lay it all out. New plan. "I'll drag the backpack behind me, as far as I can carry it. If it becomes a problem, I can leave it somewhere you can retrieve it later. There's a detachable pouch, and I'll fill it with some water and food."

His breath quickened, and color drained from his face.

"Nate."

His eyelashes fluttered. He opened his eyes.

"Take more deep breaths. And then we walk slowly. The sun's dried the path, so it's not muddy anymore like when you first got here. We can chat the whole way, nothing stress-inducing, I promise." Grabbing my extended hand and using the rocky wall behind him to steady himself, he pulled his body up.

I promised him pleasant conversation as a means of distracting him, but what could I say? Almost everything I thought of eventually led back to Nate and me. Back to our friendship and our partnership breakup. Hard feelings didn't just magically go away.

For us to make it up the cliff path, though, it was important to keep my hurt feelings in check. I swallowed my anger like a horse-size pill. Mindless topic of conversation number one. "How many Capri Suns did you drink in all?"

He took a couple of slow steps. "I drank five. And don't worry, I peed before I got stuck here." A few more shuffles forward. "How's your ankle? Is it any better?"

I bit back my sarcasm. *You mean the ankle you assumed would slow you down so you ditched me in the cave?* "It's a lot better. It's still stiff and bruised, but the bruising and swelling went down, and I can walk on it, especially thanks to those pain meds. And faster than your old granny pace."

He slowed the shuffling of his feet. "I can go slower, you know." One micro baby step. Then another. Then another.

"Hey! Okay, fine. No more pointing out your geriatric steppage."

"Good." Nate laughed and picked up the pace again.

"I won't say anything about how you might be so slow that a pedometer wouldn't register your steps."

"Good."

"Or mention that we're moving slower than those zombies in the forest we saw who had no legs."

"Good."

"Definitely not going to tell you that I hope we finish before the next annual Zombiegeddon."

"Good." He bent down to pick up some debris and tossed it behind him. The next thing I knew I was showered in dirt clumps, crunched-up weeds, and small rocks.

"Pppppfth!" He'd thrown some into my mouth. "You jackass."

He laughed. "Sorry, my over-the-shoulder aim is usually terrible." He continued inching down the path. "Are you still moving to New York? After this?" he asked, barely loud enough for me to hear.

In all my time alone in the woods, I hadn't actually thought much about my life after the competition. The zombies, my ballooned ankle, and Nate dumping me had kept me sufficiently distracted from my post-Zombiegeddon goals. Was I still moving to New York? If he'd asked me right after our make-out session, I would've scrunched my shoulders and dodged the question because I didn't know.

But now I knew. There was no good reason to stay.

I didn't want to work at Dad's company.

I didn't want to live under his roof under his rules.

I didn't want all the tracking. Or the monitoring.

Most kids at school complained about their helicopter and bulldozer parents. My dad preferred a drone-parenting approach with me, using round-the-clock surveillance to watch my every move.

I wanted a fresh start. No, I *needed* a fresh start. Far away from here.

"I have enough in my savings for a one-way ticket. After a few months of couch surfing, I'll try to get a place with roommates."

He didn't say anything. But since I promised him pleasant conversation, I continued with more questions. "And you? Going straight to college or starting your business in your parents' basement?" I kicked some dirt off the path and listened to it shower down the steep edge.

"Maybe both?" His voice lilted and cracked in that goofy Nate way. He stopped in his tracks and asked in a hushed tone, "Can we talk about money for a second?"

"Not if it stresses you out. If you temporarily lose your shit, lose your footing, and plunge to your death, that would be tragic. No thanks to all of that."

With the tops of his fingernails, he scratched his scruffy chin with upward strokes. "This is actually partly why I am so stressed. We need to talk—"

But we didn't get to talk. Because a zombie got in the way.

CHAPTER TWENTY-SEVEN

 Nate

"A ZOMBIE! OHHH FUUUUUCK!"

Stating the obvious, but it was the only thing that popped into mind when that snapping, foot-dragging eyeless piece of shit came around the bend.

"GAAAAAAAAA!"

Someone had recently fought with this zombie and lost. Between the missing eye and the freshly torn clothes, he was in really bad shape, cosmetically speaking. Energy-wise, though, he was ready to rumble. Ten out of ten on the enthusiasm scale.

And I was the one in front. First in line for a good ol'-fashioned zombie mauling.

I pleaded, "Kate? Could you hand me my stuff?"

Kate handed me a pouch, and I rummaged around in it. No stun gun. Where was my—

"Sorry, I left the backpack way back there," Kate apologized. "You said food and water only!"

The only weapons at my disposal were Clif Bars, two Camelbak water bottles, and a Strawberry Kiwi Capri Sun.

"GAAAAAAAA!" Cyclops zombie cried out again, lurching forward just enough to make me scuttle back. Feet sliding, I sent stones off the cliff.

My breathing shortened and turned into little pants. A wave of nausea hit, and my legs went rubbery. "Kate?" I wheezed. "Do you still have a stun gun?"

"Yes. But are you okay to handle it?"

Meaning, could I remain steady enough to blast Cyclops instead of electrifying myself by mistake, or losing my balance and falling to my death? Probably not. I rubbed my eyes, an attempt to clear the fear-onset blurriness.

We didn't have much time. Cyclops took firm, confident steps toward us. *Stomp, stomp. Gaaaaaah! Stomp, stomp. Gaaaaaaah!* He was maybe thirty feet away, tops.

"Kate, do you have your pyro shit?"

"What do you mean, my pyro—"

"Your fire shit! The shit you use to make fires?" This was no time for eloquence. I needed her fire shit. NOW.

Behind me, she dug deep into her backpack. "Here." She handed me matches and a lighter. My plan was to take off my shirt, set it on fire, and throw it at him. At best, that would give us more time to think. If he kept coming, I'd zap him. Who knew. I wasn't exactly in a prime decision-making state.

I tore off my outer layer shirt and put a flame at the seam, but it wouldn't light. *Stupid REI poly-techno-ultra-moisture-wick-featherweight piece of unflammable garbage!*

Kate threw me her Team Magenta shirt. One hundred percent cotton. Flammable. Disposable. And the ultimate symbol that our partnership was dead. My team shirt was buried at the bottom of my abandoned backpack. Was leaving it behind that much different than setting it ablaze? I turned my back to her so she couldn't see the sadness in my eyes when I ignited her shirt.

I held it above me like the Olympic torch and tossed it over to the zombie. It landed by his feet, stopping his movement, but not catching him on fire.

Kate shoved a bottle in my hand. "Hand sanitizer!"

"For what? Germs?"

She unscrewed the top, and it clicked. *Nate, you idiot. Accelerant.* Of course! Like a shitty Molotov cocktail.

Slightly unsteady, I heaved it squarely at the zombie's chest.

Or, at least, that's where I aimed.

The bottle clinked against the zombie's groin, splattering the disinfectant all over his lower extremities, then fell into the scorching shirt blaze. Instantly, his junk lit on fire, as did the bottom half of his body. In a cloud of black smoke, the zombie stumbled back three giant steps, then deactivated and crumpled to the ground. The inferno spread to his midsection, up the neck, and melted part of his face before it died down enough for me to stomp it out.

The putrid smell of burned plastic and electrical fire filled my nose. Tears pricked my burning eyes. Breathing deeply and steadily had already been difficult enough, and now acrid pollution filled the air. By sheer luck, the breeze changed course and blew the black smoke away from us. But the unforgettable smell was still there, in my nose, in my lungs. It would never leave me.

The zombie was too heavy to move, or more accurately, I was too weak to move it. When the zombie cooled down enough, I stepped over him. Kate took her turn, and at the exact moment she was on top of it, I scoffed, "So you could have crawled on me after all!"

She shook her head. "You're way bigger than this guy. And please, no 'that's what she said' jokes."

Damn it.

Up past the zombie obstacle, the path widened. Kate cheered, "Hey, look! We have maybe fifty yards left to go on this trail!"

We'd come this far, and so much was at stake. Winning the money and fulfilling our dreams was still top of mind. The whole fear of heights setback was a minor blip in this competition. I had to make it. For Kate.

I turned to face her. "Yeah. Apparently, the zombie distraction technique works wonders."

We approached a sizable gap between our cliff and the next cliff that lead to the end of the journey.

We needed to jump to the other ledge.

But one slip meant instant death.

Oh, hell no.

I backed up straight into Kate. The Clif Bar wrappers in my sling pouch crunched against her face.

"Owww!" she yelled, pinching her nose.

Not even a simple "sorry" came to mind. My entire body screamed for me to continue retreating. That's all I had on my mind. *Back, back, back. Go back* times infinity.

Kate came around to my side. "Oh no," she squeaked as she peered at the new obstacle.

"I know," I managed to say. *Take a deep breath, Nate. Calm down. Inhale. Exhale.*

"At least the path's wider over there?" she said, scrunching her shoulders.

BZZZZZ!

My eyes popped open. A new message.

Three contestants remaining. Good luck!

Behind us, the German came around the bend, taking microsteps with his back against the rocky wall. With grimace stamped all over his face, he was almost as scared of heights as me.

"Nate, we have to go. We can't let that guy win," Kate urged.

Oh yeah? Tell that to my hammering heart. My vomity stomach. My legs cemented to this spot.

"I can't." The mounting pressure was too much. Taking off the wristband would end everything. The rescue people would come get me. I'd still get *some* money. But I wouldn't win. But...I would also not be hanging on to a precipice for dear life after misjudging my ability to long jump to another cliff.

"You can. You will. We can't quit now." She walked up to the gap, studied it a few moments, and came back. "It's only like fifteen inches. You can do it, even with your eyes closed."

I shook my head no.

The German inched closer. A booming voice behind us yelled, "Only you two are left?"

We turned to face him. He was still clinging to the cliff wall, refusing to look outward to the forest by facing his head toward us, but he was gaining speed. Color had returned to his grayish, sunken face as he shimmied our way, where the path was broader.

Each step he took showed confidence. Arrogance. Victory. With his left hand, he fished into his pocket and pulled out a stun gun. MY stun gun, from my backpack. On his belt, my small pocketknife hung from a large carabiner. My parents had given it to me when I'd earned my Eagle Scout Award.

Kate said, "We can do this."

Anger flooded my body. *Fuck this guy.* "Okay. You lead."

We walked to the crevice, and she yelled, "One! Two!" before I could warn her that she'd miscalculated her fifteen inches. It was almost two feet.

"THREE!"

Her hand in mine, I held my breath.

We jumped.

Kate's dismount on the other side was graceful. Her feet landed nearly together. Barely kicked up any dirt. She smiled.

Me? I had to let go of her hand because my forward momentum cannoned me to the ground, and my knees skid like a plane landing with no wheels down a runway. If I'd held my arms out, it would've added the full effect.

Brushing my pants off, I assessed the damage. My knees and palms were skinned, but that was infinitely better than free-falling to my death.

"You okay?" I asked Kate.

"Yeah. Now you owe me for keeping you in the game," she said.

"I also owe you an apology. For leaving you in the cave. I was such an idiot, to think I could do any of this alone. I'm...so sorry."

My wristband buzzed. **Kate cannot win. If you stay a team and you both win, you will both be disqualified.**

That message had been for me, and only me. A reminder that he was watching me. And a reminder of what I needed to do.

CHAPTER TWENTY-EIGHT

It was time to run.

Poor Nate hadn't expected me to take off so fast. He probably was expecting something more drawn out, but there was no time for that. I didn't even accept his apology.

Likewise, I hadn't expected the German to catch up to me and take a swing. To claw at my neck and pull my hair with such force that he knocked me flat on my stomach. We were at the home stretch, a few hundred yards from the finish line, and the wind had been knocked out of me. Sprawled out and helpless, gasping for air. No longer in the lead.

But the German wasn't done with me. As I tried to catch my breath, he dropped on top of me and yanked my wristband. By some miracle, it didn't unsnap. He kept yank-yank-yanking to the point where my wrist was rubbed raw, possibly even sprained or broken.

The German's face scrunched up as he pulled. "Damn it!"

This was it.

He was one yank away from defeating me, I knew it.

I'd lost.

Body tense, my eyes squeezed shut, I braced myself for defeat. That was all I could do.

SMACK!

With the weight of the German off my torso, I opened my eyes to see where he'd gone. Nate had him pinned down, barely. The German was bigger, stronger, and angrier. But Nate held his own, staying on top of his writhing opponent. Not letting go, even with all the twisting and bucking.

This was my chance. Nate and German were rumbling on the ground. Distracted. I could run for it.

I could win.

But leave Nate? He could have just run, but he cared about me enough to push off the German. Or maybe he owed me and we were even now.

Sweat trickled down the side of my face and neck. A quick swipe of my hand across my collarbone revealed that my garnet necklace was gone. I had squeezed the pendant right before Nate and I jumped across the cliff divide. Where could it have—

The German.

Did he pull it off when he grabbed my neck?

Frantically, I backtracked to the area the German had brought me down. Sifting through fallen pine needles, underbrush, on my hands and knees. Hot tears fell, forming dark brown speckles in the dirt. If I didn't find it now, there would be no way to backtrack and find it later.

I hadn't fully understood the term "finding a needle in a haystack" until that very moment. This was hopeless.

"Kate! He has your necklace! He keeps punching me with it."

Ankle throbbing, I hopped toward Nate. At that point, both guys, with mussed hair and bleeding scratches on their faces, had gotten in good swings. And Nate was right. Sure enough, the German had my gold chain wrapped around his hand, like a really shitty brass knuckle. It was hard to see if the pendant was still attached with all the frantic punching movement.

Nate yelled, "Take off his wristband!" The German was still pinned down, but not for long. After spending so much time on his back, he figured out it would be easier to flip over and push up than lift Nate off him. "I've got his arms!"

That garnet necklace was the last thing my mom gave me. I'd worn it every day, every night since the day Raina had pulled me out of my funk and dragged me to the skating rink.

It meant everything to me. I needed it back.

Instead of pulling off the German's wristband, I pulled on his curled fingers, forcing him to give up the necklace.

"What are you doing?" Nate screamed.

But then it was too late. I'd used all my strength to open the German's hand. All of it. Slowly, his hand opened, and I pulled my treasure from his grip.

I was so ecstatic about my necklace retrieval that I didn't move when he rolled to his side and yanked a final time at my wristband.

Click.

It fell to the ground. A message flashed: `game elimination in thirty seconds`.

Nate grew weaker by the second. Soon, the German wriggled out of his hold and, in an instant, was on top of Nate.

In a choke hold, Nate strangle-whispered, "Do. Krav. Maga. Please." The German let go of Nate's neck and went for his wristband. Tugging it hard, like he did with me. And I knew five hard tugs and that was it.

Do Krav Maga? I never took it except for the few half-jokey defense lessons Nate had given me during our post–escape room hangout sessions. *All you learn the first few months is how to kick a perp in the balls.*

Ignoring my ankle injury, which happened to be in my dominant, stronger kicking leg, I pushed the German hard and nailed him in the nuts. Just like Nate had taught me.

The moment I made contact, my ankle made a loud popping sound.

The German rolled over, grabbing his crotch and screaming what I assumed were Deutschland profanities. I fell to the ground, rubbing my ankle and pulling it toward me to get a better look. The pain was worse than ever.

Nate stumbled to his feet, like a severely drunk person pretending he was okay to walk home without assistance. It looked like a cat had used his face as a scratching post. This competition had physically wrecked us.

"You need to go now." I winced and handed him the stun gun from my backpack.

An aha look crossed his face. "Wait! I was supposed to tell you something. About winning—"

The German moaned as he pushed himself up.

Nate yelped, "Holy shit! Is he one of those robots? How in the hell is he getting up—"

"Go!" I screamed.

Nate glanced at his buzzing wristband. Then he ran.

CHAPTER TWENTY-NINE

Marathon runners talk about "runner's high" a lot. The point where they hit their groove and running feels effortless. The euphoric feeling they get when their mind is clear, their body feels lighter, and they truly come alive. Endorphins kick in. When they approach the finish line, it's like an out-of-body experience. One so otherworldly that these same people keep doing marathons, to relive these moments again and again and again.

I am not a marathon runner. And those people who do them are stupid as shit. Getting to the finish line of this zombie competition was the fucking worst thing ever. No way would I ever want to do this again. Never. Ever. Again.

There was no groove. No effortless, light-bodied feeling. No high-as-a-kite euphoria. Where the fuck were my endorphins?

This was nothing like my cross-country or track meets. Gasping, exhausted, and panting like a dog in peak summer heat, I left Kate and the German in a hurry when I got the next and final wristband message. **Leave now and I'll throw in another $10,000.**

Kate had already lost, so it was just the German and me. He had a runner's physique, too, so with no time to think, I got out of there fast.

I'd meant to tell Kate I'd send her half of my winnings, but there was no time.

A quarter of a mile away, large yellow posts and black-checkered flags marked the end of the course. An ogling crowd of onlookers stood at the finish line. I was so close.

Boots stomping hard, I kept my eyes locked on those yellow markers. My heart raced, a frenetic rhythm stemming from pure panic, not from any runner's high bullshit. In the final stretch, I tried to remember my one-hundred- and two-hundred-meter race coaching. *Shoulders down and relaxed (relaxed?), hips pulled upward, knees up high, elbows driven back, pumping to the shoulder for momentum.*

What I wasn't supposed to do was turn my head, to see where the German was. Because then I'd see he was just a few paces away. Distracted, I would panic even more. Then my critical mistake would allow him to gain on me.

The yellow posts were my North Star. Staying laser-focused on them was the only way to win.

As I drew closer to the finish line, my legs nearly buckled when I came to the horrifying realization that the onlookers weren't people.

They were zombies.

And they were all heading my way.

Oh-shit-ohshitohshit!

Panic stricken, instead of running forward, or retreating backward, I froze.

A distant, familiar voice shouted from behind me. "Use the stun gun!"

Kate?

Oh right. The stun gun. The one in my hand.

To my left and right, the zombies attacked, but the voltage blasts proved effective. Each zap to any part of the zombie disabled them, frying their metal innards. With the zombie corpse fortress around me, through the gaps in the body pileup I saw the German knocking off the zombies one by one using hand-to-hand combat. Because of all of his noisy grunting and commotion, all of the remaining dozen or so robots headed straight for him.

This was my chance. I pushed myself through the stack of putrid robot bodies and tore out of there like a bat out of hell. *Go, go, go, Nate!*

Shoulders down, hips up, knees high, elbows back, and pump to shoulder.

Shoulders down, hips up, knees high, elbows back, and pump to shoulder.

Shoulders down, hips up, knees high, elbows back, and pump to shoulder.

The finish line was finally clear of zombies. Just a few yards away. So close.

Behind my left ear, I heard panting as I approached the yellow posts. The German was back, and he body-checked me so hard I flew through the air, soaring forward, legs no longer upright. Where the fuck did he come from, this German Terminator? I landed on the ground, wristband arm outstretched, like those football players did in the Super Bowl to get that "by a hair" touchdown. Titans tried it versus the Rams in 2000. Too bad the Titans lost that one.

Still robbed of my euphoria, the world went black when my head whacked the ground.

....

"Nate? Can you hear me?" My eyes opened to a gathering of people encircling me. Robbie Anderson-Steele was one of them, along with a team of medics. The stethoscope squad.

"He's awake, everyone!" Robbie shouted over his shoulder. Barely within earshot, he said to the closest doctor, "Make sure it's just a minor concussion. And clean up those scratches on his face. Get him some water and food. We need him to look good for the cameras and be coherent for the evening news."

With a steely scowl, Robbie Anderson-Steele watched me pull myself into a seated position. I was in the same place where I'd collapsed, on the finish line. The only difference was my wristband had been removed. Using my right hand, I rubbed the sore area where the band had been.

"What happened? Did I—you know—"

He interrupted. "What? Did you win?" An iciness in his voice made me shiver.

"Yes?"

He paused before answering. "We had to review our rules to be sure, but your wristband crossed the line by a few millimeters, according to the data collected." For my ears only, he hissed, "You're a lucky son of a bitch, you know that?"

The $50,000 grand prize. Plus $20,000 more for going solo. Plus the $10,000 bonus at the end. I'd won it all! A wide smile spread across my face as I ran through my mental checklist of the things I'd do with the money. First, save the house. Then, Mom's car. College tuition and seed money for my survivalist prep business were also at the top of the list if I had anything to spare. And of course, I'd give Kate her share.

The nurse wiped my face and took my temperature while the doctor examined my eyes. "Follow my finger," he said, moving his index finger back and forth.

He took my pulse and checked my tongue. "Clean bill of health," he concluded. "He just passed out from a small concussion most likely, plus he's dehydrated."

The nurse handed me a full cup of water with the Zeneration logo on it. I downed it in less than five seconds.

"Could I please have more?"

"Wow, so polite! Your girlfriend must be lucky," she said with a wink.

Girlfriend? The closest thing I had to a girlfriend was Kate.

Funny Kate. Whip-smart Kate. Lovable Kate.

Kate and her identical plaid shirts.

Kate, who saved me on that cliff.

Kate, who blasted Pete with the stun gun and kicked that other guy in the balls.

Rising to a standing position, I looked past the doctors, the corporate sponsors, the press, and searched for her. As my disorientation subsided and my mind regained clarity, I knew, with all my heart, I wanted to be with Kate. I didn't want her to leave. I wanted to tell her about the money. OUR money. To say what had been weighing on my heart for so long. It was something so unfamiliar, I had no idea how to articulate it until now.

Kate was the one I wanted to celebrate this victory with because she made it happen. Because I was in love with her. God, where was she?

Through the bustling crowd, familiar faces appeared, but they weren't hers. My dad, mom, and sister elbowed their way over to me, a mix of anger and worry etched on their faces.

Mom yelled first. "You were supposed to be at friend house! We worried sick! And you take my car!"

Then Dad. "You are grounded. Until you are graduated! Maybe longer!"

And Lucy. "I told them you leaved out of the house!" Her eyes cast toward my filthy boots. "I'm sorry you're in big trouble."

I squatted to her eye level. "Asking you to keep that secret was wrong, Lucy. That was all my fault. But when we get home, remind me that I have a gift for you."

She squirmed her way between Mom and Dad and hugged me. "A gift? For me?"

When she let me go, I cupped her face and squished her cheeks with my thumbs. "I missed you, kiddo."

I did. I missed her a lot.

I loved being her older brother.

"Can you come to my class tomorrow, Oppa? It's share day. I want to show everyone your medal and trophy!"

"Sure, I owe you that much." At least someone in my family was proud of me.

Standing up again, I found it hard to look at my parents' disappointed faces. "Mom, Dad, I'm so sorry. I should have just been honest with you about where I was going. I wanted to make you proud of me. The good news is I have enough money to make a big payment on the house. I know you lost your job, Dad, and that's because Pete Haskill got his dad to fire you, because of me. That was one of the main reasons I did this competition." I turned to my dad. "And now we have enough to hire someone to fix the leaky roof."

My parents exchanged looks. It wasn't a look of joy, like I'd expected. More like complete confusion with a trace of melancholy.

Dad said, "I don't need your money. I hate that job anyway and needed change. And I have good job now."

"Wait, you do?"

Dad smiled. "I start tomorrow. A start-up company hire me. Can you believe this old man will be working with so many young people?"

Okay, so Dad had a job now and the house was safe. "Mom, I'm going to buy a new car for you then."

She shrugged. "But I like my Honda."

"But now you can get a new Honda," I protested.

She crossed her arms. "But I *don't want* new Honda."

Surely Dad would get why she needed a new car. My eyes pleaded for him to help.

He shook his head. "Your mom like her car. I try to get new one. We test-drive new Accord every year, but she keep old one. She feel safer. She say new car with all electronic gadget thing make her nervous."

I shook my head and sighed, like how I did when Lucy frustrated me so much that I wanted to punch a hole in the wall. *Kim family rule, don't argue with them, Nate.* "Okay, fine. But we can still get someone for the new roof, though."

This time, Dad snorted like a bull ready to charge. "I learn at Home Depot how to fix. I buy better tarp and better sealant this time." A second snort, this one more sarcastic. Like a snort-cough. "If you know how to do yourself and workers come to fix, you know if they cheat you."

Unbelievable. Here I was, an ATM dispensing free money, and they didn't want any of it.

My dad gripped my shoulder. "We work hard, but we like our life."

I said in a whinier voice that I'd have liked, "But I want your lives to be easier."

The Zeneration PR spokesperson popped her head over my shoulder. Her perfect blond bob didn't move, even in the wind. "Nate, we need to steal you away in about five minutes," she said, then scurried away to talk to an eager local camera crew, adjusting her knee-length beige skirt as she left us.

My dad's stern face softened, and his crinkly eyes brimmed with tears. I'd never seen him show any kind of emotion like this. Not even when he watched his favorite movie, *Charlotte's Web*. "Jae-Woo-ya, you are good son. When I marry your mom, my mother and father—they tell me I am no longer part of family. They want me to marry someone else. Someone from family like theirs." With a fist full of tissues, Mom dabbed her eyes and walked away from us.

Dad continued. "I come to U.S. for vacation and met your

mom on airplane. She was in U.S. to study. She was so funny, I didn't sleep on the whole trip home." A single tear trickled down his cheek, but he was smiling. He quickly wiped it away.

"My family have lumber business in Seoul, many government contract all over Korea. My mother and father...they want me to marry someone from good family." He sighed. "They introduce me to Sung Jung. She was very smart, Yonsei graduate. Nice girl. We had some dating, but she was not very fun. Not like your Umma." He laughed. "I follow your mom back to U.S., and we marry at courthouse a few month later." In the distance, my mom looked over her shoulder and grabbed free energy bars and sports drinks at the finish line and stuffed them into her purse. "My parents come to visit one time, when you were just baby, to tell me I will not have any family money. I was on my own."

My heartstrings yanked so tight I barely breathed. How had they kept this from me so long? And how could my grandparents have done this to my dad? To my mom? To Lucy and me, their grandchildren?

"I give it all up." He exhaled loudly. "So, we don't have much. Everything we have is old, some is broken, but it is ours. Our family."

My mom came back and handed me a chocolate-flavored protein bar. "Use contest money for college. It is yours. Dad and I don't need. We be okay. Go enjoy your famous day." She patted me on the back and pushed me forward.

The publicist swept me away for never-ending interviews and sound bites. For over an hour, I was bombarded with "How does it feel?" and "What did you do to prepare?" and "What are you going to do with all that money?" The fame and glory I'd wanted so badly was now my reality. With a glowing smile for the camera, I rattled off talking points I'd prepared for that very moment and promoted my soon-to-come product line of survivalist gear.

Even with so much attention on me, my mind drifted elsewhere. To what my parents had sacrificed for love. To what I thought I'd gained from this competition, but what I'd actually lost.

My fake smile dimmed with the realization that I might never see Kate again.

I broke away from the press and ran to the parking lot to find her. Stiff legged but determined, my heart thumped painfully with each pounding step. I'd left the doors to Mom's car unlocked and was hoping Kate would be in the passenger seat, sound asleep, waiting for me to take her home.

But I found my car empty. I opened the driver door, and the car cabin gave off a stale, musty odor. It had been sealed shut for days.

With one bar of phone signal, I called her, but it went straight to voice mail, and she didn't respond to my multiple texts. Luckily, as I reversed out of the parking lot and headed home, Zach picked up on the first ring.

He greeted me. "Your mom called."

"I know, she's angry."

"You were on the news."

"You saw I won, right? Did I look okay?"

"Yeah."

Zach wasn't a chitchatter, so I just got right to why I was calling. "You think you could help me with something? What do you know about cryptocurrency?"

He perked up. "You mean, you want to know how the cryptography secures and verifies transactions? Or how a block-chain works? Mining is a waste of time unless you know what you're doing—"

I interrupted. "Dude. I don't need advanced tech-splanation. Do you know how wallets work? How to transfer cryptocoin from my wallet to Kate's?"

"Yes."

I hit my hand on the steering wheel. "Great! I'm heading over."

....

I stayed at Zach's for a few hours, ignoring my parents' escalating calls and threats as Zach figured out the logistics of my crypto-currency transfer. My monthlong grounding had been pushed up to six months. But it was more important to me to get Kate the money I owed her. When he finally made the transfer to her wallet and verified it wasn't traceable, I headed straight home.

Thirst and hunger gnawed at me to the point of nausea the entire drive. I took a swig of the God-knows-how-many-days-old water from the cup holder and fished around on the passenger side floor for my stash of Cheez-Its while stopping at a light. Kate's birthday present to me had fallen off the passenger seat and onto the floor. She'd used plain brown kraft paper and the good kind of tape that made unwrapping it a breeze.

Her gift? A heather-gray T-shirt, in exactly my size. A medium-ish large. Lardium. I held it up by the shoulders and laughed.

THIS GUY LOVES MAROON 5, with two cartoony thumbs pointing in. She'd left the price tag on it: "$10, originally $20."

Hands down, the best and worst gift I'd ever gotten. The twinge in my chest came back, more forceful now. This stupid gift was perfect.

A horn blared behind me, snapping me to full attention. I slammed the gas pedal to ramp up my speed, awakened to the realization that I would do anything to win Kate back.

CHAPTER THIRTY

Kate

Everything looked the way I'd left it when I got home. I took a long shower, washing the burned zombie stench off me, and carefully cleaned the scratches and scrapes all over my face, arms, and legs. After wrapping my ankle, I changed into the clothes I'd already set out on my chair the night before the Zombiegeddon competition and put on my puffy black down coat.

My roller bag was already packed and ready to go. My one-way ticket printout, secured inside the front zipper of the second suitcase. My new disposable phone, activated and prepaid for three months, in my backpack along with my flash drive loaded with all my important files. My family photos, the ones of Mom, Dad, and me, were tucked inside a padded envelope with my other important belongings. I'd left all the empty silver frames behind.

Deep inside my chest, sadness pushed its way up, making it hard for me to hold back tears. Now that the time had come, saying goodbye to my life was harder than I had expected.

Jeeves rolled up toward me as I made my way to the front door. "Good evening, Kate. It's time for me to take your vitals."

"Not now. I'm on my way out," I replied.

"Incoming call from your father," he chirped back. "A new feature with the latest software update. Video chat!" The screen on Jeeves's chest flicked on, and my dad's face appeared in high-definition color. It was something Digitools had been working on for years.

"I'll be home in an hour. Another late night at the office," he grumbled into his whiskey glass. He sat up in his chair and squinted. "Wait, where are you going? You have school tomorrow."

The lump in my throat burned. I didn't answer. I gulped instead.

"Jeeves," Dad barked. "What is Kate wearing?"

"Plaid shirt, jeans, black coat, and beanie, sir."

His eyes narrowed even more, like he had the power to look into my soul. "Does she have anything else in her possession?"

"Yes. Two suitcases and a backpack, sir."

Dad slammed both hands on his desk. "Jeeves, detain her until I get home," he growled. "Kate, I don't know what you're planning, but we need to have a serious conversation when I get there."

"No!" I shouted, my stomach in tight knots.

"You don't have a choice, Kate. My house, my rules!" he yelled.

"And that's why I can't stay," I fired back. "I can't live like this anymore. In this house, under your watch, like a prison. It's not anything like how it was when Mom was here." Every day, every minute, his overzealous overprotection left me stifled and lonely. I needed him to be my dad, not my bodyguard. My face softened a little as sadness flashed in his eyes. "I miss Mom, and I know you do too."

By mentioning her, I hoped he'd see we were both coming from a place of unhappiness and hurt. That he would be fatherly and not treat this like another hostile business transaction. Because this wasn't a negotiation. My conditions needed to be met, or I'd walk away.

"Dad, I have to go."

His face instantly rehardened. "No! Jeeves, do *not* let her leave that house. She's grounded. I'm coming home right now to handle this."

The screen went black. All the doors in the house locked at once with synchronized clicks.

What a dramatic way to have the last word.

An unblinking Jeeves stared back at me. I squeezed my suitcase handles tightly, turning my knuckles so white I lost sensation in my fingertips.

"I need to go, Jeeves," I whispered. "I'm sorry."

"You must stay," he responded. "Your father said you need to stay. He gave an order."

Each software update had given Jeeves more humanlike responses. Maybe he'd understand where I was coming from. "You've been with me a few months, Jeeves. You've taken my vitals every week. Do I seem happy to you?"

Immediately, he replied, "Based on my observations, you do not. Your frowns far exceed all other shown facial expressions."

Well, that was depressing. "Do you want me to be happy, Jeeves?"

"What I want doesn't matter."

Damn it.

Time for a drastically different approach. "Okay, Jeeves, hypothetically speaking, if I were to cut off the power in the house with the switch box in Dad's bedroom, what would happen?"

"I would still be functional, as I am battery powered. The house would remain locked but could be disabled with a manual override."

"Thanks." Problem was, hypothetically speaking, Jeeves would stop me from cutting the power.

He added, "I must ensure your safety. Keeping you out of danger is my number one obligation. You are your father's top priority, Kate."

Barely suppressing an eye roll, I muttered, "Yeah, well, I don't believe that."

"Affirmative. Your father built me just for you."

"Wh-what do you mean, he built you just for me?"

This new information about Dad left me baffled. Why would I need Jeeves?

"Your father assigned a number of Digitools engineering teams to develop and upgrade my operating system. To serve and protect Kate Anderson." He saluted me. "Keep you safe and protected."

Was this Dad's way of trying to be a good father? Or was this his way of outsourcing his parenting job because he was never home?

Was this love? Or outright rejection?

All of this was too much to process. Rubbing my temples, I tried to squeeze all of these questions out of my head. I already had a one-way ticket away from here. I had my theater and screenplay dreams to fulfill. I didn't want to follow Dad's footsteps and move up the ranks in his behemoth company. I had my goal, and Dad had his. To stop me.

I tried the front door. It was locked, of course. No one could get me out except for Jeeves or Dad.

To leave, I needed to think more like Jeeves and Dad.

"Hey, Jeeves, can you please take my vitals?"

"My pleasure!" Without asking me why I'd switched gears to enthusiastically participate in his health monitoring, he checked my blood pressure and oxygen, and pricked my finger for blood analysis, the part I hated the most.

"Your blood sugar is dangerously low. You are also dehydrated," he reported back immediately.

"That's right. Could you get me something to eat and drink? I haven't eaten or drank much today, or the last few days."

He whirred away, giving me a brief moment to run to Dad's bedroom. I shut off the main power in the house. Within seconds, the emergency lights flicked on.

"Oh dear." Jeeves's voice echoed down the hallway from the kitchen.

I unlocked the doors by flipping a switch in the control panel in the master bedroom. With my luggage in tow, I stepped out onto the porch.

Poor Jeeves. He'd be rolling around and around the house until my dad came home, looking for me with a sandwich, fruit, and juice on his flip-down serving tray. Failing in his mission to keep me confined and fed, like a round-the-clock correctional officer.

I pulled open the iron gates, which had defaulted to an unlocked position. My heart raced as each one slammed closed behind me.

Waiting for the taxi I'd prearranged to the airport, my burner phone—the one I'd be getting rid of soon—buzzed with a message. Or rather, dozens of them, all from Nate. I scrolled through them all by the time the cab pulled into the top of the driveway.

Another message from Nate.

Last one, I swear. Thanks for the shirt

I responded with five words. *Thanks for the cryptocoin*

A long text from Raina: Your dad is calling here and texting me nonstop. Daddy Warbucks sounds legit worried and sad. Are you LEAVING leaving? Bish, you better send me your new contact info if you are

My hot tears fell on the screen. *Why are you shudder-crying, Kate? You wanted this.*

I shut off the phone forever.

CHAPTER THIRTY-ONE

Subjecting myself to Lucy's kindergarten share day was one of the worst decisions I'd ever made.

That included the time I bleached my hair with hydrogen peroxide the summer of seventh grade because I'd heard Annie liked blonds. After three hours of intense soaking, my jet-black hair turned orange. I actually had to dye it black again before school started and paid Jaxon twenty dollars to help me and to never, ever mention it again. Twenty dollars in hush money so he'd shut up about my "Prince Harry" hair. I did all that for Annie.

I tried to blink away my exhaustion as Lucy introduced me to her class.

She stood next to me. "This is Nate. He's my older brother. He beat up a lot of dead people this weekend to win money." She took a seat on the colorful mat in the front row directly in front of me.

Mrs. French gasped and dropped the glue sticks in her hand. One of the boys whispered, "Cool!"

Twenty sets of eager little eyes waited for more details.

I laughed and rubbed the back of my neck. "Um, good morning, everyone."

For some reason I expected them to say back to me in singsongy unison, "Good morning, Nate," but they stared back at me with blank looks. With that introduction, could you blame them?

One boy in head-to-toe Seahawks gear raised his hand and spoke without being called on. "Were they already dead, or did you kill them to win the money?"

I rubbed the back of my neck again. "Oh, they weren't really people. They were zombies—"

"ZOMBIES?" The Seahawks boy cut me off. "I kill zombies in Minecraft."

Two of the girls in the front screamed and hugged each other. Honestly, I couldn't tell if they were playing scared or were really freaked out. Figured it was best to play it safe.

"Okay, everyone, calm down. The dead people weren't real. It's like, you know, the games you play on your iPad or pretend shows you watch on TV. The zombies weren't alive."

A little Korean boy blurted, "I'm only allowed to play chess and math games on the computer. And no screen time until I do my jujitsu lessons and finish all my reading."

Oh, I totally connected with this kid. Pint-size Nate.

"What's your name, big guy?"

"James Ejoon Cho."

"Nice to meet you, James."

The teacher cleared her throat. "Um, Nate, he goes by his full name."

James Ejoon Cho asked, "Did you really beat up pretend dead guys for money?"

Sort of? "Well, let me start from the beginning. My, um, friend, wanted me to be her partner in an outdoor competition where we win a cash prize if we made it to the finish line first. The zombies, or fake dead people, were obstacles. They were things in the way to make it harder to win."

One of the hugging, screaming girls asked, "So you didn't hurt anybody?"

Without thinking, I answered, "A few of the zombies got in the way, and I had to disable them. But they were all robots. Well, actually, I did have a few skirmishes with some real people, but they tried to hit me first. But my partner zapped one of them back in the butt, um, backside with a stun gun."

Lucy yelled, "That's not nice, hitting first!" She pointed to a sign on the wall. *NO HITTING.* "Did you fight them with your *CRAP MACAW*?"

"*Krav Maga.* And yes, Luce, I did use those moves I learned in my classes to defend myself." The kids perked up. A few parents were definitely going to be asked about *crap macaw* tonight.

The kids' comfort level grew. Soon I was bombarded with questions and comments.

"What did you win?"

"Did you get a ribbon? Or a trophy?"

"I'm going to be a zombie for Halloween."

"How did you poop outside?"

"Do you run fast?"

"Is it true that zombies only come out at night?"

"Can I see the money you won?"

Mrs. French saved me. "Class, it's hard to hear when you all talk at the same time. We have time for one more question. If you have a question for Nate, please raise your hand."

Twenty hands shot up. Lucy beamed at me. Share day success!

"Let's hear from someone who hasn't spoken yet." She pointed to a tiny little girl with purple glasses.

She put her hand down and wrung her hands. "Um. I forgot my questi—oh wait! I think I remember. Um…"

I ran through the list of potential questions and answered them. *I'll spend the prize money on college and my business. It was a great learning experience, and I would definitely do it again. Toughen up and you'll go far in life.*

With a loud clap, she yelped, "I know! Do you have a girlfriend?"

The Seahawks kid pointed and laughed at me. *Thanks, kid.* "Smoochy, smoochy, smoooooooochy!"

I'd never been so vulnerable in my life. Little kids who didn't even know me asked me the one question I didn't want to answer. Sitting attentively, they waited for my response.

Lucy came to my rescue. "Nate isn't allowed to have a girlfriend because he is grounded forever. But his bestest friend-girl is Kate."

Thanks, Lucy.

"Class, can we say thank you to Nate for visiting our class-room?" Mrs. French trilled.

"Thaaaank yoooooou!"

"Thank you for having me!"

The bell rang at the exact right time, and I patted Lucy's head on my way out. When I got to the car, I rolled down the front windows and breathed in the frigid air.

My bestest friend-girl was *Kate.*

I folded my arms on the steering wheel and put my head down.

Kate, I wanted to say. *I was an idiot. About the competition. About wanting the money. Fuck the money.*

Please, call me back.

CHAPTER THIRTY-TWO

Nate

"It's mine?" Lucy asked. "All of them?"

"Yes. All yours!" I said.

She hugged the unopened boxes of various collectible figures that I'd bought and saved over the years. The ones that she pulled down from my shelves and admired but knew better than to take out. I'd lectured her so many times on what "mint condition" meant that I'd lost count. Here I was, with a closet full of toys I'd never played with, pristine in their packaging, bringing me so little happiness. What was the point in that?

I wasn't stupid, though. There were dozens of toys I had in a foot locker by my bed that she would never touch with those Play-Doh and slime-covered fingers of hers. Those were kept safe with my two-pronged combination and padlock containers. The rare ones that did bring me joy.

It pained me to see her pull the Princess Leia and Rey dolls by their necks, taking off their clothes and swapping them with Wonder Woman's. But she was my kid sister, and this nerdy memorabilia was my gift to her. She played quietly next to the foot of my bed while Jaxon and Zach came over for my belated birthday to play VR boxing games on my new PlayStation console (no zombie games allowed). Looking super daft in those headsets that resembled oversize swim goggles, they tried to knock each other out for top score. They'd gotten good enough to unlock special game features.

"I won!" Jaxon yelled, tearing off his headgear. "Wanna play?" he asked me.

"Nah, it's all sweaty." Truth was, every spare second I had, I stared at my phone, willing it to light up.

Kate hadn't shown up for work for weeks now. They said she had put in her two-weeks' notice before the competition and assumed I had known she'd done that. Nope, but I played it off like I did. I couldn't help but think that she'd left because of me. Because of the competition. But I knew deep down that she was probably going to leave no matter what, that she'd planned it all along. I had hoped that I was enough to make her stay. That she'd stay here until we figured our shit out and made it all work. But she'd left me anyway.

"You're looking pretty down for someone who just got the early nod for valedictorian." Jaxon grabbed my shoulder and shook it a little. Our midterms had been tallied, and I'd come out on top of the class.

One person who hadn't been thrilled about my class

standing was Pete Haskill Number Four. The morning after the competition, Annie and some of my fellow skids marched into the headmaster's office to tell him about Pete's GPA scheme. He wasn't expelled or suspended from CHA thanks to his dad's influence, but he was prohibited from playing any varsity sports for the rest of the school year, which made his college applications look even worse. School-wide, all the skids mobilized. Jock skids, genius whiz skids, politically and socially active skids—all of us—outnumbered Pete and his friends tenfold, so they left us all alone.

Zach muttered while playing a new racing game, "His heart is broken." He threw the controllers on the ground, yelling, "Damn it, I'm dead too!" He took off his sweaty headset and grabbed a handful of chips.

"Ix-nay on the amnit-day," I said, jerking my head toward Lucy, who had put Leia's hair in pigtails.

Jaxon shrugged. "It's not like he said the *F* word."

Lucy looked up. "What's the *F* word?"

"Nothing!" we all shouted in unison.

"Well, look, life goes on," Jaxon said, licking brownie crumbs and melted ice cream off his plastic spoon. "You're going off to college soon, where you'll meet tons of girls. If I get into Trinity, and you go to Yale, we can hang. With Zachary too, at MIT. And you'll have tons of girlfriends when you get to be CEO of your company with a gajillion-dollar net worth."

Mom walked in with a pizza box and a bowl of grapes. She smiled at us. "They can call you *Nate Worth!*"

Oh no, more Mom jokes.

Jaxon and Zach snorted. "Your mom should be a comedian," Jaxon said. "I'm serious. Her deadpan slays me."

Mom beamed and left the room.

Jaxon and Zach lifted the top flap of the pizza box. Steam rose and fogged up Zach's glasses. Temporarily blinded, he asked, "What kind of pizza is it?"

"Pepperoni," Jaxon said, digging in.

Zach took a bunch of grapes and pulled them off from the stem one by one with his teeth. "What's it like to be rich?"

It was funny. I wasn't rich by any means, but we were so financially challenged that my windfall made it feel like I went from skid to Zuckerberg. I chewed my pizza slice and swallowed. "I thought having money would make me happier, but nope." Biggest surprise about my winnings? Having more money didn't make me feel any different. "Maybe this whole skid thing wasn't all about money after all. It was more in my head." I shrugged. "I've started to pare down my schedule, though, to make more time for fun stuff. Been doing more things that make me happy, like playing games with you plebs."

A flash memory of Kate popped into my head. *Please make sure you don't forget to enjoy your life, okay?* A long sigh escaped. "I guess the grass is always greener on the other side."

"Oh, I get it," Lucy interjected.

"What, Luce?" I asked.

"Now I know why the chicken crossed the road." She paused. "Because the grass was greener on the other side."

Jaxon gaped. "Nate, dude, I thought you were smart, but I think your sister might be a damn genius."

"Ix-nay on the amnit-day," Lucy said.

Jaxon, Zach, and I busted up laughing, to the point none of us could breathe.

Mom came back into my room and handed me a two-liter bottle of Coke. Then she pulled out a postcard from her jacket pocket and handed it to me. "Special mail delivery!"

On one side was an illustration of the Statue of Liberty in sunglasses, GREETINGS FROM NEW F*CKING YORK in bold black letters across her chest. On the other side, to the left of my handwritten address, were three words that took my breath away.

I miss Dicks

CHAPTER THIRTY-THREE

Kate

The whoosh of the crisp winter air blasted my face when I propped open the theater door. Being the newly hired stage manager assistant at the Second Street Theater in Queens, New York, had some pluses, but this furnace-like heat wasn't one of them. The place was either a blistering one hundred degrees or a frigid forty-nine degrees Fahrenheit. And you never got to choose which one.

"Do you know the theater manager's number? The heat keeps blasting during the performances, and it's hard for everyone to concentrate. It's so hot it's hard to keep my clothes on."

Zoe laughed. "I do, but he never answers. And when he's actually around, he's busy with the frozen pipes and leaky toilets. I'll call him again. I don't know why he doesn't fix it. It's wasting his electricity." She hugged me. "But aren't you happy you get to be onstage with me, even though you're losing your body weight in sweat?"

It *was* great to be onstage again with Zoe. I had been in New

York only a few weeks, and she had helped me get this part-time job assisting her, and I'd scored a small nonspeaking role in the theater's modern adaptation of *The Gift of the Magi and Other O. Henry Stories.*

While pushing a wooden prop storefront off the stage, Zoe huffed, "Oh! I forgot to tell you." The wheels squeaked with each shove. "Someone. Was looking. For you."

Who would be looking for me? Raina was the only one I'd kept in contact with from home. Dad and I had just started talking again, but he didn't know where I was staying or where I was working.

"He asked for you by name."

I asked, "It's a dude? Is it the manager or his son? Then I can yell at him. Or both of them. Oh wait, is it my dad? We've been in touch—he's in town for work this month, and he's coming to one of our performances in a couple of weeks. But...you know what he looks like."

Zoe smirked and tucked her damp bangs behind her ear. "Yeah. Definitely not your dear old dad. The guy is our age. Prep vibe. Pretty cute Asian guy."

"Now I'm curious." I peeked out of the right side of the curtain. Could it be? My stomach sank when it was clear no one was out there.

"Sorry!" a voice thundered from the left side of the curtain, nearly stopping my heart. Damn theater acoustics. "I swear I'm not a stalker or a creep. I'm just looking for—oh, Kate! It's you!"

Be still my heart. Literally. My pulse picked up the pace from zero to a thousand BPMs when I saw Nate Kim standing across the stage. *Ba-boom. Ba-boom. Nate KIM. Nate KIM.*

My mouth fell open. "How...how'd you find me here?"

With hesitant steps, he made his way over to me. "By being a little bit stalker-ish and creep-ish? Zach helped me find you. You're hard to find because you go by *Kate Hall* now." He smiled. "Your picture is on the theater's website, and Zach found you with his proprietary facial recognition software. I figured you'd find a home in the fringe theater world here. But you're super fringe. Like *way* off-off-Broadway. You're so far off Broadway you're in Queens."

I punched his arm but couldn't stifle my smile. "Jerk! So really, why are you in Queens, the theater capital of the world?"

He chewed his lip. "A wise person once told me to make sure I enjoy my life. So, I traveled to New York with my family during winter break. And because I'm me, I've tacked on some East Coast college tours too." He peeled off his coat. "Your heater's broken. This whole place feels like a boiler room. Want me to fix it?"

Behind me, Zoe squeaked, "Wait, are *you* Nate? Nate Kim? And you know how to fix heaters?"

"Yeah, Nate's pretty handy," I said.

Nate reached out to shake Zoe's hand, but she pulled him

in for a hug. "I don't believe in handshakes," she said, and then released him. "Nice to meet you, Nate! I'm Zoe."

He straightened his crumpled cardigan and smiled at her. "Nice to meet you too." Then he said to me, "I haven't eaten dinner yet. Would you grab a late-night bite with me? I'm thinking burger and fries. Maybe a milkshake too. Like old times."

I stammered, "I—I don't know. I still have to clean the seats and sweep the stage—"

Zoe elbowed me in the ribs. "She'd love to, Nate. No curfew tonight. Have fun, you two." She exited stage right.

I shook my head. "I still can't believe you're here. What colleges are you touring?"

"Columbia. Princeton. Rutgers. Columbia's here, and the last two are pretty close to New York City. I've narrowed it down to those three. You want me to work on the heater now?"

My stomach gurgled. "Actually, let's go get food. And maybe you can come back for the heater another time?"

He glanced at the ceiling, walls, and floors. "There are a ton of broken things here. And I noticed some leaky faucets in the men's bathroom. And running toilets. You might need someone to come back here a few times. Maybe even regularly. My spring break and summer breaks are pretty open right now."

I pressed my lips together in amusement. "Okay then, for future repair payment, dinner's on me tonight. There's this dive a few blocks down, Burger Basin, that's open late. We can go there.

They have handmade shakes and really great hand-cut fries. It's no Dick's, but pretty good and cheap."

Nate pulled his coat back on and put on a pair of gloves he got from his pockets. "That sounds perfect."

I grabbed my bag and peacoat and led him out the alley exit.

Our boots crunched through the packed snow. Snowflakes flurried around us as we rounded the corner to the restaurant.

He interrupted our silence. "I missed you." *Crunch, crunch.* "A lot."

I nodded. *Crunch, crunch.* "Me too." *Crunch, crunch, crunch.* "Sorry I didn't reach out. I wanted to, but I'm still finding my way here. The money's helped a lot. Thank you for that." I offered him a tentative smile.

He shivered. "And I'm sorry about how the competition ended. Your dad, he—"

"I know." I sighed. "He came clean and told me everything this weekend. We're finally talking now, adult to adult. There's a lot of healing to do, but at least we made some progress."

The Burger Basin's open sign, slightly askew, flashed in red, like it was warning us to go elsewhere. But through the steamed-up windows we could make out a bustling crowd of patrons inside. We were seated right away and hung up our coats on the coatrack by our booth.

"I'm starving," I said, snapping open the folded laminated menu.

Nate unzipped his gray wool cardigan, then flapped it open and closed for ventilation. "It was so hot in that theater! I'm still sweating."

I leaned in and peered at his T-shirt. "Wait, is that the shirt I got you for your birthday? Why does it look so, um—"

"Hot on me?" Nate interjected.

I tried to fight my smile but failed. "Um. No. I was going to say *old*."

He grinned. "I wear this shirt all the time. I've gotten so many compliments. And a ton of harassment, too, especially around the bars in Belltown. Turns out Maroon 5 is really polarizing. Like, someone threw a beer bottle at my head when he saw my shirt the other day. And another drunk guy in Capitol Hill hugged me, saying Adam Levine was his guilty pleasure. I still don't exactly know what he meant by that." He cocked his head, and his inviting brown eyes crinkled with his sheepish smile. "But I still wear it because I like the shirt. I love it actually." He closed his menu and looked at me. "I know we haven't put in our order, and I haven't tried the food yet, but can we do this again? Another...uh...date? My treat next time?"

A sigh of relief escaped me. "Sure!"

He grinned and opened his menu again. Nate looked up at the antiquated metal cash register and whispered to me, "So I guess they don't take Bitcoin?"

Instead of punching him, I nudged his knee with mine under

the table. "Nope." While we ordered, Nate kept his leg steady against mine. My skin prickled all over as heat flowed between our bodies.

After we ate our burgers, he grabbed my hand. "This is the main advantage of not having drippy sauce on your burger. It's not sticky when I do this."

I said the only thing that came to mind as I grabbed his other hand. "Roger that." A familiar feeling of contentment passed through me as Nate gently stroked my fingers with his thumbs.

He nodded and leaned in closer. "Roger that."

I didn't know what our future held, but in that moment, everything was perfect.

Acknowledgments

It took a rather large village to get this novel written and published. I've been so lucky to have been surrounded by supportive people during this exciting and (insert adjective here: bumpy, obscured, potholed, booby-trapped?) path to publication.

Thank you so much to the earliest readers of this book: Helen Hoang, my BFF and daily sprint buddy, you are the Statler to my Waldorf, and I am so happy you're in my life. Whitney Schneider, my longtime critique partner, you read the first draft and told me in the nicest way that I need to quit it with my "wildly blinking characters." I heart you. Canadian Annette Christie, my hoodie twin, you are a huge talent and a fantastic friend. Ken, you read this twice (TWICE!) for me. You are a loyal friend who always gives me valuable "tough love" feedback.

Roselle Lim, thank you for willing the universe to show me a sign when I nearly gave up on writing. Judy Lin (my late-night sprint friend and fellow horror aficionado), Alexa Martin (best co-mentor ever) and Liz Lawson (my Roaring '20s debut lifeline), thank you for responding to my messages and being there for all the flails. Danielle Paige, I can't believe our paths crossed again after college and I am so immensely happy to have you back in my life. Sabina Khan, Gwynne Jackson, Jenny Howe, Sheila Athens, Nancy Johnson, Kathleen Barber, Chelsea Resnick, Kristin Rockaway, my WFWA friends, thank you for being there for me the last few years, I appreciate you so much.

To my MAPID writers group, your feedback and encouragement really made a difference. I'm eternally grateful. To my sub support group, you are all wonderfully talented; big hugs to each and every one of you. Julia Chang, you read my very first book-like thing and taught me how to show, not tell. You are amazing. Sandra Morris, thank you for helping me when I deleted my entire website. I still can't believe I did that. My #Roaring20sdebut group, even Jeff Bishop, you were so welcoming when I felt like a latecomer to the party. Group bear hug! To the Pitch Wars Class of 2016, you are an immensely talented bunch, and I am so happy to be part of your community. Thank you to Brenda Drake for creating Pitch Wars and to all of the hardworking people who keep it running every year. Sarah Henning and Kellye Garrett, my Pitch Wars mentors, thank you for cheering me on during the highs and being there for me during the lows. You've imparted wise, realistic advice and kept me sane during the last few years.

To my fabulous agent, Brent, this book wouldn't have been written without your encouragement. You've been so supportive since the day you requested my Pitch Wars manuscript. WHAT.

A. JOURNEY (insert every single face emoji here). Thank you for believing in my stories.

Eliza Swift, my wonderful editor, thank you for championing this zombie-themed rom-com and writing so many "hahahaha"s in your track change notes. This book found the best home with the best people.

Sourcebooks Fire folks: Sarah, Cassie, Sandra, Ashlyn, Nicole, Louisa, Heather, Jacqueline, and the other sales, marketing, and publicity teams I'll have the pleasure to meet soon, thank you so much for all of your time and dedication.

Gamsahamnida to Mom and Dad for promoting my book to the elders at their Korean church. Gene, Jee Hyun, Melissa, Dustin, Lin, thanks for being so supportive during my journey. Sister Sarah, you're my bestest friend, and thank you for being there for me through everything.

A massive thank-you to Jee Jung Kang and Julie Kim, who helped me with my Korean language phrasing, specifically helping with Nate Kim getting yelled at by his parents so eloquently. To my Young Minds and Franklin moms, Microsoft gals, Anderson buddies, Columbia pals, HFA friends, ANZ buddies, NY and Seattle agency friends. Sherry, LeeAnn, Corinne, Naveena, and Naveena's parents, thank you for believing in me.

Michael at Alfred Music, Carter at Hal Leonard, and Kendrick Lamar (omg), thank you for letting me use the "Money Trees" lyric in this book. Jonathan R. and Liz (again), who helped guide me through the music clearance process, a humongous thanks to you!

Thank you to Kris C., who explained to me in detail how to use a Taser, and then pulled one out of her truck to show me.

To the Coca-Cola Company, bless you for creating those cute little ninety-calorie cans that fueled all of my drafting and revising.

Hi Maxine, Sydney, Dani, Max, and Quinn! Your auntie published a book!

Trevor, thank you for being there for me every step of the way. I love you.

CJ, thanks for being an awesome kiddo and giving your mommy time to write. I'm blessed to have a child who loves Annie's mac and cheese so much. Your suggestion to change my entire manuscript to Lobster 2 font will be shared with my editor.

And finally, to my readers, thank you so much for picking up this book. You've made my dream come true, and for that I am eternally grateful.

About the Author

© Joanna DeGeneres

Suzanne Park is a Korean American author who was born and raised in Tennessee.

In her former life as a stand-up comedian, she appeared on BET's *Coming to the Stage*, was the winner of the Sierra Mist Comedy Competition in Seattle, and was a semifinalist in NBC's Stand Up for Diversity showcase in San Francisco.

Suzanne graduated from Columbia University and received an MBA from UCLA. She currently resides in Los Angeles with her husband, offspring, and a sneaky rat that creeps around on her back patio. In her spare time, she procrastinates. *The Perfect Escape* is her first novel.